Jordan's
PENNY

ISBN 978-1-7376763-0-0 (Paperback)
ISBN 978-1-7376763-1-7 (Digital)

Editing by Write Your Best Book
Cover Artwork by Etheric Tales & Edits
Formatting by Etheric Tales & Edits

Printed in the United States of America.
Published by Stefanie Stratton
StefanieStratton2@gmail.com
https://stefaniestratton2.wixsite.com/writer

Jordan's PENNY

STEFANIE STRATTON

PART ONE:
JORDAN

CHAPTER ONE

THE ALARM WAILS and as soon as I peel my eyes open, I dread the day before it begins. Yesterday was a nightmare. I try not to dwell too much, but the mounting stress of each passing day takes a toll. I look incompetent to the partners, and I'm sick of it. That damn assistant of mine will be my career's demise. Cathy fucks up on the simplest tasks—my schedule, reports, messages, dictating, answering phones, and she even misspells her name on professional emails sent throughout the office.

With yesterday's shitstorm still fresh in my mind clouding my present reality, my elbow knocks into the body beside mine. I forgot I invited Candice over.

Wait, why is she still here?

She's sprawled out, hair splayed over the pillow and on her face. I groan, not because she's hogging my blanket, but because she didn't fucking leave.

Candice knows the drill; she's followed the rules plenty of times. Until last night. We do our thing, and then she leaves. There are no sleepovers or cuddling. There isn't even a Netflix and chill. It's only chill. She goes home and I go to bed.

But since she's still here, I soak in her lean body. Her smooth and tanned leg drapes over the sheet with the perfect ratio of naked hip and thigh to get my blood pumping again. For a moment, I contemplate going in late and feasting on her for the third time, but as satisfying as that would be, I push those cravings aside. My schedule is far too busy; two meetings, three conference calls, and a shit-ton of emails need my attention.

Candice is fun, though. My aching muscles are a reminder of that. Besides being a perfect ten—sultry blue eyes, highlighted blonde hair, augmented breasts, and the sexiest, flattest stomach—she's known her place. With her conversation rating at a three, this match suits me best since what we do requires few words. She has the pleasure of being with me, and I relieve some pent-up stress with her. No strings attached.

She remains motionless, aside from the subtle movement of her chest rising and falling with each breath. I trace the smooth lines of her frame with my gaze until my hand shifts and falls off the edge of the bed. She has damn near pushed me off my fucking mattress.

What is she still doing here?

"Hey." I nudge.

She moves, slow movements, stretching her body as she stirs, and the sheet shifts, exposing her perky pink nipples. I steadily remind myself she isn't supposed to be here and ignore the steady throb of my morning wood. Candice moves the hair from her face, and even first thing in the morning she's sexy as fuck. Her skin glows. It might be the after-sex sheen women get after climaxing multiple times, or perhaps she's glowing because she's slept on the most expensive mattress on the market. Either way, she's overstayed her welcome and needs to go.

I nudge her shoulder once more, firmer than before, and she blinks, squinting in the morning sun.

Candice rises without a word and tiptoes through my room, naked, picking up her discarded clothes. Each time she bends, I absorb the sights; specifically, that firm ass of hers. With her clothes draped over her arm, she saunters to the bed, leans down with her tits dangling over me, and kisses my cheek.

"Call me."

Once the door closes behind her, I shift to the center of my bed, fold my arms behind my head, and relax on my pricey slate-colored sheets.

Call her? I'm not the type to share pleasantries. I call for sex, and that's all. Dating isn't my forte. With my career being my priority, I haven't seen her in over a month. Plus, after last night, she'll need time to recover. I stretched her body in ways even gymnasts haven't experienced. Lucky for me, she's an exciting woman, happy to experiment with just about anything I can imagine, and she'll go to impressive lengths to please me. She's got untapped stamina for days; her hunger is as insatiable as mine.

Jordan's Penny

Begrudgingly, I get out of bed and head straight to the shower. Water shoots out of the various jets, massaging my sore body. Thanks to her, I won't need a gym session; last night was more than enough cardio. My chest and arms are tender from hovering over her body half the night as she climaxed multiple times. Even under the hot, pulsating water, reminiscing about Candice's sexy, rounded terrain sends a chill down my spine. I shake last night's images away, and I focus on work, running down the list of things I need to do. Fun time is over.

I stand in my walk-in closet, which I had specifically designed for my suits, figuring out which designer will impress the hens today. Once my eyes fall on a dark gray, fitted jacket, matching vest, and pants, I know it'll get them salivating. I pluck a new, crisp, white shirt from the rack and a black printed silk tie from the drawer. I strive for perfection and never leave the house less than perfect. In all honesty, I strive for greatness in all aspects of life—working out six days a week, maintaining a healthy lifestyle, and being the most successful partner in the firm. It's arduous work to maintain this level of success and a six-pack, but I stop at nothing. I thrive off the challenge.

As my Aunt Rose always said, "*If you're a ten, everything in your life should match.*" Even though she didn't raise me, Aunt Rose ingrained her ideology in my head. Mediocrity was unacceptable. It wasn't until I got older that I realized she was simply referring to dating gorgeous women and nothing more. But it was too late. The mantra I replayed in my mind since damn near conception was woven into my DNA now. I couldn't just date a ten and stop there. I needed to have the best and be the best in everything I do.

If I put this much energy into my perfection, I expect nothing less from someone I'm fucking. I've never brought home anyone unworthy of a career in modeling. I also don't date. Some might describe it as a sexual arrangement. I explain what I'm after and make it clear, extraordinarily clear, that I don't have time for a relationship or feelings. Neither interests me. Maybe if I got whacked in the head, suffered a concussion, things might change, but even if that happens, she'd still need to be smoking hot. I don't care if she's a moron, as long as she's a gorgeous moron with a banging body. If that makes me superficial, so be it. I want what I want, and I deserve it, too.

I stroll through the office halls, aware of what they say, not only with their mouths but with their eyes. All the women stare. Hell, even men admire me as I walk past. And I guarantee most imagine me naked. I revel in the attention; it feeds my ego, and dammit if my ego isn't one hungry son of a bitch.

Lucky for me, most of our female employees are pleasing to the eye, too. We don't require applicants to be attractive, but by the grace of God, good-looking women apply. I'm not upset by this at all; I enjoy admiring them as much as they enjoy admiring me.

Truth be told, none of the partners are complaining. Aside from Alec and me, the other three partners are family men living that mundane life. I'm sure they soak in the eye candy more than I do. If I were stuck with the same woman day and night, I wouldn't mind hot assistants running around with tight skirts on, too. I can't speak for Alec, but I don't plan on being tied down. It seems unpleasant. The bachelor's life treats me well, so I'm not trading this life for all the tea in China.

Every female employee I pass says, "Good morning, Mr. Stephens," all in different, yet sexy voices. With a fresh coat of gloss or lipstick, they smile in my direction, batting their lashes as I walk past each gray cubicle. When Tom Peters walks through these halls, they don't greet him with the same seductive tones. Their voices are airier for me, raising an octave, full of silk and seduction. I give a wink here, throw a nod there; it drives them insane.

My assistant, Cathy, the bane of my existence and biggest pain in my ass, stands at attention when she spots me heading toward my office. Cathy can't help herself, either. She's moved her desk three inches just to steal glances at me at her leisure; the indentation on the carpet was all the evidence I needed. On a positive note, I see more too. And by more, I mean every square inch of her toned, ivory legs.

She might be petite, but damn near all her height comes from those legs. They are never-ending. It's that, or her skirts are getting shorter, not that I mind either way. But those stems are her best attribute, and I can't imagine them in only heels and nothing more. Actually, yes, I can.

"Good morning, Mr. Stephens." She bats her thick lashes at me. If she keeps it up, she may levitate.

I feign indifference, offer a simple nod, and it drives her mad. She loves it as she wets her bottom lip, seductively swiping it with her tongue while I head for my desk. My pleasant mood shifts once I spot the wrong folder sitting on my blotter, yet again. I crash into the chair, and I roll back into the wall of floor-to-ceiling windows behind me. The day has turned to shit, and I just got here.

"Cathy. Here. Now."

She scurries in and sashays her hips from side to side. As hard as I focus on why I called her into my office, the chauvinistic pig in me can't stop imagining her naked. Just as that sexy image flashes in my mind, ass up and ready for me, I'm reminded why she single-handedly put me in a shitty mood.

"Owens & Co., not Cornwell Management." I shake the file and chuck it at her. Papers fly out of the manila folder and drift to the floor in varying directions. "Jesus, Cathy. They're not even in the same fucking filing cabinet."

Her bubbling morning grin disappears, and I'm sure her afternoon one will be a no-show. If I'm in a shitty mood, she must suffer with me.

I admit I enjoy the view as she leaves. Her black skirt caresses her curves, emphasizing her plump, firm ass. Even though I'd never mix business with pleasure, I can't stop imagining those legs wrapped around me in all the inappropriate yet satisfying ways. A disgruntled groan escapes my mouth and I throw my hands to my face.

The guys will twist my balls for this. Again. I've been through more assistants this year than Tom has had since he started the company. He's had Grace, a not-so-pleasant woman with one foot in the grave, for the past three decades. What she lacks in youth, she makes up for in efficiency. Needless to say, Grace takes the grand prize in the "Assistants" category. She's also the biggest ball-buster in the office, especially to me. She may get off on it if people her age still got off on things.

I massage my temples briefly and dial her extension, needing her to save my ass. Again.

"Morning, Grace," I sing with that charm she loves. "How's the most beautiful assistant on this glorious morning?"

She laughs, a tired, husky laugh, but one just as deadpan and shrewd as her personality. "Dial it down a notch, Jordan. Your advances won't work on me. I'm old enough to be your grandmother."

I chuckle while shuddering at the disturbing image that surfaced. Advances? Ugh. Never. At least Grace has a way of perking my mood back up. "Ah c'mon. You don't know what you're missin'."

Without seeing her, I sense she's smiling. "When I was younger, men smarter and better-looking than you knocked on my door to court me if your small mind can wrap itself around that."

In all honesty, I can't, but I'll let her live this fantasy out.

"Do you know why they were attractive?" she asks with a light bitterness in her voice.

"Abs of steel? Muscular arms? A great tailored suit?"

"No. It's a little thing called modesty. Look it up."

Is modesty overrated? Yes. Women love a cocky, bad boy. Open any women's magazine and you'll find plenty of studies and polls proving this. Being a conceited dick is a surefire way to keep a woman hungry for more. Women have this innate desire to fix and change a man's ways, thanks to their nurturing tendencies. I've yet to meet a woman attracted to a modest man.

Maybe if it weren't for my aunt, who voiced her opinion enough for twelve women, things might've ended differently. But having it said enough times, I believe I'm the best... every time I see my reflection in the mirror.

"I'll add that to my list. But in the meantime—"

"Let me guess. You need the file and report for the meeting, don't you?"

My eyes narrow on the receiver as if Grace has become a clairvoyant overnight. "See? It's kismet."

"No," she responds with a snarky bite. "Your assistant is an imbecile. I have one already waiting for you on my desk because I figured this might happen. Pick it up on your way to Alec's office."

"Isn't the meeting in Tom's?"

Grace laughs with evil glee, choking into the receiver before hanging up. I guess I got my answer.

Another frustrated grunt flies from my mouth. It's not the first time Cathy screwed me over. My long-legged saboteur plans conference calls five minutes after off-site business lunches. It's common knowledge business lunches never end on time. Even the elevator takes about three minutes on a busy day. With all the fancy tech gadgets I own, even I can't afford a teleportation device, if one existed.

Besides being oblivious to managing my time, her organizational skills are horrendous, too. She tried implementing colorful Post-Its to help decipher one file from another. Let's forget the fact that my office looked like a unicorn took a rainbow-colored dump on my desk, but the God damn Post-Its always fell off or stuck to other folders. Man, that was a shitty week. Also, she's rude on the phone and she never finishes her work. I'm not even one-hundred percent positive she understands the concept of basic alphabetizing.

She's kept her position because of those legs. Damn those legs, nice and slender, curving upward to beautiful calves. And wait until you get to her long, lithe thighs. Holy shit, those thighs. Just enough flesh, and not an inch more. I've spent plenty of time, too much time, fantasizing about holding those thighs open, running my mouth over her skin, sucking on them, biting them, and making her scream my name.

I need to stop.

Those fucking legs cause me more harm than good.

I grab my jotted-down notes and make my way to the extra report Grace was so generous to make for me.

"Mr. Stephens?" Cathy calls out, but I ignore her. Whatever information she's going to give me is wrong, anyway.

After picking up the file from Grace, who continued laughing as I walked away, I race to Alec's office. All eyes are on me as I'm the last to arrive, which, as of late, is my usual status these days.

"Nice of you to join us, GQ," Alec quips, rocking back in his executive chair, arms stretched behind his slicked-back ink-stained hair, with a look of ingrained snobbery.

I don't mind the moniker. In fact, I flash him my pearly whites, wearing it proudly. It's better than his title, "Office Kiss-Ass." He's got his head so far up Tom and George's ass, it permanently stained the tip of his nose brown.

Tom and George laugh at my expense, which is fine too. Let them have some fun in their old age. Both have their nicknames around these halls, but neither are unflattering. They've been partners together for decades and treat each employee with immense decency. Tom Peters is the "Office Sweetheart," and George Bennett is the "Office Gentleman." I'm not sure what is the fucking difference between the two, but apparently there is one.

They share the idea that you can get the most from your employees with "please" and "thank you." Thanking Cathy never worked for me. First, she'd actually need to do something correct for me to thank her, but I digress. Putting a little fear into her bones. Now that got the job done. Well, sometimes. Although other times, I could set her panties on fire and her motivation wouldn't change either way. After overhearing her conversation with a fellow employee about me, she might intentionally be a shitty assistant. She enjoys it when I bark orders at her. It gets her juices flowing. Her words, not mine. Kinky.

Tom and George are old-school with typical assistants—older, seasoned, and most important, competent. Grace is about the shake the grim reaper's hand while George's assistant is a fifty-five-year-old soon-to-be grandma. Their assistants are brilliant, don't get me wrong, but if I need to work late nights with mine, I can't be stuck with someone that has a face for radio or constantly babbles on about their five kids.

Appearances weren't a driving force in other facets of their lives either. Their wives are amazing women, loving and kind to the core. Either could win a Nobel Peace Prize for their charitable work and generous hearts, but time hasn't been as fortunate. Plastic surgery could help reverse the hands of time, smoothing the wrinkles that spread like road maps on their faces, and lift everything that's sagged about five inches too low. But I guess their appearance isn't a priority. Thank God I don't have to sleep with them.

Now me, I personally prefer my assistants to be attractive, fit, and stylish. She is, after all, the face they see before mine. Assistants are a reflection of their boss. A grumpy old hag welcoming prospective business owners to your company isn't a good first impression. And those are crucial. That's where Cathy fits the bill. That's also the only place Cathy fits the bill. She's no Einstein, that's for sure. She's more like that airhead from Mean Girls, Karen. Body like hers, too. Yum.

Tom gives my three-piece suit a once-over. "Someone scheduled a photoshoot today?"

I shrug with minimal effort. "Appearance is everything. Take a page out of my book, you might learn something."

"We can exchange chapters," Tom counters. "I call mine, 'Get a Better Assistant'." Tom fills the partners in about how Grace saved my ass. Again. "Perhaps the nail polish fumes make Cathy light-headed."

He might be onto something. The color is different damn near every day. I have no clever comeback, so I take my lumps like a man.

I try imagining Grace sitting outside my office. Work-wise, she'd be phenomenal, but her personality is patchy, at best. And I sure as shit couldn't stand the sight of those cankles in orthopedic shoes all day. And her perfume. Ugh. It reminds me of my grandmother's gatherings. I hated those parties, forced to perform for hours, only to be rewarded with wrapped and the occasional unwrapped pocketbook candies. She'd invite all her ancient friends over and the mixture of permed hair, moth balls, mint candies, and that horrendous heavy floral perfume would stick on me until I showered that night. And my poor cheeks. I'll never understand why old ladies love pinching cheeks.

We aren't stuck in Alec's office long, deciding unanimously on a future endeavor in record time. And for once, I'm early for a conference call Cathy shouldn't have scheduled to begin with. If our meeting ran its usual time, I would have missed this important call. And being reminded of that fact makes Cathy my least favorite person today, no matter how far she pushes her tits to her face.

The rest of my day is hiccup-free, but every time I glance at my upcoming calendar, my stress level goes off the charts; I need a stiff drink to release some steam, even after last night's festivities with Candice. But she won't get a call from me. Candice's disobedience left a bitter taste in my mouth, so she's coming out of rotation temporarily.

I undo the top button of my shirt and loosen my tie, ready to relax and stop dwelling over the gnawing pecking in the back of my mind. I'm aware of what I need to do, and I can't avoid it any longer. But maybe Cathy will surprise me tomorrow, and somehow learn Excel overnight.

Pushing that miracle to the back burner for now, the only remedy for easing my stress right now, is one of my favorite girls, Natasha. I scroll through my extensive catalog of numbers and dial. She answers on the first ring as if waiting. I tell her where to meet me, grab my things, and head to our spot when she obliges. Of course, she obliges.

When she walks through the posh bar doors, the sparkle in her cocoa-brown eyes tells me she's as frisky as I am. The seductive way she licks her lips didn't hurt either. Her short, painted-on skirt leaves nothing to the imagination, and that low-cut black silk top with her stiff nipples perked to perfection makes my strongest muscle grow. She's round in all the right places and flat in all the others. In an instant, stress from work is a distant worry, replaced with images of Natasha's naked body riding mine. And soon, I'll make it my reality.

CHAPTER TWO

PER USUAL, I'M running late for my lunch meeting. Cathy filled another day with the impossible. A conference call at 12:30 p.m. and a business lunch two towns over at 1:00 p.m. during the height of lunch traffic. I'm convinced she's got a personal vendetta against me.

I don't ask her to perform brain surgery and organizing my time isn't rocket science, just a basic office skill. Sure, I have my quirks, but Cathy has had enough time to figure it out by now. She can't even collate copies, for Christ's sake. I didn't get my position from being lax and easy-going. They offered me a partner position when I was thirty-five because I made things happen and make no apologies for how I do it. I need an assistant who can follow through with my basic requirements.

This is the fourth meeting I've been late to this month, which is unacceptable. I'm used to brushing off the partner's jokes with ease, but it's getting too repetitive. No matter how well Natasha eased my stress and helped me forget about all my work bullshit last night, this growing tension is back again, embedding itself in my neck and shoulders. I'm done. When I return from lunch, I'm calling my girl in HR and putting an end to this nonsense.

"Traffic is a nightmare right now." I settle into my seat while the partners glance over the menu. By Alec's overzealous laughter, they must be on their second drink.

Alec fake coughs. "Bullshit." He laughs again, a hyena-like snort that was too loud to be dignified, as if he's told the greatest joke in anyone's lifetime.

The others laugh too, except for Tom. I don't blame him, he's tired of my lame excuses. I lean back, frustrated and exhausted. "It's time I request a new assistant."

With his glasses perched at the tip of his bulbous nose, his strained eyes peruse the menu. Tom says, "Isn't that the seventh one you've run through this year? It's like a revolving door with you."

"I'll take Grace off your hands." I wink. "And I'll never be unprepared again."

"Jesus, Jordan," Tom scoffs, but not in a directed-at-me sort of way. "I guess Cathy never gave you that memo either." He pinches the bridge of his nose. "She is the worst, huh? Grace gave her notice. She's retiring soon."

My eyes fall to my lap. Nope. Never got that memo.

"I'll be hunting for some fresh blood myself." Tom snaps the menu closed, removes his glasses, and places them in the inside pocket of his suit jacket. "You go for the wrong qualities, that's your problem."

He has a point. Whenever I ask for an assistant, Melissa, our HR rep, knows what I like without me having to say the words. Thank goodness, too, because it breaks many rules. Being sexist, biased, and discriminatory are just to name a few. I pride myself on being surrounded by good-looking women. Now I just need my attractive assistant's work ethic to match mine, and I'll be golden.

"Perhaps you're the reason Cathy can't stay focused," Alec interjects. He sips on his bourbon and smooths down his tie. "Stop coming in like a Playgirl centerfold and she might get work done."

I'm not running around shirtless, although I'm sure they'd enjoy it if I did; my body is like Adonis.

"Jealous, Alec?"

"Once you get married, all of that flashy dressing goes out of the window," George chimes in for the first time, sipping on his usual cocktail—gin and tonic. "You'll end up with kids, a huge mortgage, and a nagging wife. The kids will get older and their crap costs a third of your salary. Fatherhood is exhausting; you won't give a rat's ass about your clothes. If you take just one piss without someone busting the door down, it'll be the highlight of your day. Prepare for that now."

Um, no. I sip on my usual—whiskey on the rocks—as Tom and Matt laugh in unison. He's not wrong about his clothing statement. George is still wearing suits he wore in the '70s.

"And that's why I'm never getting married or having kids." I toast to myself.

"Famous last words," Matt adds.

Matt Dean got hitched two years ago after vowing he'd never. He met his wife at the grocery store of all cliché places and claimed his future was in her eyes. Alec and I figured she roofied him because he loved the bachelor's life; it treated him well. Next thing we know, he's parading her around the office while she flashes an engagement ring. I'll never forget meeting her. I swore we fucked a few years prior. One pretty face blends into another, but once she opened her mouth, it was clear we never met. Imagine fucking a woman with Minnie Mouse's voice. That high-pitched voice would be memorable for all the wrong reasons.

The brown liquor burns as it trickles down my throat. Any apprehension about canning Cathy slips into oblivion. The possibility of getting an assistant that could make my job easier is a wonderful concept.

The rest of the lunch is business as usual—celebratory drinks for a successful quarter and discussing a future prospect Matt stumbled upon. Once they talk about families, I drift off into my world, ticking off all the tasks I need to complete at the office until I get everyone back on track and discuss the reason we are celebrating. There's nothing better than seeing the fruits of our labor pump an obscene number of digits in our bank accounts.

On my drive back, I call HR. Once Melissa hears my voice, she senses what I need.

"I'm trying something different. You pick this time; according to Tom, my judgment is horrible."

"It is," Melissa agrees with a definitive tone. "This will be fun."

I imagine her rubbing her hands together with a sadistic grin.

"Can I pick a man?" She jokes; at least, I hope she's joking.

I need someone I can build a rapport with, like the one Melissa and I share. She's easy to talk to and doesn't get flustered when I hover around her desk. Too bad she can't work for me; she's got the nicest rack on the twenty-ninth floor.

Every assistant I've had clams up once I'm within three feet. One girl forgot her name and hell if I can remember it either. She lasted five hours before running out, crying. My sex appeal is intimidating, I know, but c'mon already, this isn't high school. Get your shit together, ladies.

"I work better with women."

"I'd argue the opposite, but okay, Jordan." Melissa pauses for a moment. "I expected this, so I created a list of potential assistants for you. There's this girl in payroll. I already gave Charlie the heads up I might transfer her. Plus, her resume shows she's got more experience in a secretary role, so her true assets are not being utilized to their fullest potential, anyway."

Assets. My mind goes rogue. Big tits? Firm ass? Stilts as legs? I stop myself before I moan out loud.

"When do you need her to start?" Melissa asks.

"Monday morning."

A breathy sigh echoes in my car speakers. "If I don't call you by end of the day, then expect her Monday morning. If not, I'll need more time to make the arrangements. You're breaking many hearts, Jordan. It will devastate Charlie. He's losing his star employee, not to mention Cathy's poor little heart. She's been eyeing that position for three years."

I chuckle. "Then she should have done a better job. It won't be the last heart, I'm sure," I say with my cockiest tone. "But I'll try to stay positive and trust your judgment," I add, before disconnecting.

Work keeps me busy for the rest of the afternoon, and the load helps me to avoid Cathy. I'm not a total asshole, but my heart doesn't bleed for her either. She should thank me. Whatever department they shuffle her off to, she keeps her current salary. Cathy might become the highest-paid mail clerk in the history of all mail clerks.

I glance at my calendar, thankful I've made the request. Cathy scheduled my weekend like shit—making dinner plans with my parents on Sunday and arranging late-night drinks with a girl named Tracey I started seeing. Cathy is aware the partners always meet first thing Monday morning to discuss any weekend business rumblings. I punch in Melissa's extension and confirm she's squared away all the details. Hell, even if Mel hasn't been able to swing the request right away, having no one is better than this one. But once she confirms we are all set, I hang up, relieved.

"Cathy," I call like a scolding father. "Come in here."

She strolls into the office. Her navy skirt is short today as if to bribe me with thighs. She's paired it with a cream cashmere cardigan with pearl buttons and a matching necklace that hugs her throat. Cathy combines two of my favorite things—the innocence of that sweater combined with the daring length of that skirt, a perfect mix of naughty and nice. Her hair and makeup are flawless as her lips spread from lobe to lobe. But once I speak, that expression will fall.

"Today is your last day with me. HR will inform you of where you're being transferred. We're not a suitable match. Enjoy your weekend." I leave no room for interruptions or rebuttals, and then dismiss her just as fast.

And here comes the face. It doesn't matter who the assistant is, the expression stays the same. First, their head tilts down, eyes turn to slits while they fight off the oncoming tears. Then their lower lip pouts, chin wobbles, and their shoulders hunch. They're like kicked puppies. She walks out with her head towards the ground.

I can't cancel on my parents, so I pick up the phone and let Tracy down for the third time in two weeks. Her attitude spoke volumes, but I don't shed a tear; she's a dime a dozen.

When I leave my office ready to start my weekend, Cathy's work buddy consoles her while she packs her seventeen bottles of hand lotion into a Xerox box. Her friend watches as I slide into my suit jacket, offering a shy smile. Her cheeks redden when I return the gesture.

People lean on their horns, and by people, I mean me, as cars sit bumper to bumper like a herded line of cattle heading to the slaughterhouse. Or in my case, work. Some jerk-off hit a pedestrian, causing major traffic delays, but I arrive in the nick of time for my Monday meeting.

I hustle to the boardroom, showing my face, before fetching my things from my office.

"Morning." I pop my head in. Matt hasn't arrived either. The other partners nod and continue their chatter. When my eyes fall to my seat at the large Conference Room table, a folder waits for me.

Tom follows my gaze, wearing a pleased grin. "It was here before I walked in."

I thumb through the paperwork. All the information I need, a leather notepad, and a brand-new pen await me. Melissa sent me an angel. We all sit and wait for Matt, who scurries in fifteen minutes late. Better him than me.

"An accident backed traffic up for miles on Dillon Drive. Who hits an elderly man in a bright yellow neon vest directing traffic? And who's dumb idea was it to start construction on damn near every side street on the same day? Ugh." Matt shakes his head and sets his things on the table. "Should've listened to my wife and hopped on the parkway."

"Mother's always right," quips Alec while Matt clicks his teeth.

Tom passes us a list of companies we need to keep a close eye on, updating us on research he's done for new prospects, and keeping us abreast on the progress of previous take-overs. Once we settle the business aspect of the meeting, we bullshit for a few before Grace peeks her head into the conference room, ushering Tom out for more pressing matters. One by one, we follow suit.

Eager to meet whoever Melissa paired me with, I rush to my office, eager to hand out my first 'thank you' in months. It might even be a first for this year.

The desk outside my office is bare. Gone are the tchotchkes Cathy cluttered her workspace with, and the new assistant pushed the desk back to its original location, no longer visible from my office chair.

She must be here because a blue travel mug sits on the desk and her monitor is on. She's already changed the annoying screensaver of every selfie Cathy ever took back to a scrolling marquee that reads: THE LEVEAU GROUP.

Perhaps she's in the bathroom, reapplying lipstick for her new boss, as most of my past assistants did.

The moment I walk into my office, I'm taken aback. The yellow folders sit on my desk with bright pink Post-Its attached to them, waiting for my attention. Bright tabs of paper peek out of the folders with 'Sign Here' written on each one, along with an amended calendar near my keyboard.

Am I in the twilight zone or on one of those hidden camera shows? Giving no direction, she's done more in two hours than Cathy completed in two weeks. Did Tom loan me Grace as a joke? Does Grace have a hot granddaughter with a similar work ethic employed here that I was unaware of? If so, I hit the jackpot.

My phone rings and it's Melissa, just the person I wanted to speak to.

"Who is this magical being you've graced me with?"

"Isn't she great? She's quiet, keeps to herself, but she's a hard worker. Charlie fought hard to keep her, even offered to wash my car for a year. A year, Jordan," she repeats with an expressive volume. "Don't fuck up. But it's you, so…" She sighs, a groan riddled with knowing frustration. "Charlie will get her back, and my car will still be filthy."

"Real funny, Mel. The meeting lasted all morning, so I haven't met her yet. It should piss me off that she's not at her desk but," I inspect the organized piles, sorted by various levels of urgency. "So far, she's amazing. She might put Grace to shame."

"She can hold her own. You aren't as bad as some of her old bosses. You've heard about Oliver Ingrams, right?"

"Yeah. He's that cutthroat attorney that represents all those shady hedge fund executives. That man has no soul."

"That's the one. She worked for him."

Yikes.

I hang up and get to work, signing and initialing the invoices set for me. Once that's done, I ready myself for a conference call she shifted from an earlier time. I dig into my briefcase and pull my notes out, refreshing my memory about their company and the route we'd take to bring life back to their business. When I glance at my new schedule again, I'm blown away at how she's rearranged Cathy's disastrous one. I'm in love and I don't even know her name.

"Mr. Stephens," a feminine voice speaks over the intercom, delicate with a velvet edge. "Your conference call with Morgan Donaldson is on line two."

Since the desk is back to its original position, all I see of my new assistant is the eggshell-colored fabric of a long-sleeved blouse and nothing more. Dammit.

"Thank you." The words taste foreign on my tongue.

As with many calls like these, it lasts longer than needed, taking up a sizeable chunk of my day. But it's not like my schedule was full. She cleared the bulk of the clutter as if she sensed this client could be needy. I don't mind the odd coddle and reassurance gig as long as the client walks away confident his company is in expert hands. We'll revamp his business, create clever marketing magic, and let him run the company with our new operational strategy. He'll remain the face of the brand, although he'll no longer be the majority holder. The other option is to close the doors and send hundreds of people to the unemployment line. Signing with us is the smart choice. And if he plays his cards right, he could buy back his shares for the right price.

By the time I get off the phone, pinch the skin between my eyes and breathe, she's not at her desk again. She's a phantom. I dial HR.

"Melissa, I'm certain you gave me a ghost. All of this work is getting done, but I've yet to meet her."

"And you're complaining because?"

"I mean, she's here, but we haven't met, yet." I peek my head outside my office door and the chair is empty. Again. "I keep missing her."

She huffs into the phone, but I sense her grin. "I have work to do, Jordan." She ends the call right as I get an email from an old colleague, Payton Lane with an enticing subject line.

My skin prickles as an energetic hum of excitement vibrates my insides. I close my door as if under some covert operation, put my phone on Do Not Disturb, and research the company he's provided. The printer spits out page after page as I collect everything I find online about the suffering business. Just from my initial impression of the company, the first department I would fire is clear. Who puts a fat cartoon pig smoking a cigar as a logo for a company that specializes in vegan-friendly packaged goods? I'm missing the irony. If Payton's lead is solid, I'll award him a sizeable finder's fee. Too bad he's turned down every consulting job I offered him. He would be an asset to the company, and not to mention my pockets.

I've paid good money for people to keep their eyes open for struggling companies. With everyone going vegan, this one could be promising, but I'll need to investigate further before bringing it to the table.

My research consumed the entire afternoon and by the time I glance at the clock, everyone dispersed for the day, including my assistant. She didn't even say goodnight. That's rude.

When Cathy sat at this desk, her space was a disaster. Papers scattered, folders clung onto the edge of the desk, twenty bottles of different scented Bath & Body Works lotions sat in one corner while paperclips, a million paperclips, were strewn all over. But not anymore; this mysterious girl keeps a tidy space. I thumb through the stack of reports sitting in the right corner, all in order by the day of the week I'll need them. Each file has a basic company profile stapled to the front, saving me from having to flip through all the pages. She taped a more detailed sheet on the inside.

Jordan's Penny

How did she get all this done?

She left behind a few personal treasures. Two pictures sit inside a brushed silver frame. One of a beautiful woman, olive complexion with elbow-length cocoa brown hair flowing as if a swift breeze swept over her. Similar to her hair, her eyes, a brilliant shade of brown sparkles in the picture. She's stunning. My smile grows, getting my first glimpse of her. She looks as good as she sounds, albeit older than I expected, early thirties, but exotic and beautiful. With just a hint of cleavage peeking from her top, I need not see anymore; this girl is my type. The second photo is of an adolescent boy, cute, no older than six or seven, maybe eight, I'm guessing. I'm not well versed with kids. There isn't an immediate family resemblance between the two. Godson, perhaps?

Under the monitor is an engraved brass-footed trinket box, weathered with dents and scratches. It's seen better days. Hammered into the metal is an elephant with detailed scrolling foliage outlining the box. The craftsmanship is precise, and it reminds me of when I traveled to Delhi for a wedding many years ago. At the street market, this old man sang as he hammered away, crafting these trinket boxes by hand, each one unique, beveled with ornate designs and fabric lining the inside. It also reminds me of the gorgeous women I met on that trip, the colorful saris, gold coin belts, and belly dancers. Man, good times.

Curiosity gets the better of me, and I lift the lid. Black velvet cloth lines the inside with a mirror hiding in the cover. An ordinary dirty and worthless penny sits inside. A flap of black ribbon rests along the side, and I tug at it. The compartment lifts, revealing a hidden level. The second tier is almost empty too, with only a tiny scroll of paper tucked inside, begging someone to read it. So, I do. It says, "You are priceless. Don't sell yourself short."

"What the fuck? That's dumb," I mutter to myself.

I put the top compartment back and close the box. A quick pang of guilt hits my chest for invading her privacy, but the guilt doesn't last long, it's gone by the time I return to my desk.

I lean my head back. The buttery leather melts against my body after a day's work. I reflect on my new assistant. Not only did she do an excellent job today, but after seeing her picture, she's sparked my interest even further. Melissa did a superb job. Even though she's still an enigma, she's a puzzle I will solve.

I stare out my window, peering down at the city, and for the first time, I'm eager for what tomorrow brings.

The wail of my phone interrupts my thoughts. Lexi's face comes up on my screen. Now, it's my fault I'm late for our date. I have no assistant to blame this time.

With another glance at my calendar, I put on my suit jacket without worrying about the upcoming morning—free from impending stress. I relax. My new assistant will keep me out of trouble in my business life, leaving me to get into the best kind of trouble in my personal one.

CHAPTER THREE

HAS THE SEX ever been so amazing, your strides are different? Damn. Lexi was, well, what can I say? She's the type that'll let me do whatever, no questions asked. She was the workout I needed. And she left afterward; the best part of all.

I stroll into the building, ready for work. Last night's festivities continue to play in my head, but I need to stop. If I don't, I'll be walking around with my briefcase in front of my pants, hiding my hard-on.

I'm in such a pleasant mood, I let an older, heavy-set woman with AirPods in her ears take the last two spots in the elevator. You're welcome.

"Are you sure, Mr. Stephens?"

I throw a vacant nod, not giving her too much attention, too busy staring at the sultry brunette, Meredith, from our marketing department as I wait for the next elevator to arrive. I'm not surprised some random employee knows who I am. My name is infamous around these halls.

The elevator arrives at my floor, and I walk past the other partner's doors, greeting them with my first chipper morning in months. I make sure I give their assistants some attention, too. A wink here, a sexy smirk there, and a special smile just for Grace.

I'm stopped in my tracks when I set sights on my assistant. She showed no reaction in her expression when there was a sudden jolt in my stride. A noticeable lump forms in my throat. The woman standing near my office is the chunky lady from the elevator.

"Good morning, Mr. Stephens." She extends her hand. "We haven't formally met. I'm Penelope Matthews, your assistant. Let me apologize now for running out immediately after work yesterday before I introduced myself. Plus, you were so busy; I didn't want to disturb you." The sweetness in her voice is as pleasant today as it was yesterday. That upbeat and cheerful disposition will get annoying.

Now that I'm forced to look at her, I'm more confused as to her age. Besides being fat, she dresses as if she's in her forties. Frumpy. Ugh. I'm not used to the lack of care, and I'll be damned if that becomes a thing. On the flip side, if she tried to impress me with skin-tight clothes, my stomach would churn. This won't work.

Penelope is tall for a girl, an inch or two under six-foot with reddish-brown hair that's as straight as a pin, wearing make-up that's caked on.

What the fuck? Does she not own a mirror?

Her bland white shirt is boxy and unflattering, same as her two-sizes-too-big shapeless black slacks. And to top things off, she's wearing flat shoes. I hate flats. Shoe companies make flats for two reasons and two reasons only—ballerinas with amazing bodies, and soccer moms that can't wear sexy heels anymore because their feet spread from carrying. Flats are not for my assistants; I have an image to uphold.

Why couldn't she be the girl in the picture? That's who I expect as my assistant, not the oversized person in front of me.

"Uh, yes," I stutter, shaking her pudgy hand.

Why am I the uncomfortable one here?

She tilts her head with a casual grin and glances at her desk. "I hope how I did things yesterday met your approval. Whoever scheduled your time set you up to fail," she jokes, and her grin grows. A dimple appears.

She's not wrong, though. I've said the same about Cathy.

"I'm fixing it, but in the meantime," she shuffles through a handful of reports. "I pulled older files to see how you preferred them to be organized, ones that appear you organized yourself. Once I'm finished with these files, tell me if they live up to your standards. Word around the office is you're very particular." She sets the papers on her desk and eyes me again. "Can I bring you coffee or tea to start your morning?"

I stare in silence, taking her in. And there's a lot to take in. She bites the inside of her cheek, and that dimple emerges again. Penelope is correct. I prefer things a specific way, and by the looks of her, she's already failed that test. She sweeps her hair to the side, perhaps a nervous tick, although she doesn't appear uneasy.

As I make her wait a beat, her eyes, the oddest color I've seen, peer back. They are golden, as if the sun kissed her irises, flecked with darker brown spots. How do two people create a human with honey-colored eyes? What kind of genetic anomaly is this? In my thirty-seven years of life, this is the first time I've met someone with noticeable freckles in their eyes.

Her amber eyes widen, and she clears her throat, still waiting. Cathy never asked if I wanted coffee or tea. As bossy as I am, I always enjoyed getting my beverages, not only to stretch my legs but also to gather my quota of stares for the day.

"Tea. Not too sweet."

She could use the exercise, so I allow her to be my fetch girl. This will be her first test. If she comes back with anything other than Earl Grey, it'll be another failure. Hopefully, for her, she did her homework; hopefully, for me, she didn't.

As she shuffles off, I remind myself not to watch her walk away or stare at her ass. She won't survive as my assistant. She has thick skin, but not the thick kind she'll need to put up with me. Until I find another replacement, I'll resort to gawking at the other women in the office.

She isn't unattractive as a whole. She might be okay if she lost half her body weight, ditched those hideous clothes, used less makeup, and changed that God-awful shade of hair color. Does she own a mirror? She's got decent skin, fair but not the kind that'll burn and her skin looks clear; although it's hard to tell under the dollops of foundation she spackles on. Her eyes, though, that's her best attribute. The color alone is fascinating, but the shape, a mix of almond and doe-eyed, makes them stand out even more. And that is where the fascination ends.

I settle behind my desk, my computer is already on, email open and awaiting my attention. With only a four-minute head-start, she's accomplished all of that and organized the mess I left last night.

Within moments, she taps the door with two quick knocks and enters. "I overheard you prefer Earl Grey, but the kitchen ran out, so I brought something different." She places the steaming mug in front of me, careful to not spill a drop. "I'll buy a box during my lunch break to hold you over until they restock the kitchen." She stands for a moment as I push the black mug to the side.

I accepted the tea, but more than likely, I'll end up dumping it in my private bathroom. Earl Grey is the only tea I'll ever drink.

"That is all, Ms. Matthews."

"Penelope is fine," she adds before exiting without another word.

I thumb through the folders on the top of the pile, skimming their contents before organizing them myself. Without thinking, I take a sip. The heat masked the initial flavor, but once the mint hit my nose, it was too late to spit out, so I swallow instead. God, I hate mint.

"Hmm." An automatic reflex hums in my throat, and I stare at the mug, bewildered. "What the actual fuck?" I'm not repulsed.

Why am I not repulsed?

All my life I've despised candy canes, mojitos because of the crushed leaves, mint-flavored gum, hell, even toothpaste all because of those damn pocketbook mints. I sip again to make sure. The flavor is subtle, but refreshing, awakening my senses as I continue to sort my work. In no time, the cup is empty, and I'm left wanting more. But I refuse to tell her this tea might be better than my Earl.

I roll my chair to a nearby cabinet and steal a hurried glance at Penelope. She's hard at work with a white AirPod in her ear, just like this morning. She must sense eyes on her because she tilts her head up and gives an awkward yet warmish smile.

Is she listening to music while working? Who the fuck does that? Angry and aggravated, I slam my door closed while she holds my gaze. An unknown shiver tickles my spine and for a moment, I miss Cathy. Imagined that.

I dial Melissa. "About this Penelope…"

"She's great, right?" Melissa's chipper mood radiates through the phone, but my mood doesn't change. "No need to thank me."

"This won't work," I add with simple fact.

"Jordan," she warns, scolding me with my own name. Melissa is the only person I'd allow to talk to me in that tone.

"She isn't fit for the position if you catch my drift."

"I don't. Tell me why."

She knows damn well why, and why I can't say the words aloud. And I really can't say them to someone in Human Resources.

Melissa clears her throat. "Because if you do—"

"Come on, Mel." I make my tone fun yet pleading, hoping our history will win her over and she'll bend my way.

"Our handbook states a thirty-day probationary period unless there's severe misconduct. And I doubt she's done anything warranting termination, Jordan. Give her thirty days and then we'll talk."

I'm not sure where Melissa keeps her enormous set of brass balls, talking to me as if I'm a mere colleague with no power to fire her ass, too, but I concede because I like her. "Thirty days." I slam the phone down.

The chair doesn't make a sound when I sit back, kneading the skin on my neck. Thirty days. Thirty days. I've willingly gone longer without sex. These thirty days might be worse, though. Thirty days would be a breeze if she were the girl from the picture, even if she were dumber than dirt.

"I'm having an adult tantrum," I confess aloud.

A sly grin sets over my lips as I birthed the idea. Melissa underestimates me. I'll give Penelope thirty days, but if she quits before, Melissa will have no choice but to find a replacement. I'll channel my inner Oliver Ingrams and make her life miserable. She didn't survive him. She won't survive me. I won't let her.

CHAPTER FOUR

WEEK AFTER WEEK, I tried my best to make Penelope miserable.

"Come on, Penelope," I'd shout, slamming my fist to the desk, then toss the document in her face. "Remove the God-damn gridlines."

She didn't flinch. She didn't cry. This woman's skin is as thick as a gator. Penelope would return, lines erased, and I'd shove the page back in her face, demanding them added again. I was relentless.

Each time, she'd wear an impervious grin, nod in long, ponderous lines, and prepare the spreadsheet as I commanded without calling me on my bullshit. Not that I expected her to, but a normal human might defend themselves at least once. Penelope wasn't normal. I berated her, and she took each reprimanding like a champ. Maybe she and Cathy had a lot in common. Who knew getting chewed a new asshole was sexy?

Through everything, she never budged, only did as I ordered. I reamed her, berated her for losing a call I dropped on purpose. Nothing. No reaction. I expected her to run to the bathroom in tears, return with red-rimmed eyes and all that caked-on make-up smeared, but no. She stood her ground as if my tone didn't faze her. She must shit diamonds with the amount of pressure I put on her each day.

Penelope is full of determination. Nothing will stop her from finishing her probationary period, I'll give her that. She's impenetrable and immune to me, not to mention borderline indifferent. Could Melissa have suspected my motives and warned her? Maybe that's why she's putting up with my antics. She must sense I'm trying to break her.

Every day she arrives extra early, fires up my computer, sorts through the work, bangs everything out in record speed, all while maintaining a smile. That smile never wavers. Her dimples burrow into her cheeks with each pleasant yet annoying grin. Some days, I want to smash those indents further, but the minute I set my eyes on her 14 karat gems, my anger pauses. They are like kryptonite. That might be the reason I hate her so damn much. Those powerful fucking eyes. And that voice—sweet and silky—grinds on my nerves, mainly because it doesn't match the rest of her. Who smiles while getting chewed out by their supervisor? Sadists, that's who.

Workwise, she's on point, and dare I say… perfect. The partners appreciated the effort put forth, too. Ninety percent was Penelope's doing, while I take one hundred percent of the credit. She's a younger, more efficient version of Grace, even sharing the same frumpy fashion sense. Frightening.

On the positive side, she's the first secretary to take initiative, doing work I didn't ask her to do, and nailing it every time. But I'll be damned if I tell her that.

"Penelope. Office. Now."

Her chair skids outside the door and in moments, she scurries to the front of my desk with a pen and a notepad in hand, ready to jot down whatever I say.

"Sit," I demand.

Why does she dress like a retired flight attendant?

The powder blue button-down blouse and a navy scarf tied at her neck do nothing for her. Or anyone. I'm aware wide-leg is a style of women's pants, but hers are wide everywhere. Too big. But where Penelope's fashion sense lacks, she makes up for it in her work. She creates a sexy ass spreadsheet, color-coded, and arranged in an aesthetically pleasing manner. The sexiest reports I've ever seen. Sexier than Grace's.

She takes a seat in the black chair facing my desk, ankles crossed, left over right, readying her pen. Her dimples are in full swing as she waits for me to speak, tattooing her grin in place.

"May I say something first?" she politely asks.

Her eyes find mine, and my plan turns to shit. Like literal shit. I can't fire my mug across the office like a psychopath, hoping to scare her away when she points those eyes at me, so I give a clipped nod instead.

"I've been working for you for three weeks, doing all you ask, and then some." She straightens in her seat, voice void of inflection, but one wrapped in warmth, a tone she's never spoken in before. She inhales and continues. "I know you're used to someone… more specific. But I do exceptional work. If you need to yell, go ahead, but I'm not quitting."

Well. Fuck.

Penelope shows no fear. Not of me, at least. She must have a set of brass balls dangling inside those humongous pants of hers. She sits in silence with her doe-eyes, carefully watching me with a stare. I have no logical rebuttal, not without appearing insane, but I haven't gotten this far in my career without being quick on my feet.

"You're right, Penelope." I cross my arms in front of my chest and lean back on my executive chair. "For you to remain in your position, I needed to be certain you could handle me. My earlier assistants couldn't handle me at my best, let alone my worst."

I rise from my seat and close my office door. Time to try a new technique. I sit along the edge of my desk, eyeing her from above. My dashing sex appeal and proximity intimidate most women, causing them to stumble over their words, making them uneasy. One slip-up is all I need. Once she lets her guard down, I'll be able to penetrate through that dense skin and tear her down from the inside out. My own Trojan horse.

Those amber eyes stare back, dimple puckering her cheeks, and she says nothing. The sun beams through the glass windows and the light catches her eyes as if harnessing the sun's strength. When my stares become too much, she peers down, girding her pen, taking the sun with her.

Frustrated, I groan. "You're joining me for lunch."

She studies me again, eyes immense, offering a clearer glimpse into the windows of her soul, even though I swear the woman must not have one. She feels nothing. "Uh," she fumbles, and her forehead wrinkles. One dimple digs deeper as she chews the inside of her cheek, one of her few signs of apprehension to date.

I snatch the keys off my desk. "Grab your things. Let's go." There's no time for a debate and I wait by her desk while she shuffles for her handbag, leaving her phone.

"Leaving your cell?"

"What?"

I point to the phone with my chin.

"Um." Her movements are stiff and shaky. "I'm working, so I won't need it."

With her purse slung on the crook of her elbow, I hustle to the elevators to make our way to the garage. She matches my long strides. If she wore four-inch heels, she wouldn't be able to keep up, but because she's got those hideous yet sensible flats on, she's hot on my tail.

Tabitha was the only other assistant I brought to a business lunch. I enjoyed watching her squirm across from me, fidgeting with the cross she wore on a gold chain around her slender neck every day. My Benz impressed her, and I admit, she was impressive getting in and out of it, too.

When we get to my car, she gets in without complimenting my ride. Most women are impressed by the custom interior, but Penelope isn't most women. She gets off on being indifferent toward me. I hate that about her. I hate a lot of things about her.

If I said the drive to my favorite bistro was uncomfortable, that would be a gross understatement, no matter how short the ride was. Three people traveled in my car: Penelope, me, and the stifling silence between us. Every radio station I clicked on had a commercial, and now I have that fucking Kars4Kids song stuck in my head.

We walk to the hostess stand but we don't wait. She seats us at my favorite table on the back deck of the cozy bistro.

The planks of wood above, wrapped in ivy, break up the sunlight in patches, offering us a hearty mix of sun and shade. Being a gentleman, I pull out Penelope's chair while the server's helper fills our glasses with Perrier. In classic Penelope fashion, she doesn't react in the usual way I'm accustomed to. She offers no seductive glance over the shoulder, finding my eyes as I glance down. Penelope thanks me with a quick head nod. That's it. And again, she digs into her purse and pulls out her pen and pad, waiting for me to give her a rundown of tasks to do upon our return to the office.

"Enough with the working, Penelope. Jesus. Try to relax for once. We're at lunch."

She does a casual roll of her eyes, but nothing I could alert HR about as she tosses her supplies into her handbag before glimpsing at the menu. When the waitress comes for our order, I'm not surprised by her choice—salad. Most women don't eat enormous meals around a man; especially when they're with someone that thrives on a healthy lifestyle. She'll most likely pick at it, too, trying to be modest, even though she could eat me out of house and home.

Where Penelope's indifference lacks, the waitress makes up for it, offering a prolonged glittering stare that sent a rush of desire coiling through me. I have no doubt her number will be on the bill later.

Penelope surveys her surroundings, admiring the rustic bistro, so I glance around with her. Vines of ivy cover the distressed brick building where scattered paintings are hung. A crisp, white tablecloth covers each table, a small bouquet of pink flowers with unlit tea-lights surrounding the short vase sits in the center. During the day, this section of the restaurant is comfortable and quaint, but at night, the ambiance draws your breath away. Intertwined in the ivy and beams above are white pixie lights and mason jars filled with softer yet warm lighting. You're transported to a fairy's garden surrounded by fireflies; at least, that's what the ladies I bring here have said.

In the pit of my mind, the nagging churns. As hard as I've tried to crack her surface, she's held strong, fighting back with silence and determination.

"I owe you an apology." I fix my tie and adjust the silverware, finding it difficult to make eye contact.

God, I hate apologizing.

"You're a terrific worker and as tough as nails. I need someone like you in my corner."

Her face, more rounded than the diamond-edge cheekbones I'm used to, softens as if finally relaxing. "Thank you, sir."

I wave a dismissive hand. "You've earned my respect. Call me Jordan."

"Okay."

Penelope gives only what's necessary, as if words cost money, and she's pinching pennies and clipping coupons.

When the food arrives, I'm thankful. The awkward bout of silence became deafening. I tear into my salmon while she meticulously cuts her lettuce into bite-sized pieces. At this rate, she'll end up eating only five dollars of that twenty-dollar meal.

"Tell me about yourself," I order between bites.

She fidgets with her fork, pushing the food around, and discards most of the ingredients to one side of her plate. "Um... what do you want to know?"

I shrug, not sure myself. If Penelope ran this show, she would have an alphabetized list of questions ready on hand. No doubt color-coded by order of importance, too.

She swallows and takes in a bigger breath. "Like the basics?" The confused expression makes me grin, but I dip my head, accepting any ammunition I can use against her later.

"Um... I'm 31. I've worked here for about a year before being transferred. I love music." The end of her sentence goes up an octave as if she asked a question, still unsure of what information I seek.

Well, I was wrong about her age. How is a woman her age able to look both older and younger, all at once? Her fashion sense ages her decades, but she has a young spark behind her golden gaze that drops that age bracket back down.

I recall my sporadic visits to her department. There's no recollection of her whatsoever. "I don't recall seeing you."

She laughs and then apologizes, covering her mouth as she finishes chewing a cucumber. "You wouldn't have."

Now it's my turn to be perplexed.

She sits back in the chair, relaxing into a position, but her shoulders stay high and tense. "I blend into the background."

"I'm sure I would have remembered you," I add, without missing a beat. The lie is as smooth as sin, and it comes naturally.

"Really? That's funny." Penelope's lips form a dry grin. "You used to sit on my desk until Charlie got off the phone. A blue ceramic cup of paper clips sat near the corner," she says, and still, I've got nothing. "Yeah, you didn't notice that either. They spilled everywhere, and my cup shattered into a zillion pieces."

Oh shit. I inhale a quick breath as bits of memory surface. She's right. I always sat on a desk, her desk. There was this intern down there filled with so much saline. Her tits were near her chin. That's where my focus stayed.

Penelope shrugs it off, much like everything else. But that woman's eye contact game is strong, maintaining an unnerving focus on me. Just one stare can pierce through me. Add that to the running list of things I dislike about Penelope Matthews.

Without a question or prompt, she says, "Melissa warned me about you, but I've dealt with worse."

So, I was right. Melissa figured out my plan. I laugh. Penelope hadn't seen me at my true worst. Sure, I've tried to break her in these past few weeks, but me pretending to be mad is far different from the actual thing. Wait until I tell her she'll be stuck doing a research project with me, cooped up in the Conference Room late at night. Research projects always stress me out and I take it out on whoever is nearby. She'll be begging for a transfer.

"What'd she say?"

Penelope sets her fork down and watches me for a breath before answering. "You have a bad reputation. I don't consider you difficult, but I suspect many of your previous assistants lacked focus while others were under-qualified." She sits forward in her chair and leans in toward me as if to whisper. "Your last assistant, Cathy, might have been dyslexic."

No matter how hard I try, I don't stifle my laugh.

"I'm serious," she adds. "I used to tutor dyslexic kids."

Fuck.

Now I feel lousy. She lifts her fork again, moves the hard-boiled egg to the side. Her face remains unchanged. I yelled at Cathy a lot for filing stuff incorrectly, entering information wrong, and screwing up phone numbers.

Slowly, the corners of Penelope's mouth turn up, and a smile blooms.

"I'm joking. Well, not the tutor part, but Cathy lacked experience. Her search history was full of How-To's."

Relief fills my chest, and I crack a smile. She had me for a moment. "So why did everyone else lack focus, and why are you so different?"

I'm aware of the answer, but I will relish her stumbling response.

Without flinching, she says, "Pretty women don't need thick skin. People fawn over them, and they are used to getting treated kindly. Then real-life smacks them in the face, and they don't handle it well." When my dissatisfied expression forms, she knows she didn't fully answer the question. Penelope lets out a frustrated breath, and her cheeks turn rosy. Answers are coming. "If you need me to feed your ego, I'll do what you ask, but I won't be like the others; you're my boss and I know my lane, so I stay in the lines. My focus lies in one place—work."

"Go ahead," I beckon. "Feed my ego."

Her head shakes from side to side as it falls toward her lap. Her auburn hair hides her face like a curtain. When she lifts it again, she stares me straight in my eyes and says, "Your looks distract people, and you enjoy that fact."

I lean back and keep our eye contact until she fiddles with her fork again.

Besides the partners, Grace, and Melissa, no one has been this blunt before. I asked her to be, but I never expected her to do it. Or to be able to do it. I might like this. Penelope can feed my ego on command and do excellent work. Any way I slice it, I win.

"You're one of the few assistants that can form complete—," I pause for a moment and rephrase my wording. "You're the only assistant I've had that can form a complete sentence around me." I pick up an asparagus spear and bite the steamed stem. "Charlie isn't having you back," I decide aloud, although silently, I'm still weighing my options.

A slight chuckle escapes her lips, and in its wake is a lovely smile. Her full, dented cheeks blush again. While my stomach digests, my brain needs to consume more information, hopefully incriminating information, about Penelope so I can get rid of her after her thirty days are completed without Melissa giving me hell for it. Maybe I'll give her forty days just to prove a point.

"So, do you have a boyfriend? Girlfriend?"

She eats at a sloth's pace, discarding the onions and egg to the side, cutting her cucumbers in quarters, and does the same to the cherry tomatoes. Penelope doesn't slather the dressing over her salad either, she's a dunker, using a little with each bite. She must drown her food in ranch dressing and gorges in the comfort of her own home.

"Yes."

Unsure as to which part of the question she's answering, I try a different approach.

"Serious or new?"

She doesn't appear bothered by the inquiry, still focused on her plate. "We've been together for a while, since high school."

"Well, I hope your significant other won't mind you spending late nights in the office with me, tons of overtime. We'll be commandeering the Conference Room, basically living in there."

In the few weeks she's been my assistant, Penelope has kept her composure. But one mention of late nights and she flusters instantly. She fidgets with her fingers, eyes wide, and appears apprehensive. Even though she said she doesn't get distracted by me, something is distracting her now. I can't have an assistant be unavailable when I need them the most. This may be a real window of opportunity for me.

"It... that shouldn't be a problem."

The waitress brings my digestif, along with one for Penelope. As I raise my glass, she eyes hers, still sitting on the table.

"What is that?" she asks, pointing to the glass with her chin.

Sensing her apprehension, I reassure her. "I promise, it's not a trap. You're allowed to have a drink if we're having a business lunch. You don't have to finish the whole thing if you're not comfortable."

She lifts her shoulders with indifference, but I egg her on to try it.

Why do I care if she tries it or not?

I urge her. "You might love it."

She raises the glass to her nose, inhaling the cherry-fused brandy before taking the tiniest of sips, and instantly, her nose scrunches. Her tongue grazes over her lips and Penelope bobs her head with moderate approval. "It is sweeter than I thought, but that's some strong stuff," she declares.

Penelope introduced me to her mint tea, and now I introduced her to something new. We may complement each other after all.

As we leave the bistro, my mission to get any information, incriminating or otherwise, about Penelope was a bust. I didn't even chip the surface, let alone crack it. Perhaps when we work late, side by side, she'll divulge things, whether she's aware of it or not. I'm eager to discover something of value. Secret drug addiction, perhaps? Maybe she'll get comfortable around me and say something out of line or inappropriate that I can use as my reason to send her packing. But I hate to admit it. Right now, I enjoy Penelope's ability to hold a conversation, although minor.

And how sad is that?

The ride to the office was less awkward than before. Penelope settles back at her desk, thanks me for lunch, and pops in her AirPods. I've allowed no assistants to listen to music, I distracted them enough; they didn't need another excuse as to why they pumped out shitty work. But Penelope bangs out one flawless spreadsheet or report after another as if the music drives her. I don't understand how she creates the spreadsheets as fast as she does. Her fingers enter information at lightning speed. She makes it seem easy.

My curiosity is getting the better of me. What does she listen to? Whenever I peek out of my office, she's bobbing her head, mouthing lyrics, tapping her sensible flats on the floor as her pen dances in her hand. I caught her humming once, too. Her cheeks burned as if she sat in the sun too long; on the rare occasion she became embarrassed. Other than a handful of times, she's done little for my self-esteem, though. Her indifference towards me is aggravating, to say the least. If left to her, my ego would die of starvation. Add that to the list.

CHAPTER FIVE

PENELOPE AND I started working on my research project. We park ourselves at the Conference Room table surrounded by boxes of files sent to us by Oakfeld. Reams of paper for printing, a pile of pens, highlighters, and neon Post-Its sit in the center of the long, oblong table.

As Penelope tries to organize our work, she tapes various documents on the glass walls for easy viewing and starts a checklist on the dry erase board. The more I help organize, the more chaos I create. So, I do what I do well—spit orders, stare at my laptop, and investigate some ideas further. My notepad has the insane ramblings of a madman as I haphazardly jot ideas on new sheets of paper.

Most of the information we need is sitting somewhere in this room, shoved into mislabeled folders in mismatched boxes. This is one reason their business is failing. Organizational skills were not their strong suit. Penelope has a ton of work ahead of her before I can figure out a game plan that'll resurrect this dying business and create a mind-blowing presentation that'll convince the partners to invest the money and energy. Since she's the ninja master at organizing, I leave that to her. She asks random questions here and there, but never the same one twice. For once, I don't have to micro-manage anyone or repeat myself.

Within only a few hours, Penelope's headway sifting through the mess is impressive. And I've skimmed my fair share of documents, too.

There's no question why this company is barely treading water. If we don't rescue Oakfeld soon, the company will drown beyond resuscitation. Penelope sits with her legs crossed as she sorts through another box. She licks her chubby finger and flips pages, putting them in various piles in front of her with her head bobbing to whatever music is bumping in one ear.

"Having fun yet?" I ask.

"So much fun," she deadpans with a sturdy, stoic tone. "When I finish sorting and organizing, I'll summarize the info into the computer."

"I can help."

She giggles, but all laughter drops when she sees my reaction. "You're a paragon of helpfulness. Sorry, but I've seen your spreadsheets," she jabs with what appears to be a saucy smile.

I'd have hurt feelings if what she said wasn't so true. Using Excel is like second nature to her, so why waste my true talents doing tasks for people beneath me. "I'll just sit here, stay handsome, and brainstorm my approach."

"You do that." She licks her finger again and thumbs through more pages, placing the last paper in a short stack.

I'll take her response as a subtle compliment to feed my emaciated ego.

I continue my tasks while Penelope finishes organizing. She's a well-oiled machine, sifting through each file with precision. We're only one day in and already, this experience is nothing like previous projects. I'm not babysitting anyone. I have confidence Penelope is doing what's needed and will continue to be an asset.

After my extensive Google search on similar businesses, I keep coming across the same information, exhausting my efforts.

"Give me one," I demand, summoning a stack of my own. My eyes need a break from staring at the computer.

She pushes a pile across the table. "That's their marketing records. I'm arranging each by year. I'll issue color codes when we're done for easy reference."

Jesus, she's thorough. While I copy her style, I speculate what this would have been like with Cathy. More than likely, I'd toss myself out the thirty-story window.

One by one, Penelope sorts through the piles, scoots her chair on the carpet, moving down the length of the table, repeating the same process with each pile until she's finished. I'm still sorting and reading the small stack she gave me.

"You almost done?" she asks.

I stumble upon an invoice for an advertisement package purchased by Oakfeld. I'm dumbfounded. It's one thing to advertise on a billboard, but to buy the space, not rent, simply because it gave them a two percent deduction off the cost. Who does that? Two percent?

"Let me ask you a question." I raise my face to hers and she's already focused on me with her pleasant resting face—the corners of her mouth naturally turned up, eyes big and curious. "Would you pay for a billboard near an old-age home?"

"If I sold life alerts, probably," she answers. Her eyes fall to the document she holds in her grasp. "But not organic, vegan-friendly products. Elderly folks aren't about to change their eating habits." She tilts her head to the ceiling. "The only reason I can come up with is they were hoping to catch the eyes of the children and grandchildren visiting their loved ones. You know, Millennials, Gen Z, Gen X, whatever they refer to themselves as. But even that's a stretch."

Color me impressed. I didn't even consider that aspect of it. She makes a brilliant point, but there's a downside to that too. "And how often do kids check in on their elderly loved one?" I ask.

She makes a hybrid sound—a mixture of a laugh and a snort. "They're targeting the wrong audience. And what's with the pig mascot?"

I laugh so hard my shoulders shake. "If we take over this company, I'm slaughtering that pig."

"They should play on their name, use a silhouette of an oak tree or leaf, something along those lines."

I don't hide my elated expression. Her pros might outnumber her cons now. If I said Penelope Matthew is thorough, that would be an understatement. Box after box, she's organized years of documents in a matter of a few hours. But she doesn't stop there. She's already started plugging the information into the computer and printing out detailed spreadsheets. I'm a little turned on.

For someone stuck in payroll for a year, I'm unsure how she's figured out this position. While she's hard at work on the laptop, I grab a dry erase marker and start a pros and cons list. We both agree on where the pig stands.

I pinch the bridge of my nose after reading up on their numerous failed re-branding attempts. Did they hire Cathy's sister to lead their advertising department? Tension builds in my brain as I flip page after a boring, white page. I glance in her direction, watching her bob her head to some unknown song while entering information a mile a minute on the keyboard and flipping over the corresponding paper. She's in her own world, oblivious that I'm in the room. I don't enjoy this feeling.

I crumple a piece of paper and toss it. Since she's paying absolutely no attention to me, she doesn't see the ball of paper flying toward her and it bounces right off her head. Startled, she jumps in her chair, and I almost fall out of mine, laughing.

She rips the headphone from her ear, less than pleased, but within a few moments, her mouth softens, and her dimples reappear. "I'm almost done with 2005."

I stand, stretching my arms, legs, neck, and back. My entire body cracks and pops. She finishes up with one less earbud in her ear as I walk to her side.

"What are you listening to?"

She watches as I grab the unused earpiece and hold the white pod close to my ear. Her shampoo aroma still lingers even though it's late in the day—mint or eucalyptus, or both.

"That's rude."

"Don't act like you're surprised," I respond with indifference. She's listening to some Electronica or EDM crap. "This is what you listen to all day?" I rid my eardrums of the noise, returning the shitty music to her, plant my ass on the table, and soak in the intriguing Penelope Matthews.

"No. I enjoy a variety of things."

Melissa warned me Penelope kept to herself, but Mel never mentioned getting information from her would be harder than pulling teeth.

Why do I want her to talk?

I hated when Cathy babbled. Most of it was incoherent as she stuttered through her words. But why is Penelope different? Do I miss a flustered and uncomfortable assistant?

I stare at her, eyes wide with wait, willing her with my mind to supply me with some resemblance of information. When she provides nothing, I ask. "Such as?"

She sinks back in the chair, a move she makes before she's about to share information, but right before that, I got a quick glimpse down her shirt. I regret nothing. Without the support of a damn good bra, those tits must sag really low.

"Take movies, for example. When a big action sequence happens, the scene demands loud, fast-paced, or thunderous music—quick drumming—something attention-grabbing. When there's a love scene, they play more sensual music. I'm no different. I listen to music that fits the energy I have or need. If I have to bang out a ton of your obnoxious reports, I play upbeat songs to help motivate me to work faster."

Without a beat, I smile. "Obnoxious reports?"

She shrugs and takes a sip from her travel mug.

"Refill? I need something to wake me up."

"I don't drink coffee," she blurts as I grab her travel cup. When she sees my expression, she adds, "Blueberry juice."

Information comes from her in dribs and drabs, but I like when she knows her answers don't satisfy me, adding a little more detail until I am.

I set the blue travel cup back in front of her. "And you use an insulated travel mug with a giant coffee bean on it because?"

"Keeps my drink cold, for starters, but like you," she eyes me with a peculiar stare, "I go to the kitchen for office gossip." As if she doesn't think I will inquire further, she picks up a folder, thumbs through the contents, and types on the laptop.

I twist my waist; the tension is tight. A loud pop freezes us both. Damn, that felt good. "Anything juicy besides that blueberry juice?"

Most of the office gossip is only tantalizing when I'm involved. Alec likes to believe he's the center of the best gossip, but he's a fool. The only time anyone speaks his name is when they are poking fun at his cologne. Consensus says his cologne should replace smelling salts. He's not an ugly guy, but he's a little too cocky for someone that doesn't pull in as many ladies as I do.

"Some ladies can't stand that I've lasted longer than a day. They prayed you would have transferred my first day. Is there, like a waiting list of women who sign up to be your assistant or something?"

If I could've transferred her that day, I would've, but the latter part of her comment sends me laughing.

She shrugs again. "People are funny sometimes. They talk about me like I'm not in the room, but hello, with my size, I'm noticeable; still, no one watches what they say around me even if it's about me."

I feign shock when she alludes to her breadth. Sure, I took a quick note of her weight the minute I lay eyes on her, but I'm a superficial bastard.

No one expects anything different from me. While much of today's society judges people based on outer appearance, most don't judge by appearance alone, except for me. I do.

"That's rude," I utter with mock disgust. Her shoulders rise in one lazy gesture. "No, I mean, you shouldn't say that about yourself."

"Says the oblivious man who sat on my desk on more occasions than I have fingers." Her brows arch. She's become impervious to my stares, and I hate that about her. "I've been like this damn near my entire life. I'm not blind and I'm aware of what people see." Not a millimeter of anger coats her voice, and she doesn't appear hurt or offended, just says it with acceptance. Her golden gaze narrows in as if trying to pierce my soul. "Has anybody ever told you about yourself?"

"Like told me off? Pffft, many times. Just this past weekend this lady demanded I go f—"

"No, not like that," she groans, rolling her eyes back. "Has a stranger made a rude comment based on your looks?" Her invasive eyes make me nervous and uncomfortable, but I can't figure out why. "No?" she answers for me when I don't respond.

Now I shrug with lazy satisfaction.

"No, I guess they wouldn't have much to insult, huh?" Her indirect compliment was an amuse-bouche, but it satiates my ego's hunger. "For me, it happens all the time. I didn't get this thick skin overnight. I know my lane and I stay in it."

That's the second instance she's repeated that statement. The first time she said it, I assumed she was referring to a boss/assistant relationship, keeping things professional. Which with her, I'm more than satisfied with. But she didn't mean it that way at all. I'm more curious now than ever to see who is in "her lane."

"Well, if I hear anything about you, I will rectify it."

Her eyes dance behind her lids again, as if my kind gesture would be futile.

I walk into the kitchen and prepare a mug of tea—my usual Earl. When I return to the Conference Room, she's back to bobbing to her tunes, ignoring me. I compel myself to finish my drink even though it's not as satisfying as the peppermint tea she offered me on her second day. When her crap music stops enchanting her, I must ask her to buy me some for the office.

I sneak a peek at my watch, understanding why my eyes burn and why my body aches. Penelope and I covered more than enough groundwork on our first night. If we maintain this momentum, I don't see why we couldn't finish by the end of the week. Under different circumstances, a project of this size would last a good two or three, maybe even four weeks.

I release an audible moan and it gets her attention. "Let's go home. My brain hurts."

She gathers her things like the building is on fire while I lean back on the chair, eyes closed. Even though my head throbs, it's not from stress because I have no doubts Penelope will help make this project a breeze to get through. I open my lids just as she approaches my side, setting a tea bag on the table and a packet of Tylenol.

"Use honey, not sugar."

As she exits, I sniff the peppermint bag, and somehow, the tension fades a bit. This woman might be alright.

CHAPTER SIX

USINESS MEN CROWD the restaurant, all donning designer suits, expensive watches, and cufflinks just as pricey. There are enough business cards in here to gift wrap a Suburban. Random office chatter, snobbish laughs, and egos fill the room as we feast on the over-priced but well-deserved meals and booze.

Empty plates and wine glasses clutter our table. Not a single scrap of food remains on anyone's plate, and it shows. Tom loosens his tie and undoes his top button. Matt methodically rubs his belly, releasing deep exhales. While I blot my mouth, finishing my last bite, Alec wipes his glistening brow.

"Meat sweats?" I ask, and they nod in unison. I eye my dish, thankful I opted to dine on a healthy salad instead of the heavy rib-eye special.

While they digest, I let them feast on the positive news—the amazing progress Penelope and I have made in the few short days working in the Conference Room.

Alec rests his sights on me. "Let me take Penelope for a spin. I found this awesome start-up project in need of investors, but I need to do a thorough background check on the creators. If she's as good as you claim, I'll work Penelope for a day or two."

"Fuck off." A long sigh escapes my mouth, and the rest of the partners narrow their eyes toward me. "What? She's not a fucking car. Last week, you bragged your assistant asked you to grab a drink after work. She's more than willing to hang out after hours, just put the work in front of her and make her do it."

Tom shakes his head. "I'm astonished that you two haven't been subject to any harassment suits." He turns to Alec. "What's the investment?"

"Picture This," he boasts and says nothing more.

We wait with little patience for him to finish the sentence. When he remains silent, only staring at us with his big bug eyes and mouth open, I mutter, "Picture what?"

"That's the name," he adds. "A selfie stick for dogs. Imagine your little pooch snapping photos of himself. Twitter and Instagram servers would explode."

Tom releases a low moan while Matt sits at attention.

"Research further and see if this concept is worth bringing to the table. The idea is marketable. I can't imagine they will need a tremendous investment now, but once things take off, the demand will force them to expand production. That's the best time to dig our claws in," Tom advises.

Tom has always been a ruthless businessman; although, you'd never tell by his grandfather-esq appearance. He's like everyone's grandfather—white hair rims the sides of his head, aged skin, bulbous nose, and ears too big for his face, but oddly enough he's got a gentle pair of eyes. Sometimes. With business and money, those gentle eyes turn soul-less and bring grown men to tears. I've witnessed him tear down the strongest of men.

Over the years, Tom settled into a less abrasive approach, putting his yelling days behind him. He handed that torch to Alec and me. But sometimes he's louder when he's quiet than when he yells.

"Exactly." Alec grins, flashing his silver tooth. "But researching would be easier with efficient help," he eyes me, but he's not prepared to test my resolve. Not today. "So, Penelope," he starts again with a wider, snobbish grin. "The office halls are still buzzing. She's not your typical eye candy." He eyes at each of us. "You surprised everyone when you didn't send her wide ass back to Charlie."

George pinches the bridge of his nose as he bows his head, shaking with disapproval.

"I lost fifty dollars," Matt admits.

"I won fifty." Tom lifts his head back up, flashing a guilty grin.

Astonished, I scan each of them and laugh.

"Unless your tastes are boundless." Alec sips his wine, observing me over his glass.

"Get the fuck out of here." My voice booms, louder than intended, gaining a nearby table's attention. "She is not the eye candy I'm used to, but she whips up a sexy ass file."

"Imagine that ass in a miniskirt?" Alec retches.

We all laugh at her expense, except for Tom. In an instant, guilt hits my middle, and I take a hefty swig from my glass. After our conversation last night, I failed the moment I entertained this conversation.

Why do I care?

"Pluck a nerve?" Alec questions.

I purse my lips, but then put on my best poker face to use. "Keep that shit up and I'll have Grace prance around in a miniskirt by your desk," I start. My brows dance with excitement. "She's got a soft spot for me. She'll do it."

"Soft spot," Tom repeats, confused. "If by 'soft spot' you mean a palm to the face, then yes, she would love to smack you." Tom chuckles.

George laughs, too. "I'm almost positive she's threatened to do it several times. We're just grateful you're prepared for meetings," he adds. "I don't care who your assistant is, what she wears or looks like. Ms. Matthews is a keeper."

He has never spoken truer words. Penelope isn't my typical assistant; this is a fact. But work-wise, she exceeds all my expectations.

Penelope is nothing like the stereotypical overweight woman. She's the opposite of all those generalizations. She's active, always fetching files or papers for me around the office; lazy isn't in her vocabulary. Sloppy is not a characteristic of hers either. She might organize things too well. Her appearance, on the other hand, is a toss-up. Sometimes she cares about her appearance, while other times, she looks as if she's dressed in the dark. And it is never clear which version will show up to work the next day.

Since her first day with me, she has changed, and I've seen every subtle transformation. I pride myself on being a self-proclaimed female connoisseur, so I pick up on these things. And although I don't compliment her on the little tweaks she makes, I notice every one of them.

On some days, Penelope has toned down her make-up, and with that change, I've discovered she has freckles. When she's not hiding them, she looks as if she could be in her twenties. I get a glimpse of her youthful and jovial side. But when she's packing on the foundation, her make-up compact is always in her hand, making touch-ups throughout the day or adjusting the scarf she sometimes wears around her neck. She wouldn't need to adjust anything if she'd ditched that God-awful scarf altogether, but I guess scarves are her thing.

Her hair is different, too, nixing that unflattering auburn shade for a more natural brown with lighter streaks framing her face. This color suits her better. Even Penelope's wardrobe has changed too, wearing clothing more suitable for her body shape with colors that complement her complexion, like the color red. I'm praying those flats are next to go, but I shouldn't complain; she's quick on her feet in them.

As quick as she forges on the path to being fashion-forward, she resorts to her unflattering ways in a matter of a few days. She cakes on her make-up again and wears clothes fitted for people three times bigger than her. No matter how many versions of Penelope I see, the one consistent is her happy and professional disposition. Rarely have I seen her in a foul mood.

I am fortunate, but even with everything available at my fingertips, I wake up on the wrong side of the mattress once in a while. Not Penelope. She wakes up on the right side every day.

Not even the whispers or loud chatter around the halls dampen her mood. She's like Scotch-Guard. Nothing penetrates her surface. The worst part of all is she doesn't deserve the shit she gets, even from me. And she sure as shit doesn't deserve to believe there's any veracity to what's said about her. Penelope is an excellent worker and a friendly person from what I can tell. Not only is she intelligent and nice to the core, but she's funny in subtle ways.

And her eyes. Not one man could denounce her captivating stare. The way her golden glow catches the light, they can fill any room with immense warmth.

Sometimes when she talks, my mind disappears like I'm swimming in honey. Eye contact was never unnerving until Penelope started working for me.

Penelope has many endearing qualities, qualities that half the office lacks in, including some men sitting at this table.

Why the hell am I even thinking about this?

Jordan's Penny

I stare out the window, peering down at the buildings below. The view is breathtaking at night; like a festival of lights with a blanket of stars above us, nothing but the city skyline as far as the eyes can see. The city is so peaceful from up here, not buzzing with people and honking cars. As serene as things seem, the music that's bumping behind me is anything but.

Penelope's music plays in the Conference Room on full volume, nothing but nineties hip-hop. This genre is one I can stand behind. It reminds me of simpler times, dicking around with my friends, drinking, and partying, way before I became serious about my future. As long as she doesn't put that EDM trash on, she'll get no complaints from me.

She wasn't wrong when she said the music helps. I always assumed it would be more of a distraction, but I was wrong. We're getting more accomplished tonight than last night. Well, that's not true. She listened to her music in her earbuds and single-handedly finished most of her work for the night while I, music-free, did minimal by comparison. If she shared her music, maybe I would have been more productive.

With hip hop beats filling the background, it revived my energy, keeping the boredom of relentless numbers at bay, and adding some pep to my step.

The vicious growl of my stomach rumbles and if this music was at a lower volume, Penny and anyone left in the building might have heard the ravenous roar, too.

"What do you want for dinner?" I ask, scrolling through my phone for options as I wait for suggestions.

"I brought my own, but I'll order yours."

All day I've been hankering for a turkey wrap with avocado and a side salad, so Penelope places my order. She must sense my irritability and urges the deli to put a rush on it, even offering a sizeable tip if they deliver in under twenty minutes. She laughs into the receiver as if familiar with the person on the other end. It's a delightful laugh, one she's never given me when I cracked a good joke.

As the clock ticks away, my hunger eats me alive. I shift in my seat, too eager for food to focus on the task at hand. Being hangry is a real medical condition.

Our attention diverts once the elevator dings in the distance. There's no way they'd be able to prepare my meal and deliver to the office that quick without breaking a few traffic laws.

Penelope glances at her watch. "With a minute to spare," she says, extending her hand to mine. "Don't be a cheapskate either."

"That could be anybody," I reply with a bit of snark.

Barreling around the corner races an unfit man with a backpack slung on his back, dripping with sweat, out of breath, and holding out a brown bag.

Penelope wears the grin of a woman sure of herself. With her arm still extended, waiting for payment, I dig into my wallet as my stomach unleashes another loud rumble. She eyes my middle as I pull out my wad of bills, finding a Benjamin. This should impress her.

"That wrap better taste good," I warn.

She laughs and takes the bill, not impressed, per se. "No turkey wrap will ever taste $100 good. But," she smiles wide, "you'll brighten someone's day, and that is what's most important."

She walks away, fanning herself with the money, inhaling its scent, and hurries toward the out-of-breath delivery man. Again, she's right. He flashes me every crooked tooth in his mouth when she handed him the bill and told him to keep the change. The two exchange wide grins as she turns back toward me. The delivery man bows, very thankful. Perhaps she's a little impressed by my generosity.

I head to the kitchen and moments later, Penelope arrives with the most expensive deli wrap and salad I'll ever eat.

The cleaning crew has already cleaned the tables, but Penny wipes down the table again, cleaning the surface with a wet cloth. She's anal with certain things and cleaning the already clean kitchen table is one of them.

"Sorry," she mutters under her breath after noticing my odd expression, as she takes a dry paper towel and wipes the table down one last time. "Force of habit."

Penelope takes her insulated lunch bag out of the fridge, grabs a ceramic dish from the cabinet, and plates some of her meal. While she waits by the microwave, she stares off into space, and I dive into my overpriced dinner. It tastes okay, not as good as I imagined it would, but whatever Penelope is heating smells divine. There's enough garlic in it to shoo away any vampires that might try to attack her later tonight.

My chewing slows as my mouth salivates, but not for my food; I'm drooling for hers.

As she sets the dish down, my eyes feast on a plate of steaming whole wheat pasta and vegetables. The plate pops with color—diced Roma tomatoes, grilled chicken, zucchini, and squash. As boring as pasta and veggies can be, the scent entices all my senses.

"Is that basil or spinach?" I ask.

She pushes her fork around a noodle. "Basil." She jabs a piece of chicken with her fork. "Fresh from my garden."

"Hmm."

I stare down my dry turkey wrap before eyeing her food again. She notices, too.

"Want some? You're drooling."

Before I answer, she rises from her seat, grabs a plate from the stocked cabinets, and dumps the rest of the pasta onto the dish. With turned-up lips, I count down the timer on the microwave and discard the wrap back into the recyclable container. Penelope grabs fresh silverware from the drawer and pushes them across the table along with her already heated but untouched plate.

"But that was yours."

She shushes me. "Just eat."

"Who's the boss here?" I deadpan but do as I'm told and jab a forkful of food and swirl the noodles into the light sauce. Is that a lemon butter broth? Once the food hits my taste buds, my first instinct was to shout, "flavor town," despite how stupid that sounds.

The microwave beeps and she places her steaming plate in front of her chair before going back for two smaller plates, offering me one.

"Divvy up your salad," she orders.

Without hesitation, I follow her orders and give her a fair share. She, too, digs into the leafy greens as if it's an award-winning entrée.

"Aren't you going to eat what you brought?" I ask.

In one subtle movement, she lifts her shoulders in a shrug. "I'm not in the mood for it anymore."

Before I realize, my plate is empty, and my stomach is barely full. My only regret is not eating slower, so I could taste how amazing it was. All that's left is my portion of boring salad and the bland, half-eaten turkey wrap. As if she senses my disappointment, she pushes her plated food toward me.

I wave off. "You eat it."

What she doesn't say with words, her eyes speak volumes; she's insisting, almost begging me to take it.

Like a starving savage, I go to town on the second helping. Everything is so flavorful. "This is amazing," I admit between bites. My mouth waters with every forkful. There's a perfect amount of seasonings and vegetables, with a precise ratio of broth—not too much to classify as a soup, and not too little to be dry. Even her reheated chicken isn't chewy or overcooked. The entire meal is light yet filling. "Maybe you should cater dinners from now on."

She picks at the salad, playing with it more than eating it. "How many more nights will we have to stay late?"

The mental checklist runs through my head. Thanks to her, the list isn't long, but I'd be lying if I said I didn't enjoy working after hours with her. She has this innate ability to turn work into a fun project.

"A couple more nights I guess."

"My boyfriend gets worried about me leaving so late, but that shouldn't be a problem."

Jackpot! New information—she has a boyfriend. Maybe that boy in the picture is their son. Some of their features are similar—the skin tone, nose, and freckles. Nah, that can't be right. Moms love to brag to other people about their kids, shoving school pictures in people's faces or asking others to buy overpriced candy to support their sport's team. Just another piece to the Penelope Matthews puzzle that is still incomplete.

"If we finish up their expenses for the past five years, we can leave earlier. Do you need help to input anything?"

Penelope chokes on a lettuce leaf. "I've seen your typing skills, so, no. We'd be here until tomorrow if I let you help. You sit and stay pretty while I do the heavy lifting."

Although she's joking, I don't laugh. Penelope is doing most of the work. While I have an eye for the bigger picture—spotting vital details and figuring out the best way to salvage any company—she works on the mundane tasks I need to complete the job. She plugs all the numbers, organizes the documents, and prepares the spreadsheets in a way that's pleasing to the eye. Can't have the partners half asleep because the presentation isn't interesting.

I shoot her an unconvinced expression. "Not everything is about the looks, Ms. Matthews. Brains matter, too."

She squints, and her mouth forms a straight line. "Is that the same motto you follow in your personal life?" Her mouth parts for a beat, waiting for a rebuttal, but her expression shifts back to her professional stare. "I'm sorry. I shouldn't have said that."

"No," I wave off, grateful she's coming out of her shell. "Don't be sorry." I lean back, much like she does when she's relaxing into our conversations, and rub my full, yet still flat belly. "I don't date," I answer with simple satisfaction. "Not into the whole dating thing. But, since you asked, brains aren't an attribute I pay much attention to when cutting loose. I'm just having fun. But brains are important in other aspects."

She dunks a cucumber chunk into the dressing. "I get it. Why not, right? You're remarkably successful, driven, determined, and as the twenty-ninth floor calls you, 'Sexy Stephens,' so get it while you can."

The exposed part of her chest turns rosy, having said the words out loud, but that's the only sign of her embarrassment.

"Sexy Stephens?" I do little to hide my disappointment. "Where's the creativity?"

She shakes her head, and her eyes close. I'm guessing they're rolled back into her brain. "You're so conceited."

Penelope grabs the empty plates and brings them to the sink and washes them.

"I know." I move beside her, grab a towel, and dry the plates. "If I make excuses for being this way, that's admitting guilt, but I'm not guilty of anything except exuding confidence. If I don't want the best for myself, who will?"

"Oh, I don't know. People that care about you, maybe?"

I don't respond. What she's referring to revolves around emotions and I don't have time for that, nor do I care to. If I choose to self-reflect and analyze the women I've been with, I can point-blank state that I don't care what they think about me because the fact of the matter is, I don't care about them. Not in that way, at least. The arrangement is straightforward.

The only thing that matters to me is my job. It affords me the lifestyle I desire.

Growing up, I wasn't surrounded by love. My family wasn't bred like that. Nannies took care of me while Dad worked hard, and Mom tried balancing being a wife and mother, all while maintaining a full-time job because she missed being a part of the workforce.

When I was younger, I wondered why they had me if neither of them spent time with me. Dad never showed up to any of my various sports games, but was quick to drag me into the office and parade me around to his coworkers as if we had some amazing father/son bond. Mom showed me love, just not in the typical doting way everyone else had; at least not when I was younger. She's changed a lot since, but sharing feelings wasn't a thing in our home unless dinner was bland or overcooked. Early on, self-sufficiency was an important lesson I learned, relying on *numero uno* and no one else. And I also learned that if someone beats something in your head long enough, you believe it.

If it weren't for my aunt implanting her superficial beliefs in me and me expanding on them to the twelfth degree, maybe I would crave something different. But I enjoy bedding some of the sexiest women in this city. Am I a superficial, conceited, womanizing workaholic? Most definitely, but what's so wrong about wanting success and enjoying meaningless yet thrilling sex with attractive women?

Is there something wrong with that? Is there something wrong with me?

"I mean," Penelope starts and then shuts her mouth. She scrubs the sponge over a plate with force. At this rate, she might wear down the ceramic. "What the hell do I know? Don't listen to me. I'm the last person who should talk about relationships and love."

"Take it easy on the plate, chief. You're fine, don't worry about it." I wave away her worry. "We're having a conversation. I mean, you're the one in a relationship, not me, so you have more experience in that department."

This time, she waves me off. "No. I overstepped. It's your life, only you can live it." Penelope pauses again as if in her own world, letting the water clear the suds. "Whatever makes you happy and makes you complete, that's the path for you. Life is too short. Take what you can from it and don't let someone else dictate your happiness. From what I know of you, you are doing just that."

An amused chuckle escapes my mouth. "Damn straight."

I'll be damned if I live for someone else. I do what makes me happy—working hard and playing harder. A smile must've crept on my lips because when I glance at Penelope, a shy smile spreads on hers.

But why does she look sad too?

"Um… we should get back to work," Penelope urges.

As I observe Penelope's expression change, I can't help but feel a little judged, even though that wasn't her intent. With this unsettling wisp of guilt in my gut, I follow Penelope back to the Conference Room. Once we get back to work, all friendly chatter ceases and we plug away at our tasks.

Of course, Penelope finishes what she needed to do earlier than I expected so she packs up her belongings and heads home for the day, while I struggle between my work and whatever the fuck it is that's happening in my head.

An inkling of anger builds. Why am I harboring on what she said in the kitchen?

Of course, I'm happy. People envy the life I lead. Hell, even Alec tries to live through me, begging me to talk about my latest conquests. He even went so far as asking me to hook him up with friends of the women I talk to.

Penelope may not be passing judgment, but a part of her must wish she could have a chance with me. Of course she does. Why wouldn't she? I'm the complete package.

The ding of my phone quiets any further chatter in my head. A text from Francesca. She's in town for the night and begs me to meet up.

Don't mind if I do.

CHAPTER
SEVEN

AS FIT AS I am, these late nights are kicking my ass. My evening sexcapades with Francesca didn't help either. This morning, my blankets have taken me hostage, and for once, I don't mind at all. Too tired to work out, I succumb to their demands and stay in bed. A few extra minutes of relaxation couldn't hurt.

With the high thread count sheets pulled to my chin, I'm curious if Penelope struggles to get up. I've been working her like a dog, not just with my regular work schedule, but with the Oakfeld project, too. While most of my energy goes to analyzing the data she's prepared, she handles everything else. Hell, I've been working her to the bone since she became my assistant, and she's never complained or looked stressed or overworked. She must have an energy battery pack stored somewhere.

Unable to fall back asleep because of some unknown nagging sensation in the back of my brain, I drag my ass out of bed and ready myself for the day.

On my way to the office, I stop at a bakery, pick up a few pastries, and a cup of fruit for her, a little something to show my appreciation. She appreciates me in little ways—leaving a box of her tea on my desk or stealing all the good pens in the supply room for me. She may not fawn over me like my other assistants, but she takes care of me in other ways.

I drop the bakery box off at her desk and I'm blown away at how tidy her space is even after all the work she's done. After setting the goodies by her keyboard, I trudge into my office, ready to tackle a few emails before Penelope and I retreat into the stuffy Conference Room. After I send out a couple of responses, I glance at my Rolex and peek out my door.

No Penelope. She's late.

Just as I realize she's not on time, the morning greetings ring from cubicle to cubicle like the wave in a stadium as she hustles past her coworkers. In the past, I would chew out my assistant for being late. Cathy was late one time. Once. But Penelope is different. Just as I was about to rag on her for her first tardiness, the hardened expression on her face stops me.

"Morning, Penelope."

"Morning." Her curt tone catches me off guard. She doesn't glance in my direction. Instead, she focuses on setting her things down, or should I say throwing her things down.

"Are you okay?"

She hums and nods, switches on her monitor, and pushes aside the boxed pastries and fruit cup aside.

When she first started, she didn't make a peep and only spoke when spoken to, but always maintained that polite and professional manner. As our working relationship became more familiar, her true personality shone through. She smiled more than usual and even showed her sarcastic sense of humor. I assumed those quiet days were a thing of the past, but watching her pursed lips silently curse out her keyboard after jamming in the wrong login password. It's going to be a long, silent day.

Without a joke or an excuse for why she's late, she places her AirPods into her ears and gets straight to work. Even her typing is aggressive. She doesn't have long nails per se, but she clicks the keys like the words owe her money. Her attitude isn't the only thing off, either.

For such a beautiful day, she's dressed for the weather we won't expect for another couple of months. Who wears a neck scarf and cardigan when it's sunny and seventy-five degrees outside? She also resorted to her old makeup habits, wearing a thicker coat of foundation than yesterday. Not a freckle in sight. I try hiding my off-putting expression, but what the hell is her process in the morning?

I leave her to it and retreat to my office, skim through various emails, tending to the most crucial ones and make some calls. She grunts with what sounds like frustration or aggravation and even drops the F-bomb as she struggles to fix a paper stuck in the printer. Perhaps she woke up tired as I did. At least I'm not alone.

The rest of the day does not differ from how it started—quiet—aside from her moans, groans, and loud typing. I leave her be as she works on parts of the PowerPoint presentation for me while she's in her own world with an intense focus. I busy myself. But the nagging sensation tickles the actual question in my head.

My internal struggle prevents me from getting anything done.

Ask her? Or don't ask her?

Fuck.

Either way, something needs to change because her mood is fucking up my entire day. And just when I started enjoying having the music in the background, she's keeping it all to herself again, only playing it in her earbuds.

Her glossed lips press together, eyes focused on the laptop monitor, hard at work while I observe her like a creeper. If I could read minds, hers would be my first. She's so wrapped up in her tunes, I could leave the room for three hours or streak naked in front of her and it'd make zero difference. Whatever she's listening to is helping her type like The Flash, but it's doing little to improve her shitty mood.

After a few minutes, she moves, pulling her silky hair off her neck, fanning herself with a stack of papers. If she took her cardigan off, she wouldn't be so damn hot. She shrugs the dark blue cardigan off, exposing her bare shoulders, but she stops once she glances toward her arm. And just as fast as that sweater almost came off, she pulls the thick material back up, as if, in a matter of seconds, her body reconsidered and was no longer hot anymore.

Penelope eyes the monitor again, frustrated, and stands from her chair, pushing it away from the table. The empty chair skids across the floor behind her and crashes into the glass wall. The force alone should have shattered the glass. She tosses the pods onto the table.

"You hungry?" Penelope shoves papers into a folder and slaps her palms onto the table.

She hasn't spoken for so long, the two words she utters sound unfamiliar. Or maybe her tone is foreign.

I nod, fearing any fast movement or noise might set her off the deep end. "You okay?" I ask again for what seems like the hundredth time today.

She storms out of the room without an answer. I'm about to follow her, but my phone rings.

George.

"How's the proposal coming along?"

"We are making great headway. Penelope is a godsend. If this goes well, I'm submitting a bonus for her."

"She's giving Grace a run for her money."

We laugh, but he's right. "Penny has youth on her side, but she's as diligent as Grace. I'm hoping we complete all my specs by the end of the week, then I'll prep the graphics and proposal packets for a sit-down."

"Sounds good. Tom scheduled an impromptu meeting tomorrow. Something about that startup Alec won't stop going on about. It should be quick one, so it won't take you away from your project for too long. From what you tell me, I'm sure Ms. Matthews can manage without you. See you tomorrow, Jordan."

The call was brief. But by the time I'm halfway to the kitchen, the aroma hits me, carrying me like a scene from a cartoon with my body floating and my nose leading the way. If I wasn't hungry before, I am now.

Whatever she brought in today smells better than yesterday. Penelope stands in front of the microwave with a fork in her hand, waiting for the time to tick down. She taps her foot angrily.

"Need any help?" I loosen the top button of my shirt and roll up my sleeves, ready to give a hand or both.

"Please," she snaps back. "I can operate a microwave."

I pride myself on being able to read women. But Penelope Matthews is one female I'm clueless about. I remain silent. I can't tell if she's trying to be funny or if she's just being a bitch. Once I glimpse at the time, its most likely the latter. That's not very professional.

I grab two plates from the cabinet and put them on the table for us.

"We're eating in here again?"

"Penny, aren't you claustrophobic in the other room?"

She cleans the already spotless table and dries it as she did yesterday.

"You missed a spot," I point like a drill sergeant and she's quick on her toes, and rushes over, scrubbing the spot. She apologizes. "I'm joking, Penny. Jeez. Germophobe much?"

"What? No. Sorry. I've been conditioned to—" She shakes her head as if cleaning her thoughts too. "Sorry. Habit."

She puts the food in the center of the table, family-style—brown rice in one dish, and peppers, onions, and shrimp in a light lemon butter broth in the other. Penelope sets my plate in front of my chair.

I salivate as the steaming food awaits. Starved all day, I dig in. The saying is true, a way to a man's heart is through his stomach, and at this rate, I just might fall in love.

"I need to marry you. You're an amazing cook."

"Hmmph. And all this time I assumed marriage was about love," she grumbles. "Silly me." Her lips, the only real feature that'll give anything away, show her true cards. The corners of her full lips turn up, but only a smidgen. Her eyes remain hidden under her thick lashes, half-closed.

In a matter of minutes, I polish off the plate, but before I swallow the last bite, she grabs my empty dish and gives me the remaining food. Talk about hospitality. Everything she touches is perfection, from spreadsheets to dinners. She can do no wrong. What else is she good at?

"You sure there's nothing wrong?"

"I'm fine." Penny replies with just the right amount of 'stop fucking asking me' in her tone.

Why do I keep asking? Why do I care?

She takes small bites and offers a half-smile, the first hint of a smile I've seen all day, but I'm no fool. Penny would never ask for help if she needed it. She would rather keep everything to herself—her music, struggles with work, or whatever's bothering her now. Her private life is private, and she does a magnificent job of keeping it that way. But that won't stop me from trying.

I try a different tactic. "I'm curious about your music obsession. What soundtrack is your favorite?"

Penelope lifts her head and stares at the ceiling, tugging on her bottom lip with her teeth as she sinks back into the chair. There it is, the classic lean, her signature move. Even if only for a second, she'll drop her guard down and I'll get another piece to the Penelope puzzle.

Satisfaction creeps onto my face as she loosens up and engages instead of just answering me with professional courtesy. God forbid she goes over her allotted words for the day, which today is about forty in total.

Jordan's Penny

"The Gladiator score, not the soundtrack. That movie was fantastic, and the music," she gushes, "so powerful."

I stare in awe; her features soften as she disappears for a moment, trapped in a scene. All tension she held in her body minutes ago disappears, if only for this moment. I can't recall a single movie that wields enough power to de-stress me like that.

She rests her pointer finger on her lips, frenetically tapping as if trying to conjure up another. "The two Kill Bill soundtracks, and don't laugh, but pretty much all the Twilight ones, too. Even the scores."

I use God's pure will to stifle my laughter. Twilight? But I don't dare judge, not today, not with the mood she's been in. So, I sit back and listen as she shares a little more about herself, grateful that she's talking at all. Penelope Matthews is still an enigma; one even Alan Turing couldn't crack if he tried, and I've been trying since day one.

"I always found a piano piece can evoke so much emotion with no words spoken. I mean, I guess any single instrument can do that, but the piano is one of the more powerful ones, in my opinion."

Without pausing, I divulge something about myself that few people know. "My grandmother forced me to play piano in front of all her white-haired friends when I was younger. I hated every second."

Her golden eyes widen with delight, and her mouth shows her shock. "Do you still play?" With both elbows on the table, she rests her head on her hands, hanging on my every word as if my little secret flipped a switch and lit up her face. This new mood is a vast improvement.

I shake my head to the sides and stare at my hands. Damn, I hated practicing day and night, but I couldn't disobey my mother or grandmother. Everything always needed to be perfect, including me. They didn't approve when I stopped playing. My grandmother turned her nose up at me for months after she found out.

Even though I keep a Steinway in my apartment, I never lift the lid anymore. My ass would grow numb sitting on the bench while the ivory and black keys ached to be stroked. I would wait and wait with my fingers hovering over the keys, hoping for some string of notes to form in my head, but nothing came. The music inside me is gone. Now, the piano sits in my apartment because it is sexy near my floor-to-ceiling windows. My long, slender fingers are no longer used to create beautiful music. I use them to entertain women in other ways.

"What other hidden talents do you have?" she asks.

I refrain from sharing the one that just popped up, but the longer I think, nothing else comes to mind; none work appropriate, at least. I pull at any minor ones I can grasp.

"Um, I used to juggle." I recall spending the day home from school simply because I wasn't in the mood to go. I sat in front of the TV watching The People's Court with three oranges and kept tossing them until I got the hang of it. "You?"

She bites the inside of her cheek, and that dimple digs deep as she eyes the ceiling again, as if the ceiling holds all her answers.

"I bowled a three hundred once." Although she says the words as if anyone can do it, she beams with pride. The first authentic smile today. "I was fifteen. My parents threw me a party. That was one of the happiest days I can remember. The bowling alley gave me a plaque, but my boyfriend threw it across the room during a fight." She flinches, almost as if reliving the moment her plaque got destroyed. Her hand slides the scarf back and forth along her neck until she catches me staring at her.

I try to come up with another talent to keep this conversation going. Hell, I'll do anything to stop us from going back to the stuffy room. Plus, I'm hoping she'll offer more bits and pieces about herself, pieces that won't put her back in the mood she had before.

Penelope shares her hatred of snakes and spiders, gushes over cheesy young adult novels and films, fears zombies even though they aren't real. She also shares her theory, with an impressive amount of details, might I add, about how they will be real one day. Her expression takes a sudden turn for the worst when she shares she hasn't seen her family in over a decade.

I tell her about my Twizzler obsession and how I became the youngest partner in the firm a few years ago. But when I told her I kept my favorite blanket from when I was a baby, she laughed so hard, water trickled from her nose. Even when I added that I no longer sleep with it, that extra tidbit of information did nothing to stop her laughing fit.

After bullshitting for longer than we should, she demands we get back to work, but this time, she plays the music for us both. I never realized how much music helps my productivity; it births my focus all over again, but every time I glance in her direction, she's checking her phone.

I look at my Rolex and it's close to ten p.m. "Penelope, get out of here. It's been a long day."

She accepts and packs up her things, straightens out some paperwork before taking her music and exiting the Conference Room, fast. Boy, did she leave in a hurry. Is she afraid I'll change my mind and call her to come back? She's practically running. Damn, those flats are functional.

With the music gone, so is my focus and drive. After reading the same sentence twelve times, I call it a night, too.

After the jets in a steamy shower tenderize my skin, I lay in bed, still stressed about work. I keep a running list of what I need to finish to stay on course. My approach to the proposal is stressing me out more than anything else. In all fairness to Penelope, I shouldn't worry, considering how amazing she's been. She's thorough, more thorough than I've ever been in previous proposals, but I can't stop harboring on which angle to pitch. I make a mental note to run my ideas by her first. She'll give me the advice I need.

My mind won't shut down as much as my body needs it to. It continues to fire on all cylinders, and I'm left tossing in bed, unable to fall asleep.

I contemplate calling Candice for a quick video chat. It wouldn't be the first time she did things in front of a camera, but that idea doesn't sit right either. She'll babble, ask generic questions, and the more I contemplate it, the more agitated it's making me.

I switch on the TV and search for Gladiator.

CHAPTER EIGHT

THE CONFERENCE ROOM shrinks while the work surrounding us grows, but we will cut the strings that tether us here at some point today. The idea alone is freeing.

The printer spits out the last pages of my presentation. I do a dry run using Penelope as my audience, implementing all the visuals we created together. After offering solid advice and ideas, we've put together one hell of a presentation. A single bow of her head is the only confirmation I need. We have a home run on our hands, and I'm positive the others will want to sign this company on as a client. She gives me a high-five and releases a breathy sigh of relief.

"We can finally move out of here," I exhale as I straighten the stack of packets we've created.

"Thank God," she hollers and stretches in the high-back chair with a renewed glow highlighting her cheeks.

A tinge of disappointment resonates in the pit of my stomach. It's inexplicable, like a gnawing sensation, not annoying, just bothersome. In the past, the late-night projects drove me insane. The help I had wasn't helpful at all. And it wasn't just the projects that sent me over the ledge, work was unbearable too. Having Penelope as an assistant forced me to dig deeper within myself. Sure, I had nice eye candy around the office, but my preferences for assistants only created more work for myself because I was so, dare I say it; superficial.

Work is so different now. Man, I am lucky Melissa paired me with Penelope; an assistant that not only does her job but does her job well. She goes above and beyond for her position, and not only has these past few nights been enjoyable, something I never dreamed possible, but Penelope makes every day easier. Because of her tremendous effort, I could devote all my focus to the work and not worry about what the hell my assistant was fucking up. I couldn't imagine doing back-to-back projects, but now, I can't wait for another one to fall in my lap.

I glance toward Penelope as she tucks the remaining papers and pens against her chest before she heads back to her desk. Thank goodness her mood is better than yesterday. She's probably relieved our late nights are over, happy to sit at her desk again and do anything that doesn't involve the name "Oakfeld."

Once my ass hits my office chair, it's like I've returned home from a weird, semi-stressful, but yet enjoyable vacation. I sink into the buttery leather with my eyes closed and take a few soothing breaths.

"Candice Michaels is here," Penelope's cool cadence chimes over the intercom.

Confused why she'd be at my office after not returning any of her calls in the past few weeks, I tell her to send Candice in.

Candice closes the door behind her, grinning from one dangling earring to the other. I haven't seen her since I booted her from my apartment, yet she acts as if we've spoken every day since. She's got something up her sleeve, I can tell. Her short, slinky white dress shows off her spray-tanned, toned legs, the ones that travel to her heaven. Her fake tits overflow in the low-cut, draped neckline, reminding me of what I've missed. With my nights freed up again, Candice might rejoin my roster and give me a good workout later if I choose to put her back into rotation.

"I was in the area. I miss you."

She saunters around my desk, dragging her manicured nail over the shiny black surface, stands by my side, and sits her firm ass on my lap. With her this close, I've got front row seats right down her dress. Her perfume fills my lungs. Orange blossoms and vanilla waft off her skin, tempting me. Candice hooks her arm around my neck, pulling me close. My eyes obsess over her ample chest as I drag my salivating tongue along my lips and inhale her alluring pheromones.

With work being my primary focus, I left my sexual urges to simmer in the background, but now with Candice this close, the needs I deprived myself of flood to the surface. My balls ache. She moans in my ear as she shifts on my lap, sensing it, too.

"I've been a busy man," I manage. With my eyes fixated on her round tits, my mind churns, recalling how her hard nipples taste while I graze my tongue over them. And the way her ass sits on my lap now, I'm surprised any words I spoke were audible. All blood flow is heading south, pumping into my pants. She leans in again, pressing her sticky, glossed lips to mine, allowing me a quick taste.

There's a fast knock before the door opens. "Excuse me, Jordan, I found a few discrepancies on the 2013 budget spreadsheet. We need to—"

I tear myself away from the kiss and toss Candice off my lap as if caught by my mother. My hand flies to my mouth to wipe away the sticky gloss left behind.

Candice straightens her dress and fumes. "I closed the door for a reason. What are you? An idiot or something?"

"I'm so sorry," Penelope rushes, her eyes focus on mine and her cheeks burn as her embarrassment engulfs the room.

"Uh, hello?" Candice adds, "Take a picture or something, so you can fantasize about him in that lonely life of yours?"

My eyes never leave Penelope's. If she's bothered, she says nothing and does even less; she places the packet with the bright pink tabs sticking out on top onto my desk, and hurries out, closing the door behind her with a thud.

My mouth goes on autopilot, a rushed and annoyed autopilot. "What gives you the right to disrespect Penny like that?" I boom, voice ricocheting off the walls. "You can't just come here, unannounced, and expect the world to stop for you. I have work to do and I sure as hell won't allow you to talk to my assistant, let alone any of my employees like that. You need to leave."

Without a word she storms out, swinging the door open so fast the handle smashes into the wall behind it.

I stand in the doorway, stretch my arms on the top of the door frame and watch Candice rush past the row of cubicles. Every pair of eyes stare in my direction. I shrug. In seconds, they turn their attention back to the seething blonde rushing down the hall as if her panties were ablaze. Penelope is the only one ignoring the surrounding disruption. As disinterested as ever, she's listening to her music and ignoring the drama and my lingering presence.

And then I catch her.

Penelope glances toward Candice right as she trips on her heels. Candice's ankle wobbles back and forth before she rights herself. The timing was impeccable, almost as if Penelope willed Candice to falter. Penny tries to stifle her laugh by fake coughing. I hide nothing and laugh as Candice turns around, cheeks reddened, before straightening her spine and dress, storming off to the elevators around the corner.

Penelope takes out one AirPod. "I'm sorry. I should've waited until you called me in."

"You did nothing wrong. She's the sorry one. You caught that wobble, though?" I ask with raised brows. "You should let her borrow your shoes."

Her lips turn up, but it's not enough. I need a genuine smile, one where her dimples press deep into her cheeks, and she shows teeth. Penelope is the best assistant I've ever had, and she needs to know it.

"Friday. Lunch." I point to the two of us.

Her eyes sparkle like a star stolen from a night's sky and I get what I came for. A glorious grin. I'm unsure if the elated expression is because she's having lunch with me or because we're celebrating our project's completion. Either way, I'm satisfied with my efforts, so I head back into my office, smiling from ear to ear, too.

CHAPTER NINE

MOM SET THE table to the nines as if she's being showcased by Home & Garden magazine. She places a large floral display in the center, lights white candles, and adorns fabric napkins with gold napkin rings that rest on a tier of white plates rimmed with gold. I love the woman, but this is excessive for a Sunday dinner, even for me.

Like the table display, Mom wears her Sunday's best—a lovely blouse printed with large pink roses, black slacks, and a gold-chained belt adorns her waist. Even her light brown hair is perfectly coiffed—as if expecting royalty. But it isn't until Aunt Rose waltzes through the door that all this effort makes sense.

Aunt Rose has been MIA for months, too busy jet-setting around the world with her fifth husband—some guy that hopped on the Bitcoin train at the proper time. She's always dressed to impress, with not one strand of her golden-streaked hair out of place. Aunt Rose is the only reason my mother put this much effort into the presentation and the meal. That I can guarantee. Although her effort is noteworthy for most, the gesture falls flat for Aunt Rose. Nothing is ever to her standards.

Aunt Rose makes one disappointed noise after another, displeased with something in front of her. The spacing between the wineglass and plate is perfect. Her gripe couldn't be that. Mom measured the distance with a ruler. Her dissatisfied groans could stem from the white hydrangeas in the floral arrangement or the temperature of the chilled soup; she's never been a fan of either. But with Aunt Rose, one never truly knows what her fuss is about. She's always been a mystery; at least that's what most of her previous husbands claim.

My mother does her best to ignore the not-so-subtle grunts from Aunt Rose's throat. Her stare in my direction continues. It happens so frequently; it is a distraction.

"Something wrong, Mom?"

"Can't a mother just admire her son?" She scans me once more, wearing a beam, ear to ear as she eats. "Talking to anyone special these days?"

"What? No." My response came across defensive, way more than I intended.

All she replies with is, "Hmm," before eating a forkful of cauliflower mash. Her eyes stay on me, still donning an awkward yet knowing grin. That motherly stare is unnerving.

"Work's been great, though. I'm presenting next week for a new company, a three-generation family-owned business that made horrible financial decisions and hasn't been able to recover. Penelope and I agreed we need to forget the conservative-middle-of-the-road philosophy and outmaneuver the competition by—"

"Penelope? Who's Penelope?" Aunt Rose interrupts.

"She's my assistant, and she's phenomenal. If not for her, I'd be at the office cursing someone out."

Memories of the last company I proposed taking over whirl like a tornado. Tabitha offered little help. She struggled to get all the financial information organized in two weeks, and it was only seven years. I would consider baby pandas more helpful, and all they do is stumble around like drunken toddlers.

For almost a full month, I lived in the office to get the project done. After the first three weeks, I no longer harbored any guilt about making her fetch things like a dog. That was the worst research experience to date.

"I know my nephew; he's got someone good-looking under him." Aunt Rose winks. "Isn't that right? Tell me about her."

My mother is quick. "She's his assistant. Appearances shouldn't matter. And why is it always about appearances with you? I swear you're the reason he only associates with nobodies."

"Beautiful nobodies," Aunt Rose interjects.

Mom huffs. "They may be beautiful, but that's all they offer. Beauty doesn't last forever, yours included, hence the reason you nipped and tucked every square inch of your face and body."

Mom's barb causes me to choke on my food until Aunt Rose shoots me her death glare.

"None of those women are marriage material," Mom finishes.

I've told my mother countless times marriage isn't for me. Women are like leasing a car. Once you put enough miles on them, it's time to trade her in and get a newer model. This works for me. And from the looks of it, I'm following in my aunt's footsteps, minus the marriage part. Every husband she finds gets younger, more handsome, and richer while she uses their money to freeze her face and body from aging. She's jabbed more needles into herself than a junkie. But besides medical procedures, she leads a healthy lifestyle and always dressed to the nines and never leaves the house looking a mess because, as she would say, "*You never know who you're going to run into.*" I learned from the best.

"No nephew of mine will date someone ugly. Look at him," she says, pulling me toward her and pinching my cheeks. "That face should be on the cover of magazines. Look at his jaw. Do you know how much a doctor charges to create this level of perfection? I warned Jordan if he married an ugly girl, I'd cut him out of my will. Then comes the ugly babies. Ugh."

"Whoa," I exclaim. "Babies?" No thanks. With the number of horror stories at work, that is a road I don't plan on traveling.

"Don't sell yourself short, Jordan," Mom scolds, dismissing my apprehension about kids. "There's more to life than gorgeous women who can't give you the love you deserve. And you have a lot more to offer than what eyes can see."

She sounds like Penelope. My aunt rolls her eyes with dramatic flair and exhales just as loudly. But my mother presses forward. "Are you and Candice still seeing each other?" Mom does not try to hide her disapproval for the ladies I associate with.

"No. God, no," I confess. Our last encounter still leaves a bitter taste in my mouth. As subtle as my mother's grin was, there was no mistaking her elation upon hearing the news.

"She was attractive though." Aunt Rose's angled brows rise.

There's no denying Candice's outer beauty, and maybe her flexibility, but she offered nothing of substance. Her warranty wore out. The office incident with Penny was just the icing on the cake. She had many infractions before that. The most crucial one was breaking my cardinal rule: do not get attached. Once she committed that crime, she signed her one-way ticket out the door.

"She was a bitch," I admit.

Aunt Rose chuckles with enough effort, her shoulders shake, but her hair doesn't move an inch, frozen in perfect flips and curls by an entire can of hair spray. "Honey, all the pretty ones are. You have your moments too."

Mom waves her off. "So, tell me about Penelope."

I have little to share, only some random facts she spoon-fed me, not enough information to piece together a complete background story. I still know next to nothing about her except I enjoy talking to her when she's in a talkative mood.

"She's 31, hardworking, punctual, calls me out on my shit, which is pretty funny. And she loves music, she's always—"

Mom interjects. "Did you tell her you play the piano?" Excited that Penelope and I share a love for music, although our tastes differ, Mom claps.

I chuckle at Mom's enthusiasm. "I don't play anymore, Mom. And tone down the excitement. I'm not dating her, but we work great together. She's nothing like my other assistants," I admit. "But she's a sweet girl."

My aunt's eyes widen as if I've admitted a juicy secret. "So, she's fat."

The fork falls from my grasp, hitting the plate with a sharp clank. My annoyed exhale soon follows.

"So, she *is* fat," my aunt reiterates.

Now it's my mother's turn to moan and groan. "How are we related? Looks do not equate to beauty," Mom adds while I figure out how to get off this subject altogether.

My aunt sucks her tongue, and her eyes roll so far back into her head, only the whites of her eyes show. "That's what ugly, fat people say."

Aunt Rose is relentless and makes no excuses for the way she views the world. Or people. She's all about the surface. Nothing more, nothing less. Well, maybe money, too. She loves money.

Sure, Mom doesn't have the same body as a teen, a little rounder in the middle, but in her defense, she's refused plastic surgery, accepting herself the way mother nature intended. She's beautiful and has aged gracefully. It doesn't hurt that we also have excellent genes.

I rub my temples as the two women argue back and forth like old hens cackling. This conversation took a turn down a dead-end street and I need to get everyone back on track.

"Mom isn't ugly or fat. And Penny isn't unattractive, but she's definitely—"

"Fat," Aunt Rose finishes.

The dishes and silverware clank beneath the force of my fist on the table. "She is my assistant." I reiterate my point with just enough "shut the fuck up about it" in my tone. "End of story."

My mom mumbles, "You're a stubborn man, but I'm hoping you'll get out of your own way sooner rather than later." She shrugs as if she hasn't just insulted me. "You smile when you talk about her is all."

"What?" My voice goes up an octave or maybe three. "She's the best assistant I've ever had. She does her job well. That's all," I finish for what seems like the seventh time.

"Ugh," Aunt Rose groans with frustration. "Let's not talk about this girl anymore, which leads me into the perfect segue. I met a model at Saks the other day. At least, she should be a model if she's not already. I mean, I didn't care to ask either. She was just a pretty face that made me think of my nephew. Here's her number." Aunt Rose shoves a piece of paper in my hand. Bridgette is scribbled on it. She even drew a heart above the "I," just like girls did in middle school. "She's waiting for your call."

Aunt Rose is infamous for getting numbers of random women she thinks I'd find attractive, like a glorified pimp. She has great taste, I'll give her that. I appease her and put the paper in my pocket, but I have little intention of calling after the last woman she matched with me. Slept with the girl one time, and the following day she's at my apartment with a bag stuffed with her belongings, ready to move in. If that wasn't scary enough, every time I turned a corner, there she was, waiting for me. Stalking wasn't just her hobby; it became her full-time job.

I lean back and listen to the only two women in my life arguing. Their voices turn into white noise as I scarf down the delicious meal my mother prepared. As the love versus looks debate continues, the throbbing in my

78

head intensifies. I can't take much more of this. Not tonight. I slide the chair back, kiss them both on the cheek, thank my mother for another lovely dinner, and leave before they drag me back into the conversation.

Too engulfed in the bullshit, they don't even take a breather from their arguing to say goodbye.

For a long time, I'd sit in front of the piano and stare. The black and white keys would remain untouched, but not for a lack of trying. A part of me missed making music. I'd place my fingers over the keys and wait for the perfect tune to come to mind. When nothing surfaced, it became infuriating because, in my life, things always came easy. Music used to come easy for me.

I played nonstop for hours when I was younger, not just from sheet music, but from whatever flowed from my heart to my fingers, and it was beautiful.

But none of that has happened in decades. Sure, I could play a memorized piece, but I never connected to that music. Those notes meant something to someone else. They were someone else's masterpiece. As beautiful as it was, it didn't belong to me. Too afraid to create something awful, my hands would shake in fear. So instead, I would sit in silence and wait for something perfect to present itself.

At this moment, I sit in front of the Steinway, yearning to play. The pull is like a magnet, and I rest my fingers on the white and black keys. All I can do is pray the music rescues me from this dull yet noticeable ache in my chest as I press down on them.

Like a timid child learning for the first time, forgetting everything ingrained in me, I play until I remember, regardless of how bad it might be. Still afraid to hit the wrong key, I continue with caution. I correct my posture, excited when a melody hums in my bones, as clear as if written on paper. The tune is slow, a soft, melodic song.

Penny comes to mind. No matter how hard I fight it, that conversation by the office sink still weighs heavily on my mind. It's infuriating. Mom has brought up my dating on many occasions, but it took Penelope, a relative outsider, one time to get me to analyze what I'm doing with my life.

So, I continue playing, playing the perfect score of my story. The idea seems fun enough, except what I'm playing isn't a fun or exciting tune. The keys translate what my words cannot, mimicking my emotions with the music. I play no high-pitched cords, only low, slow strokes over the ivories as it rings through my apartment. For some, the song is depressing, and maybe it is, but it's accurate. And it's all mine.

I end the piece, close the lid, and see the hard outline of my jaw on the glossed, black surface. Never one to dwell on emotions, my hectic days didn't afford me the time, I allow myself just one moment to feel. I can't deny the discomfort in my chest any longer. It has been taunting me for what feels like months now. Emotions get discarded like yesterday's food, but I can't shake this gnawing sensation; I must indulge it if only for a moment with hopes it'll soon pass.

As I dissect my emotions, this hollowness intensifies. Am I just a shell of a man? With women at my fingertips, that fulfillment has only brought temporary pleasure. Granted, it has always been my choice to sleep alone, but suddenly, the idea seems so... lonely.

Thinking of all my previous female companions does nothing to lift my spirits. None of those women are intelligent or funny, let alone decent human beings. Candice is a prime example of that. Most are like me, conceited, superficial, and acts as if everyone is beneath them.

"Jesus Christ."

I can't bear the sight of my reflection for once.

My mother and Aunt Rose's invading voices send me spiraling, arguing what qualities are right for a partner. As my mother spits out her bitter truth, my aunt's mantra, fuck, my mantra replays on a loop.

"That's why you cycle through husbands," Mom barbed before I closed the door behind me.

Penny's voice rings through my mind too, sharing her experiences and how they molded her into the person she is now, making her believe she's less because she's not society's version of beautiful. While Aunt Rose conditioned mine, society did Penelope's dirty work. All their opinions battle one another like one chaotic mosh pit of arguing voices. I suppress my screams.

Jordan's Penny

I've always led a shallow life, and all it has done is give me a perpetual status: single.

Angry at the piano and irate at Penelope for fucking up my entire life's existence, I rise. I feel sad. Bone-deep, soul-crushing sadness.

This is fucking ridiculous.

I do what's familiar, something that will erase this hurricane of sadness, and pull out the number shoved in my pocket, and make the call. I'm not sleeping alone tonight.

It isn't long before Bridgette shoots me a picture of herself while we're on the phone. My aunt told the truth. She's gorgeous. Once Bridgette agrees to meet, and I grab my coat off the hanger and head to a nearby lounge.

When she strolls into the dimly lit lounge, her dress rides up with each stride her long, smooth legs make. The black dress is as short as it is tight, letting everyone in the bar admire her slender curves. Not a single strand of her blonde manicured hair is out of place and her makeup is flawless, the little she wears. The way her hips move has me shifting in my seat. She's like walking sex with a confidence that could push all my buttons in a big way.

"You're handsome." Bridgette wraps her tanned and lithe arms around my neck. "Mm, and you smell good, too," she whispers as her lips brush against my ear.

She sits beside me, resting her knee against my leg as she slides her tongue over her enhanced lips. Bridgette tucks a lock of her flaxen hair behind her ear and drags her finger south, knowing my eyes will travel along her sexy terrain. Her taut nipples strain against the thin fabric as I strain in mine.

The stumpy, middle-aged, balding bartender takes our order, and we sit in uncomfortable silence as we watch him make our drinks.

"So, tell me about yourself?" I ask, needing to break the stifling silence. Her seductive stares make my hair stand on end.

Her finger grazes over my knee with a wanting deep within her eyes. She says, "Like my measurements?"

"Um." I watch her finger dance higher up my thigh. "I was referring to likes or dislikes. I don't know... something about you."

"Well, I like what I see." She giggles, a timid yet enticing sound, but she's far from shy as I grab her wrist, stopping her from creeping any higher up my leg. She pouts when I place her hand back in her lap.

"What do you do for work?" I ask. I swear if she says modeling, I might scream.

For the first time, I'm hoping she has a tiny spark of intelligence behind all that sexiness. Is it far-fetched to hope she's an art purveyor or something that'd require remnants of an education? This new concept makes all blood flow south. Hell, I'll even take her being a model if she has a secret passion for all things Civil War-related. Something, anything that shows a deeper spark of substance.

"I model."

Damn.

The disappointment consumes me, but my poker face remains strong. "Figured as much. Model for anything in particular?"

"Different outlets."

I take a hearty sip of my drink. And then another. She doesn't go into further detail, and her lack of disclosure reminds me of Penny's old habits before she realized I craved more. But unlike Penny, Bridgette doesn't pick up on my cues and go into further detail. She gives what she gives, and that's all. I guess I'll need to yank the details out of her.

"Like?"

"Print ads."

I take another long sip as she continues undressing me with her eyes and wetting her lips. Realizing she won't give me anything specific, I switch topics.

"What kind of music do you like?"

"All kinds."

"Any specific?" I ask.

"Nope."

I take another sip. "What do you do for fun?"

Her prolonged stares continue to pierce through me. "I'm sure we can come up with a few common interests." Her blood-red manicured nail circles over my knee.

I take another sip before she grabs her drink. Her tongue dances along the rim of the glass, a show just for me before tasting her cocktail.

"Ugh, this is disgusting." She slams the martini glass onto the bar, spilling most of its contents. "Bartender," she shouts. "Do you even know how to make a Cosmopolitan? Or are you an idiot?" She shoves the half-spilled glass toward him, spilling more.

The bartender's cheeks flush as he apologizes profusely. I gulp the rest of my drink, enjoying the burn as I glance at my watch, indifferent to the time.

"It's time to go."

"So," she leans in and whispers, "your place, or mine?"

Now, I undress her with my eyes. I drink her in. Since most of her is already on full display for everyone in the lounge, there isn't much else to imbibe. My focus turns to the bartender, recalling his light-hearted expression morph the moment she called him a foul name. I put a fifty on the bar, offer my deepest apologies, and eye her up and down once more. The guttural moan that escapes me oozes wild sex.

She plays into it as I dig my teeth into my bottom lip, daydreaming about her naked body on all fours, glistening with sweat in front of me or maybe on top. I rise from the stool, getting a marvelous view down her dress and admiring her silky skin. I bet she tastes good too.

"Hmm." My throat vibrates as I walk past her and out of the quiet lounge with Bridgette hot on my trail.

"Should I follow you?"

I'm stopped in my tracks when I spot something on the pavement near my shoe—a penny. The weathered copper coin stares back. When I reach for it, Bridgette huffs with disapproval and suggests it's not worth the effort to retrieve. But she's wrong. I hold the aged coin in my hand and scratch the crusted dirt off one section with my nail. This penny has been to Hell and back and for a moment, my mind wanders, dreaming up a million made-up tales this penny could tell. Underneath all the gook, although it may not be shiny or new, it's still worth something. With the penny clutched tight in my grip, my feet don't slow and by the clicking of her heels, Bridgette can't keep up. I don't turn to her when I answer.

"Nope. You can't give me what I need."

CHAPTER TEN

I WALK THROUGH the office halls, still in a mood from last night's dinner at Mom's and my subsequent meeting with Bridgette. The newfound disappointment in realizing I've been an asshole my entire existence doesn't help either. That shit still sits like a truck on my chest. Then again, I always knew I was an asshole, but that fact never bothered me until now. Making no apologies for my behavior came naturally, and now this overwhelming guilt and regret sit tight as a vise. If I brought Bridgette home, would this ache dull or be worse?

Her sex appeal and the way she wears that dress forced my strongest muscle to stand at attention. Although the dress wasn't see-through, her perky nipples pressed against the material, and the mini length gave away all I needed to know. But after her outburst and what little she brought to the conversation, her appearance, although still enticing, became irrelevant. I craved something... something more.

What the fuck is going on?

With clenched fists, I trudge to my office, and the moment she smiles, my mood lifts.

Penny sits straight at her desk, almost as perky as her high ponytail and neat curls that drape over her shoulder. The hairstyle slims her rounded face a bit, flattering her. Her new hairstyle isn't the only difference she's sporting.

"New glasses?" I ask.

"You noticed."

How could I not? These frame her face better than the ones she's worn in the past. She looks nice in them, but more importantly, she thinks she looks nice in them, too; it's written all over her face.

"I bought you another box of peppermint tea. You were running low. And a little something extra."

I stand in the doorway to my office and spot the work she's placed in neat stacks on my desk. At the top of the pile is the box of tea and a pack of Twizzlers. There's no shielding my appreciation.

"Honey."

I turn to her. "Yes, Penny?"

She giggles, covering her mouth with both hands as her cheeks burn a brilliant shade of bright red. Perhaps she's not immune to me after all. Penny snorts before composing herself. "Use honey, not sugar. For the tea." She shakes her head, and her ponytail whips her face.

"Oh." Now my cheeks warm. "Yes. Thank you. We're still on for lunch, right?"

"As long as you're paying," she teases.

I grab a peppermint tea bag out of the box and head into the kitchen, suddenly thirsty. After cursing whoever oversees the kitchen's inventory because we're out of honey, I grab a handful of sugar packets and walk back to my office. The calming, minty steam fills my lungs as the bag seeps.

"What are you doing? No sugar." Her stern tone scolds me like I'm her truculent four-year-old.

"If we had honey, I wouldn't need sugar. Would I?"

And with that, I take my steaming mug into my office to start my workday and tackle my duties as a partner. Penny waltzes behind me without missing a beat and slams her bear-shaped bottle onto my desk. She's passionate about her tea, I'll give her that.

At that moment, for the second time today, I catch something else different about Penny. She's ditched her flats and is wearing pumps, tall ones too, making her almost my height. Shit. She might be taller than me now.

"Use mine."

I try hiding my smirk while I steal extra glances at her fresh digs. I'm impressed.

"Can you make it?" I ask with sugary politeness. "You make it better than I ever could."

She scoffs, but does as I ask. "You're useless, ya know."

"You must be a 'Save the Bees' fanatic. Is honey a passion of yours?"

She puckers her lips and shoots a knowing glance while squeezing the thick amber sweetener into my mug.

Once she's finished creating the perfect cup of tea for me, she catches me eyeing her clothes. Busted. I close my mouth and divert my eyes to the first folder on the stack as she exits my office. Man, I love our banter. How amazing is it that we can chat, joke around, and I don't need to worry that work isn't getting done? It's fucking amazing.

Once I tackle the pile, my mind wanders with none other than Penelope sitting center-stage. Each day, it baffles me how badly I wanted to transfer her. Man, was I an idiot or what? Watching her work under pressure, I'm blown away by how at ease she is when I bombard her with tasks and lose my cool, through no fault of hers, of course. She's got nerves of steel because she never flinches or seems bothered by my temper. Hell, I've tested her to see what she's capable of, not only for my professional benefit but for a personal one, too. Penny is one tough cookie and I like that about her. Maybe her stint with that attorney was like a boot camp, prepping her for office combat.

I lean back in my chair as she heads down the hall, ready to get another glimpse of her attire without her catching me. Everything she's wearing differs vastly from her usual. Where one day she'll wear clothes ten times bigger than her, and other days she'll throw on something slightly more fitted. Today, she's strutting around in clothing on the complete opposite end of the spectrum.

She's rocking a black power suit. The black jacket remains unbuttoned, but it fits as if tailor-made for her with seams that dart at the waist, slimming her middle. Underneath, she's wearing some sort of plunging V-neck lined, black lace bodysuit with a black semi-sheer insert keeping her decolletage modest and work-appropriate. Only a hint of her ample cleavage is visible compared to some things the other females wear around here. Now, this is how my assistants should dress.

Before today, I just assumed round was her shape, but that was her fault for wearing tents as clothes. Now that she's strutting around in clothes fitted to her body, man was I wrong. Penny has a nice hourglass shape, thinner waist compared to her fuller hips and bust. And for someone that doesn't wear heels, she looks like she can run in them, sure and steady on her feet. I've never been compelled to take inventory on what an assistant wore before, but this woman keeps me on my toes.

Like everything else, the tea doesn't disappoint. Pure perfection; the perfect ratio of honey, water, and tea.

With the amount of effort we've put in last week, I've become conditioned to that fast pace, and breeze through my normal tasks in half the time. With little to keep me busy, the only thing that'd entertain me now is to bother my assistant. It's entertaining to watch her side-long glance drop as her dimple forms from turned-up lips. I rearrange her desk, moving a slotted bin so I have room to sit and face her, stealing an AirPod from her ear. She doesn't even bat an eyelash anymore. I'm still debating if her lack of a reaction is bothersome or comforting.

Today's mix is dance music.

"You like your variety, huh?"

She shoots an unthinking nod, not allowing my presence to interrupt her workflow. I sit for a few, tethered to her music. The frenetic, not-so-silent tapping of my fingers on her desk drum to the beat. I sit through another song, drumming on her desk harder than the last.

Her fingers stop typing and her eyes shift to mine. With one hard exhale through her nose, it must be working. That side-eye is moments away, and then those dimples will appear. How far must I push before she pushes back?

"Hey, Penny," Danielle says as she walks past her desk. "Afternoon, Mr. Stephens."

We respond in unison, and Danielle continues, but her stride is different now that I'm paying attention. She shifts her hips with more exaggeration, as if on a runway. It's a show just for me, but because she expects me to watch, I stop.

"Where are we going for lunch?" I inquire.

"You're paying. You pick."

A different song kicks on and the familiar beat plays. "I used to love this song." I continue my dance on the corner of her desk. "There was this club I used to frequent. I'd buy a few bottles, bring some females into the VIP section, have the greatest time," I brag. Penelope flips me a wicked side-eye, but no dimple follows. Too much bragging, perhaps. "Turn the music up."

She hands over the other AirPod and I pop one in my ear, jamming out on my own. I stay seated at her desk while she works, somewhat bothered by my presence. When the phone rings, she tells the callers I'm unavailable and to call back after lunch.

Penny can type quicker than I've ever seen anyone type before, but today, she keeps having to backspace every third word. That's my fault.

"Go," she demands, holding her hand out, waiting for her music back. "You're keeping me from getting my work done."

"Let's go for brunch instead. Whatever you're doing can wait."

"Mr. Peters needs this by lunch."

"Fine," I drone, retreating to my office. I reserve a table at a new restaurant I've been eyeing and return a few calls. It's better than stalking the clock.

Thankfully, she's the fastest typist in the west and finishes by noon. I hover around as she gathers her things, resting her key fob on the desk. The emblem calls my name like a siren song.

"You have a Jag? We're taking your car," I spit out fast. She turns to me for a moment, hesitating but agreeing.

I follow her to the elevator and we both press the button, but she presses the button to go up while I press the button to go down.

"You park in the garage across the street?" I question. "Why not park in the one downstairs?"

The elevator dings and we get inside. "I like to walk."

We use the sky bridge to our building across the street, then take the elevator to the garage. I make a mental note to never let her walk to her car alone if we stay late again. Penny walks fast for someone in heels, and I quicken my steps to match her stride. I never imagined she'd be so quick on her feet, but Penny has a knack for surprising me.

As she gets closer to the car, the headlights flash once. My strides slow, and my mouth drops open. This isn't just a Jaguar, she has an F-Type, and the car is brand-spanking new.

"I'm paying you too much."

My mouth could catch flies as I trace the sleek lines of the dark gray coupe, well worth over a hundred grand. She has twenty-inch five-spoke rims in glossy black accented with carbon fiber, and bright red brake calipers peaking behind. Even the wheel nuts have the Jaguar logo on each. It's sleek and sexy, like the body of a gorgeous woman. I open the door, and note of the personalized treadplate that says, "Penelope." Inside is just as arousing. I slip onto the red and ebony leather performance seats and admire the interior. Holy shit. Now I understand why my car didn't impress her. Penny's car is nicer than all the partner's cars combined.

"The car was a gift. No need to act crazy." She moves her finger to my chin, pushing up. "Stop drooling in my car."

She might be too late, though.

"Your boyfriend must love you."

Penny presses start and the engine purrs to life and so does her music, to a deafening level, but she's quick to lower it.

"Trust me, if I could get rid of this car, I would. I prefer the simpler things in life. But..." she starts, and I can tell by her tone she loves this car. How can she not? "It's soundproof, so I can blast my music, and no one is the wiser."

I cock my head to the side and lift my brow, skeptical.

"Get out, I'll show you."

She cranks up the volume to an obscene level. The sound system is flawless, customize for her and her alone. The music blares through the Meridian speakers and echoes in the quiet garage. I shut the door and the screeching of someone's brakes in the distance is the only sound echoing in the garage, and not a single decibel more. I open the door again and Penny's music is still as ear-piercing as before. She lowers the volume as I slide back in.

"And you hate this car because?"

She buckles herself in. "Because the trade-off isn't worth it. Simpler things could make me just as happy."

"Like what? Flowers, jewelry, cards, mushy shit?"

"Where are we going?" she asks, and I tell her.

She repeats the name of the restaurant into the car, and the directions come from the speakers. I sit back and sink into the seats, enjoying the smooth ride, and in complete awe at how well she handles this beast of a vehicle. She presses a button on the wheel and says, "Uncle Jack." The car dials a number as we drive toward the parkway.

"Hey, Pen. What exit?"

She laughs, a genuine laugh with her mouth turning up on both corners. Even her eyes smile. "Exit 54 North clear?"

"Should be clear, kiddo. ETA?"

"Hmm," she hums. "Let's try four and a half." She presses the button, and the call disconnects right as he began speaking again.

I ask, "How fast can this car go?"

She hops on the parkway, merging with grace. Penny's arm reaches across my body and tugs on the seatbelt, tightening the strap along my chest and lap. "You're about to find out."

My eyes turn back to the interminable stretch of road ahead and there are no cars in sight. She guns the gas and my head jerks back onto the headrest.

In five seconds flat, we reach sixty miles per hour. She maneuvers like a professional. It's both terrifying and exhilarating. We are well above the legal limit and when I make the mistake of turning towards Penny, my fear rises. She has no intentions of slowing. While we fly on the parkway, my heart races faster than the speedometer. I might get sick.

I make the grave mistake of looking at the gauge. "Maybe you should ease up now, Penny. There's always a speed trap ahead."

"Stop gripping the seat," she barks. Her eyes burn with intensity as she remains focused on the road. "You're creasing the leather."

No sooner than she finishes scolding me, I spot the trooper hiding on the shoulder and panic. She'll get one hell of a ticket and lose her license. Worst-case scenario, I'll Uber her to work each day or pick her up myself.

Her car rings.

"Hey, Pen-dreti. That was three minutes. Better than last time."

Penny laughs as she eases up on the gas. "Pen-dreti? Really?" The guy on the other end of the call laughs, too. "My boss will fire me if I don't get him to his lunch meeting."

"Yeah, yeah, yeah. Be safe and do the speed limit on the streets."

"I'm always safe."

"Yeah, okay," he mocks with disbelief. "You'd be safer if you left J—"

"Okay, Uncle Jack," her voice booms, silencing the rest of his sentence. "I'm hanging up now."

"Should I tell them you said hello?"

She focuses on the road, eyes far off into the distance as she eases up on the gas. Her whiskey eyes move from the road then to her mirrors, surveying her surroundings with cool confidence. At a mere eighty-five, she's as calm and confident as someone driving fifteen.

"Uh, yeah. Sure."

She gets off at our exit and turns the corner. The tires grip the road, hugging the pavement like a mother to a newborn. The car handles almost as flawless as the way she handles the car itself. The one thing in this car that isn't handling well is me, fists in the shape of snowballs with knuckles just as white.

"Both my dad and uncle are cops. And…" she starts through weighted breath, "my dad moonlights as a stunt driver. He teaches actors how to drive and do some of the easier stunts for roles, helps choreograph action scenes with cars, all that fun stuff. I've been driving since I could reach the pedal."

I sit back, impressed. And I hate to admit, but turned on as well. Once we get on a normal city street, she takes it easy on the gas and follows the GPS instructions. I enjoyed the adrenaline-inducing driving demonstration, but I enjoyed this new bit of insight into Penny way more. Her wide-eyed innocence is merely a smokescreen, for she is the holder of many intriguing secrets.

CHAPTER ELEVEN

PENNY VALETS THE car and we're seated immediately. I pull out her chair again. This time, she glances over her shoulder, thanking me with her eyes.

That's what I'm talking about.

We settle into our seats and peruse the menu with some light office chit-chat. I mention another company I've been keeping my eye on, one that the partners might be interested in investing in. They loved the work we put together for this last one. All our information was spot on, and my presentation, flawless. Because we impressed everyone so much with our work, I volunteered to do it all over again. With Penny's help, of course.

"Don't worry, it wouldn't happen right away. I'm still waiting for the right moment to strike. Plus, you need some time to recover from this last one."

She presses her palm flat against her heart, relieved. I'm relieved too, but it's her own fault for reinvigorating my love for this job. All that tedious typing, sorting, and organizing is now taken care of, leaving me to focus on what I need to do.

I watch her review the menu and there's something else about my assistant that's caught my attention. Penny is relaxing more around me, revealing more tidbits about herself, and to others, too, making new friends on our floor. Besides all her changes, I can't deny my own.

My lifestyle brought me happiness, or what I assumed was happiness. Sure, I had fun, but I refused to dig deeper and admit I had nobody. All my phone contacts are either business associates, immediate family, or women I've bedded. No friends. That depressing realization left me lonelier than ever. And the person I have to thank and be livid with is

Penelope Matthews, changing the way I view fun, changing the way I view life. She's easy to get along with and talk to, qualities past assistants and all of my hook-ups have deprived me of.

In the limited time we've spent together, we've built a genuine friendship, and I'd be lying if I didn't admit it feels nice. Different, but nice. Infuriating, but nice.

"Seems like you're making more friends at work these days."

Penny's stare turns dubious. "They're nice because they want front row seats to Sexy Stephens and I'm holding their all-access pass." Her new frames slide down her nose as she continues to read the menu. She pushes them back up, only to have them slide down again. "I was friends with a handful of girls before my transfer, and none expected me to survive the first day." She lifts her glass of water, toasting herself. "But I'm the best assistant you've ever had, so…"

While her glass is still up, I bring mine to hers until they clink. "You are," I agree, and not just to her but, to everyone I talk to about her. "What did Tom need you to do?"

"His new assistant brought over the Meill Management file. I couldn't have Tom waiting until after lunch for the expense report. Someone must've deleted the original file, so I needed to create it all over again."

As she focuses on her menu again, I sit back, perplexed. Why Tom would ask Penelope for anything? That's what his assistant is for. Penelope is far from dumb, yet she did the work anyway.

The waitress arrives to take our order, signaling Penny to order first.

"I'll have the grilled chicken special, please." She offers her menu back to the woman.

"And for you, sir?"

I give the menu a good once-over. My eyes keep drifting back to one item on the long list of options. "I'll have the Farmer Kev burger, medium rare, with the works. And a Coors Light. Thank you."

Penny's eyes widen as the waitress takes my menu and leaves.

"What?"

"Never pegged you for a burger and beer kinda guy. IPA, maybe, but not Coors Light." Penny contorts her face as if tasting something sour.

"There are many things you don't know about me, Ms. Matthews."

"At first, you were an open book, but now, I'm re-evaluating everything. You've got a few chapters you've yet to publish, I see. How do you go from a seared salmon on a bed of couscous with a balsamic drizzle to a ten-ounce burger with pulled pork, fried onion strings, cheese, and God only knows what else? And a beer."

"Tomatoes, lettuce, bacon, coleslaw, slathered in barbeque sauce and ranch dressing. It comes with fries too."

"I can't wait to watch you eat that," she amuses. "Are you going to use a fork, Mister Fancy Pants?"

I can't help but laugh. Little does she know I lived off of beer and burgers in college. They were the perfect go-to fuel when I crammed for tests, or just because I was hungry. I've eaten more burgers than I've bedded women. And that's saying a lot. It is still currently my favorite go-to late-night snack. Not the best choice for someone that likes to stay fit, but I work it off at the gym or bedroom.

"There's only one way to enjoy a burger. With a beer and your bare hands. Forks are reprehensible."

Amused, she takes another sip of her lemon water. "I'm going to enjoy watching this."

"You act as you've never seen anyone eat a burger before."

She laughs. "No one of your caliber. I imagine you eat gourmet meals with expensive utensils, careful not to use the incorrect flatware. And definitely not a domestic beer."

Sure, I give off the vibe she's referring to, but there's more than meets the eye when it comes to me. I just choose not to show it to everyone. Hell, I don't really show this side to anyone, but there's something about Penelope that makes me drop the facade. I enjoy cheap beer, greasy burgers, tees and sweats, and the occasional mindless reality television. What else does she imagine about me that I could debunk?

I shrug lazily.

"You might be the most intriguing person I've ever met," she adds.

"I could say the same for you."

She laughs a demure laugh. "Well," she starts, and her brows rise, a sure sign she's about to fire some sarcasm my way. "That's hardly a compliment, considering the ladies you deal with are as deep as a puddle. Anyone outside of that, hell, anyone that can spell might seem fantastical to you."

And there it is.

I nod in agreement. "True. But back to you. Now I find out you're a secret race car driver. Add that to being an expert bowler and having the ability to adapt to any position you're placed in the office. What can't you do?"

She glances at her lap as an indescribable expression forms. Most likely, she's fidgeting with her fingers, too. Penny lifts her head again, flashing a smile that makes me take notice. "Have you seen my resume?" Her plump lips purse. "I've worked many jobs before this one." Her head tilts to the side, making her grin lopsided. "Yeah," she starts after careful calculation. "I've been with this company the longest."

I recall an earlier conversation we had. She admitted to working for the company about a year before being transferred to me. One year isn't long at all.

"Please don't tell me you like to move around because then I'll need to move with you, and I'm rather attached to my apartment. The view is magnificent and…"

She giggles, shielding her mouth to prevent me from seeing her pearly whites. But I spot the most important part of her reaction, one reaction no one can control—her cheeks turn rosy again. She's blushing and blushing hard.

"Why not stay in one place?" I ask.

"Oh, you know, the cliché love trysts with bosses. So many broken hearts," she deadpans. "They can't handle the rejection, then the stalking ensues. Ugh. Once that starts, I move onto my next victim… I mean job." She maintains a straight face, takes a drink of her water, and bats her thick lashes over the glass.

"Should I stock my freezer with some pints of Häagen-Dazs for when my time comes?"

"Mm-hmm," she purrs.

The waitress delivers our meal, and I might have overdone it with the works. The burger is piled high with pulled pork and coleslaw. There's enough bacon on this to serve an entire continental breakfast at the Holiday Inn. A thick layer of fried, crispy onion strings is sandwiched between a wedge of lettuce and two thick tomato slices, with some dangling off the sides. And the melted cheddar cheese. Oh. My. God. It oozes out the sides from all angles. The brioche bun is toasted perfectly, held into place at the apex of this mountainous burger by not one, but three toothpicks.

Penelope mouths the words, "wow" in silence.

"I'll let you rescind your fork statement."

I'd like to, but I won't.

I grab the burger monstrosity with both hands. Juices, sauce, and half the toppings fall out the back as I practically unhinge my jaw to take one bite. Penny hasn't eaten her food yet. Too busy watching me.

"Mmm," I moan, and my eyes roll to the back of my head. This is what heaven must taste like. My fingers are coated in grease, barbeque sauce, ranch dressing, and slaw juice as I take a long sip of my cold beer. Perfection. I smear a fry in all the sauce that's dripped onto the plate and devour that too.

She eyes me, impressed, and starts on her plate.

"You should try this." With the big burger pressed between my hands again, I hold it out to her, offering her an untouched section. Juice continues to drip down my hands and onto the white linen tablecloth. "Come on. Live a little."

Penny giggles and waves me away. "That's all you, boss. It's dripping all over the place." She cups her hands under the burger and catches a chunk of pork that falls out.

Disappointed she didn't take me up on my offer, I pull the burger back to my mouth and continue indulging. It's nice to let loose for once and not worry about appearances.

I'm not disappointed for too long, though. She pops the pork in her mouth, closes her lids, and moans with approval. Penny turns to the table behind her and steals two white cloth napkins and offers me one.

"Instead of a side of fries, it should come with a box of wipes."

"Mm-hmm," I hum.

After I devoured the burger and most of the fries, we talk for another two hours, longer than any business lunch I've ever had. Honestly, I wouldn't mind if we sat here all day, but Penny deserves a reward.

"Let's hit the road. I'm giving you the rest of the day off."

With a few snaps of my fingers, the waitress returns with the bill, and I hand her my exclusive black card. The waitress, an attractive woman, does little to hide her intrigue; her expression speaks volumes. While Penny and I wait for the car, she glances at me and shakes her head.

"What?"

"Mm-hmm. Don't think I didn't spot what you did back there."

"What are you talking about?"

She clicks her tongue. "You don't even know when you're doing it anymore. It's like a second skin with you. The way you handed the waitress your fancy-schmancy black card exuding cockiness. That card is just a status symbol for you. You're not even using it for the travel perks; you never travel. The card, your car, your suits, none of that defines you. You know that, right?"

Her Jaguar rolls up and I hold my hands out as if showcasing her flashy vehicle on The Price Is Right. "Says the woman who owns this brand-new car." I toss the latter half of the sentence with my own Bob Barker spin.

She rolls her eyes and shakes her head. "I park in a different garage to keep people from seeing that car. The exact opposite of flaunting."

"C'mon, Penelope," I say, incredulously. "This is you, all you—the custom system, your inherited need for speed. The damn thing even has your name stamped on it."

She scoffs. "This car suits you more than me." She turns to the smokey gray ride before us. "Wanna drive it?"

No words are necessary, but I suck my teeth at the offending question. I toss the valet attendant a $50 bill, open the passenger door for her, and wait until she slides in. I position myself behind the wheel, adjust the seat, secure my belt, and fix the mirrors.

Penny settles in beside me and buckles herself in. Her teeth sink into her bottom lip nervously.

"Don't crash my car. He'll kill me and make you watch." Her normal voice is rather soft, almost rounded at the edges, but this time her tone is as sharp as a blade, void of sarcasm.

And with that, I pull away from the curb and enjoy my turn behind the wheel of her luxurious vehicle. I don't take this opportunity or Penny's trust me in for granted. I head onto the parkway, but I don't push the limits as she did.

Damn, this car is a beast but purrs like a kitten. In what seems like a few blinks, we are back to our building and my playtime is over. I found my next lease.

As I exit the car, my heart sinks. This is why I never settle down with a woman and I don't buy cars. I lease both. But this piece of machinery is different. I could drive this forever. Walking away from it feels like a breakup.

I make my way to the passenger's side and open her door, startling her as she rummages through her handbag. After she clutches her chest, she burst into laughter. I'd be lying if I said her beaming smile didn't bring me a bit of joy. It's as infuriating as it is welcoming.

My hand extends to hers, helping her out. The way her skin—silky soft—warms mine, and does something completely unexpected. It was like a zing of electricity zapped through my veins. Nervously, I jerk it away with one quick motion, and the delicate smile she wore sinks like a brick in water.

"Well," she says, flustered. "Thank you for lunch." The words rush out as her eyes dart to her watch.

I made the moment awkward by dropping her hand abruptly, but it's her fault too, making all these unexplainable emotions and sensations rise to the surface.

It was just her hand, Jordan. Get your shit together.

"Thank you again for all your hard work. Enjoy the rest of your day off, and thanks for letting me drive."

She shoulders past me and a mixture of her perfume and mint shampoo blows in my direction as she eases back into her car and slams the door shut.

"Enjoy your weekend, Penelope," I shout while I wave goodbye like the jackass I am.

The tires burn rubber as she pulls away like she's running from something. Once I see my reflection in the glass doors, it's obvious what she's running away from.

With that nagging sensation still pecking at my gut since lunch, I head to Tom's office, determined to get answers.

Tom's desk used to be polished and empty, as if he did little work. Grace was a godsend, a well-oiled machine that kept Tom organized and on track. Now that she's retired, his desk is a nightmare. Post-Its line his monitor like a neon pink frame of things to do, with files scattered along the surface of his desk, some opened, some closed, and some on the verge of falling to the floor. He's one sneeze away from a paper tsunami.

Grace would roll over in her retired La-Z-Boy if she saw this pigsty. She would bark at him for not using a coaster, so she sure as shit would lose her mind if she walked into his office. This man is drowning in paperwork.

Thinking back before Penny came into my life, my desk lived a similar fate, and it wasn't just my office that was a mess. My brain was equally disheveled. The only time I wasn't stressing about something work-related was when I was having sex. I spend every moment of my day worrying. If I lost Penny now, I'm not sure I could survive one day.

I sit in the armchair across from his desk, waiting for him to get off the phone with his son. From what I can make of it, his oldest son forced his little sister to sit through a zombie movie.

Crying. That's all I hear, and the call isn't even on speakerphone.

Penny would freak out if I did that to her. I'd love to see her reaction if I turned on a zombie movie, and the devil inside me is poking at the idea. But I'm almost certain she'd tell me to fuck off if I invited her to a movie with me. Well, maybe she wouldn't use as much profanity, but she'd laugh and assume I was joking.

Tom's new assistant stalks the doorway a third time and leans her head in, smiling at me. "Can I get you something to drink, Mr. Stephens?"

"No."

While Tom reams his son a new asshole, she bends near the filing cabinet outside his doorway, giving me a free show of her shapely ass for the umpteenth time. When she glances over her shoulder to confirm my sights, she winks and shifts her hips.

Jesus. Is subtlety a lost art? She has zero shame. After we share a few more awkward glances, I rise from my seat, give a fake smile, and shut Tom's door right as he hangs up his call.

We shoot the breeze for a few, bouncing prize ideas to raffle off at the upcoming holiday party. Once we tick a few items off our list, I brief him on some mundane work details I've been meaning to discuss with him.

"Like my assistant?" He raises his white, bushy brows.

"Meh. But what I don't like is this desk. What's going on here? I'm having PTSD flashbacks."

"No. Your previous secretaries had one thing in common, but they were all horrible at their jobs. This one gets the job done. I asked for a detailed expense report this morning and it was on my desk before lunch, color-coded and all. Once I get this mess organized again," he gestures to the file orgy sitting in front of him. "I'll be fine."

I nod, able to appreciate a hard worker, but my screaming gut is telling me something isn't right.

"Be right back, Tom."

I throw the door open and hurry to Penny's desk with a purpose, retrieving the last report she created—an expense report for a company Tom oversees.

Once the printer spits the paper out, I snatch the report and hightail back to his office. My pleasant mood from lunch is obliterated.

I break the news to him—his assistant is pawning off her work and taking all the credit. Not only is that unprofessional, but it's shady as fuck and I won't tolerate anyone taking advantage of Penny.

"Why would Ms. Matthews do it?"

"She's too nice to say no. Tom, if this happens again—"

He waves me off before I can finish, shaking his head. "I'll apologize to Ms. Matthews on Monday." Tom tosses a file on his desk and huffs with annoyance. As I suspected earlier, the sliding file causes a domino effect on the rest of the papers dangling off the edge, sending papers and folders tumbling to the carpeted floor. He strings together a colorful mix of cuss words while his face turns red, and the vein near his left eye bulges.

I do some tossing too, sending his assistant a dark scowl as I stalk past. I'll be damned if I let someone take advantage of my Penny.

CHAPTER
TWELVE

I ARRIVE AT the office early Monday morning and Alec takes a seat, resting his heels on the corner of my desk as he brags about some random weekend tryst. I let him do all the talking since my normal routine of cycling through women is on hiatus until further notice. Hell, Candice was the last person I kissed before I tossed her ass out.

"So, what's going on with you? Who's your latest fling?"

Ugh. I should have known Alec would ask. I swear he lives his life through my conquests, so I give him dribs and drabs.

"Met up with another model."

He takes his feet down and leans in, elbows on his knees with his chin resting on his hands, ready for story-time. "Nice. Tell me, tell me," he begs.

"Nothing to report, honestly."

His big, but still somehow beady, eyes narrow in on me, unconvinced until I offer the details he craves.

"The usual: tall and slim, blonde and perky, legs for days. She could give any Victoria's Secret model a run for their money. Feisty, too."

"And?"

I don't even have it in me to lie. "And nothing. I left her on the sidewalk. She still might be waiting; you can go get her."

"Down to fuck and you left her on the sidewalk?"

I slump in my leather chair, hands tucked behind my head, imagining her expression as I walked away. I smile.

"Yup. Tried a different approached for this one. Tried talking, but she's a human pile of saltine dust, bland and salty."

Alec, less content with my version of events, leans back with his arms folded in front of him.

"Who cares? She was D.T.F."

I shake my head. "I tried to talk, at least before we fucked. And then she was rude to the bartender, so that set a foul tone to the night. She seemed like the type to be clingy afterward, so it was for the best in the long run. Did you hear what happened with Candice?"

His eyes widen like when a puppy sees a treat in its master's hand. I've told him all about my fun with her, never one to mince details, especially because there was no future with her. Alec shakes his head.

"After talking shit to Penelope, I kicked her out of my office. She stormed out of here, fast. Haven't found her replacement yet."

"Ah," he exclaims. "That's what all that chatter was about. What about Natasha?"

Oh, Natasha. She was perfect—lithe legs, satiny black hair I would grab from behind, and a chest worthy of sleeping on, pumped with so much saline I'd never need a real pillow again. But every time I think about her now, the strongest memory she leaves behind is her whining. Talk about a miserable person. She was always complaining about something—food too bland, the temperature too hot, too much laughter coming from the table behind us. Or my favorite. It was too airy out. She may have meant windy, but who the hell can tell with her. If she can dream it, she'll complain about it, and she did. Often.

I'm not saying I'm any better. Everything revolved around my wants and needs too, but she was worse. Way worse. And now that the correct head is steering my actions these days, all the qualities that mattered before no longer do. Life was less complicated before, but as frustrating as dealing with my emotions is, no matter how hard I try, I cannot revert to my old ways.

"I cut her loose."

Alec's jaw drop. The disappointment radiates off him in waves. "You're far from a mid-life crisis, so the only thing I can think of is that assistant of yours." He leans back, resting his hands behind his head. "She fucked up your game. Got the hots for her or something?" His smug smile reappears, and I'd love nothing more than to slap it off him. "You wanna hit that, don't you?" He spanks the air, mimicking doggy-style sex, but with his arms stretched out wide.

She's not that big.

Alec contorts his expressions, showing me what I'm assuming is his orgasm face. It shifts and morphs from one grotesque expression to another, making my stomach turn. I'm glad I didn't eat breakfast yet.

"Ew. That's gross." I unleash a foul retching noise, hoping to never witness his climax face again, and my sympathies go out to those that do. "I mean, since she's worked for me, I have changed. She's kept her position because she's an outstanding employee. Plus, I enjoy working with her."

That sly grin doesn't leave his lips. The only thing stopping me from reaching across my desk and yanking his tie tighter is the lawsuit Alec would file against me.

"I feel bad for her," I blurt, letting my unease get the better of me.

"So that's why you're extra nice?"

I suck my teeth, but not because I said anything untruthful. I felt bad, just not in the way Alec interpreted it, and lord knows I can't explain it myself, not to him. "Yeah, but—"

Penny's chair skids across the floor outside my door. Alec and I exchange stunned expressions. My insides become warm, churning with worry. And guilt. God, I hope she overheard nothing that was just said. Alec shrugs his shoulders without care. What an asshole. That concludes our morning gossip session, and he exits without a worry, while I feel like I swallowed a brick.

"Good morning, Penny," I chirp, and put a little extra sugar to my tone to compensate for anything she may or may not have overheard as I sit on the edge of her desk. "Did you enjoy your weekend?"

"Morning." She takes out her phone, cues her music before placing one pod in her ear. "Yes, thank you. You?"

She's back to her old ways of answering. Her responses are brief, curt, and too polite to be friendly, not the warm responses I grew accustomed to. I hate when she's like this, but it's my fault, talking about her with my door open. Shit, talking about her period.

"Let's just put it this way, I'm glad to be back at work." I beam, praying it smooths over any damage that was done.

Shit. What if she asks why I'm glad to be back at work?

Awkwardly, I drop the smile, cough into my fist, and pretend something other than my size twelve shoe is lodged in my throat.

"Oh, before I forget," she interrupts my fake coughing fit and reaches into her purse. In her hand is an envelope. "For you."

I reach for the teal envelope while she offers a modest grin, a hint of something sweet and warm.

"This better not be a resignation letter," I warn as I drop my hand, refusing to take it.

She shakes her head, one quick shake; random strands of hair stick to her nude lipstick, but she's fast to remove it. "Consider this an early birthday/Christmas present."

Taken aback, my arm freezes in mid-air. No assistant ever cared when my birthday was, let alone gotten me anything to commemorate the occasion. She holds the envelope and wags it. I eye her, but take the envelope and break the sealed flap. It is a card meant for a toddler and her grin spreads as I open it. Somehow, she found a card about a boy's favorite blankie, and my laughter bubbles over. On the inside flap, she wrote a web address, a date, time, and street address.

"What's this?"

"My father is teaching a class soon. I begged my uncle to get you a spot, so be on your best behavior."

With my mouth drawn, eyes wide, I stand frozen. "This is amazing, Pen. Thank you so much."

I beckon her to stand, and I wrap my arms around her. She pats my back in slow motion, timid of my touch. I sense her unease. Her body stiffens against mine, but I don't let go. She'll get over it.

Her hair tickles my cheek, and per usual, her dark locks smell like fresh mint, tingling my senses as I fill my lungs. My cheeks cramp from smiling so hard as I sway us. Her hold on me tightens a smidgen. She got over it.

The embrace is comforting and warm, genuine and caring. It's been ages since the last time I hugged someone and didn't regret it and break away.

Her chin rests on my shoulder. With her warmed cheek pressed against my neck, a zing of energy hums in my veins. Knowing Penny's lips are near my ear, my pulse quickens. Her lips part as she takes in a timid breath. The hair on the back of my neck stands on end.

"Um. People are staring," she whispers.

"Oh, sorry." I release her and straighten my tie and toss all the uncontrollable thoughts running wild in my brain into a locked box that will stay in the unattainable depths of my subconsciousness. I shake the momentary chill out of my bones and hold the card in front of me. "No one's gotten me anything before, let alone something this cool."

"After seeing your eyes light up like the Fourth of July the other day, I figured you'd enjoy this. The class is the Saturday after the holiday party, so don't party too hard."

"You're coming, right?" I blast with no room for debate. "For you, the party is mandatory. You're coming," I demand. "Keep me company, make sure I behave myself. You don't want me making you look bad, do you?"

I lay the emotional blackmail on thick, but I want her at the party. With her there, I could have fun instead of forcing myself to smile and play happy host.

She rolls her eyes. "Fine, but not because you're blackmailing me or anything. Some of my coworkers are cool, besides you, of course."

Content with getting my way, and with Penny thinking I'm cool, I leave Penny and jump on my computer, eager to research her father's website. Just from browsing his webpage, the experience looks thrilling, but I'm more excited to meet her dad and uncle. She mentioned she hadn't seen her folks in years, and since she hadn't been forthcoming with information, maybe he'll shed light on some of her dark secrets.

CHAPTER THIRTEEN

THE PARTNERS AND I stand together in the enormous banquet hall, clinking glasses in celebration. We mark another successful year in the books, and with my eye on some new companies to take over, the upcoming year will be just as promising.

The banquet hall looks as if elves came from the North Pole and decorated the room. They sprinkled little touches of holiday spirit in every nook. White-lit garland drapes in the crook of the ceilings with red and gold bows at each arch. A twelve-foot tree sits in the corner with the biggest star I've ever seen sitting on top, surrounded by fluffy white cotton and oversized wrapped boxes with festive bows underneath the tree. They adorned each table with rich red tablecloths, gold dinnerware, and beautiful yet festive glassware. The centerpieces are simple white birch branches wrapped in fairy lights and stuffed inside tall hurricane vases with glittering gold mesh bows around each glass.

Since we've taken over this hotel, we've upgraded the entire staff and brought in a world-renowned interior designer for a complete remodel. The payoff has been phenomenal; the business has never been better.

I stand in the corner and breathe in the festive sights again. I'm always amazed how each year the decorators bring a part of the North Pole into this one room. And it's always a new theme, whether it's an idea or a color scheme; they repeat nothing.

The bar is open and employees trickle in. We mingle around the hall, schmoozing with everyone. Our company wouldn't be where we are in the industry if it weren't for everyone here tonight, doing their part. For once, I don't mind seeing these people outside the office; it's not a chore. My newfound appreciation for everyone is all thanks to one woman making every day stress-free. I'm no longer swimming against the current.

Everyone dresses in their holiday best with husbands, wives, or significant others on their arms. In the past, I've brought dates but this year, I'm turning over a new leaf and I came stag. Besides the fact that I can't make it a late-night because of Penny's amazing gift, in all honesty, there isn't anyone worth bringing tonight.

Tom's wife rambles on about how stressed he is now that Grace has retired and moved off to Florida. I try to reassure her he'll find a suitable replacement sooner than later when the rest of my sentence escapes me.

Standing in the doorway are Melissa and Penny with their coats still on, eyes soaking in their surroundings. Penny stands in the doorway, hesitant, ready to change her mind and bolt.

My mother has told me frequently I was oblivious to the world around me unless something were to affect my daily life. But with a woman, especially one I'm fucking, I spot all the subtle changes. Not that I'm sleeping with Penny, but every time she changes something, I take notice, like right now.

Penny has changed her hair again. Bangs frame her face and she's pulled the rest of her long brown hair into a high, sophisticated ponytail with loose waves toward the ends. She's sporting her glasses again and wearing festive red lipstick.

My entire face spread into a smile once I spotted her, knowing my already pleasant holiday spirit will brighten once we joke, laugh, and mingle. This will be a magnificent party.

Penny unbuttons her long, black wool coat, and I'm stopped in my tracks. She's dressed like a secretary from the fifties, sporting a long, body-hugging, black pencil skirt, skimming just below her knees with a white silk blouse and red suede pumps. And sitting at the base of her neck is a lovely strand of white pearls.

A lump in my throat forms and no matter how hard I swallow, it doesn't budge.

I excuse myself and walk toward them with this unexplained bundle of nerves in my veins. I'm never nervous around anyone, but I'm nervous now, as if I have everything riding on this greeting.

"Just the two ladies I was waiting for," I greet, and almost trip over my two feet.

"Waiting for me?" Melissa asks.

"Yes, Melissa. Santa got you something extra special this year." My smile broadens. She'll gush over her gift. "It's under the tree. A little thank you for finding Penny for me."

"I gave you what you deserve, not what you think you wanted."

Melissa surveys the tree in the distant corner of the room before scurrying to fetch her present.

Penny fidgets with her fingers, dimples dig deep, and her cheeks blush as she remains silent. She better snap out of that soon. Her eyes go on a winter wonderland journey as she canvases all the decorations on display.

"This is breathtaking." Her full, red lips part and she takes it all in. I follow her eyes with mine, reliving it with her. It is amazing, and that Christmas is my favorite holiday doesn't hurt either.

"You look amazing. Did I tell you that already?"

"No," Penny answers just as awkwardly as I asked. "But thank you. You clean up well, too. I'll be beating the ladies away, maybe even some guys," she quips before reaching over and shifting my tie. "With it off-kilter, you look less formidable and more human. Let the real you show. For once." Satisfied with her adjustments, she places her flattened palm against my chest and focuses her whisky eyes on mine. "But remember," she points a warning finger, "you have an important lesson in the morning, mister."

I throw my hands up, surrendering to her. Misbehaving is not in my plans tonight.

"I saved you a seat at my table… that's if you don't mind sitting with your boss."

She shrugs.

I take her coat, give it to the coat check, and retrieve two glasses of champagne from the tray of a server circling the hall.

"May the upcoming new year bring us both happiness and success," I toast, holding my glass to hers.

"And may you have a safe lesson tomorrow."

Our glasses clink and we take a sip of the bubbly, all while sharing a magnetic gaze.

Once Penny walked through the door, I ignore my duties as partner and stay with her at the table. We fall into our usual routine of bantering and goofing around. She slaps my arm and laughs until no noise comes out of her mouth, only wheezing. Either I'm killing it with the jokes tonight, or she's a lightweight and is feeling the buzz. Either way, I'm enjoying the attention a little too much. She becomes out of breath after a strong bout of laughter and her hand stays on my bicep until she gasps for air, holding her stomach with her other hand. It becomes infectious and I laugh uncontrollably, too. She's the only person who can make my cheeks hurt from laughing.

"Looks like someone is enjoying herself."

Our eyes drift upward and her hand falls. A tall, muscular guy stands in front of our table holding three red roses. I'm unsure if all the eyes are on us because Penny and I were laughing too loud or because this random man is standing by our table. Once I read the room, all eyes are on him, not me. I suppose he's decent-looking if swollen muscles wedged into a shirt two sizes too small is your thing.

"Did I interrupt something?" His eyes drift to me before settling on Penny with a strange intensity. "Not happy to see me?"

Penny straightens in her seat, back as straight as a ruler, and she clears her throat. "No." She shakes her head and rewards him with a smile of beautiful satisfaction. "No, don't be ridiculous." She jumps to her feet and throws her arms around his swollen, tatted neck. "I thought you were coming home tomorrow, had I known. . ." her voice drifts to silence as he squeezes her middle before pushing her away.

"Aren't you going to introduce me?" he asks, almost like a demand.

"Yes, Jord-Mr. Stephens, this is my—"

"I'm her fiancé, John."

"Fiancé?" My eyes dart from him to her in an instant. "I didn't know you were engaged." The confusion hardens my words.

"Really?" John asks aloud as Penelope sinks back in her seat. "Not surprised, actually," he amuses. "She's good at keeping secrets." Although his tone seems curt, his broad smile says otherwise.

John takes a seat beside Penelope, handing her the flowers and placing a kiss on her cheek. All the laughter between us disappears, sucked from the table by the man holding Penelope's attention now. Her knee bobs under the table, bouncing and rubbing against mine. She's dancing with excitement now that he's here, no longer forced to hang out with her boss. Once she notices her jumpy knee is grazing mine, Penny shifts in her chair, moving closer to her fiancé, snuggling against him. I shift my weight as the chair becomes uncomfortable.

John leans into the crook of his fiancé's neck as if to share a secret. Penny closes her eyes and her lips curl upward, forming a passive smile, and tilts her head to listen.

"Where are my manners? Let me get you a drink. What's your poison?" I ask, rising from my chair.

"I'll get my own, but thank you, Jordan."

Without another word, I leave the table and give them a moment alone. I didn't care for the way he said my name, but then again, maybe that's just how he talks—pointed. Even though I shouldn't, I head to the bar and order a whiskey on the rocks for myself; my mouth has gone dry. It's one thing to hear about him in the few conversations she's shared, but it's another to have him here.

Danielle and Patricia gawk at Penelope's fiancé nearby and make some rude comments about how he's too good-looking for Penelope and they can't fathom what he sees in her. I'm sure they'd say the same thing if we were together. We live in a fucked-up world.

What?

I shake my head, unsure why that even popped up to begin with, and return my sights to the table, sensing Penelope's stare. Her expression is one I don't quite understand. But before I could decipher it, John takes his finger and pulls her chin toward him, making her break our connection. His lips travel near her ear for another time, and she agrees to whatever he's said before he brings his lips to hers. It's a kiss so deep, it's possessive. I should turn away, but I don't.

Once he lets her up for air, she takes a rushed sip from her flute. Her eyes fall toward her lap before searching for me again. As I down the whiskey double in my glass, she catches me, cursing me with that fire in her eyes for not behaving myself. But I need to take the sudden edge off.

Before she sips her champagne again, John reaches for the glass and pulls it away from her mouth, placing it in the center of the table before heading to the bar in the opposite corner of the hall.

"You've got some competition," Melissa discloses as she taps on my left shoulder but approaches from behind on my right.

"Huh?"

"You're no longer the hottest guy in the building. Penny's man is giving you a run for your money. He's been here all of what, five minutes? The entire hen house is squawking."

"What are people saying?"

"Enough to make me dislike most of the staff on your floor." She sips her wine, and we both cast our eyes in the same general direction. Melissa genuinely likes Penny and whatever was said bothers her. "Look," she gestures toward Alec. "Even he's jealous of the guy."

She's right. Alec is scoping out Penny's fiancé, standing straighter, fixing his tie, sucking in his stomach, and puffing out his chest. Melissa and I share a light chuckle.

"But fuck them," Melissa adds with conviction. "He's the lucky one. Penny is awesome and a saint, especially if she can deal with you. I don't care who he is, or how big those muscles are, she's the real catch. Not him." She taps her glass to my empty one, toasting Penny without her knowledge. "Thanks for my present. Maybe Penny will be my plus one for a fun, girl's getaway."

I imagine Penny traveling with Melissa to the all-expenses-paid spa resort. She'd have fun, and who couldn't use a weekend getaway now and again? I could use one right now.

"I'm glad you let her prove herself and didn't transfer her like everyone assumed you would. You seem happier now, less stressed than before." She pauses for a moment, steals a glance at Penny and then me, placing her flattened palm over my heart, tapping twice. "Well, 'seemed happier' is more appropriate now." She leaves to go chat it up with Matt's wife and I'm alone again.

A few of Penny's office friends, her actual friends, not the fake ones that chat with her just to catch glimpses of me, sit at the table with her and her fiancé. I do my best to stay away. Sitting there now might be inappropriate and awkward.

Out of all the conversations we've had, Penny only referred to him as her boyfriend. Why keep that a secret or downplay the relationship?

And why the fuck do I care?

With temptation running an all-time high, I steer clear of the bar and busy myself mingling. It was easier to put on a cheerful face before, but now the effort to maintain a smile is painful. I need to get through the rest of the party, but in all honestly, I'd rather go home, sit in front of the piano, and play.

I head into the hallway for a breath of different air. The jolly surroundings are like a tourniquet on my chest until I spot Penny exiting the restroom.

"Hey," I say, throwing my hands in my pockets, fiddling with the loose coin inside. I rub the rough surface between the pads of my thumb and index finger, hoping it soothes me.

"Oh, hey." Penny startles and takes a step back.

"You having fun in there? That was a pleasant surprise for you, having your fiancé show up like that." I put extra zing on her secret. Maybe a little too much.

"Yeah, everything is great, he's great like that," she blurts. Her rushed words are almost as frantic as her eyes as they dance over my shoulder, refusing to make eye contact with me. "He's expecting me back at the table."

I eye her up and down. Not one limb of hers stays still. She must sense my confusion, seeing her so wound up to get back inside.

She leans in closer, but not too close. "He thinks we have a thing for each other," she confides with a hushed volume. "I keep telling him you're my boss, you only date models, and blah blah blah. I mean, yeah, we're friendly, but we kind of have to be so we can work well together, right? Um…but if he catches us talking alone, you know, away from the party, it'll just add fuel to the fire he created in his imagination."

The sting of her words brands me. I've never been friends with any of my assistants, and I never assumed I needed to be just to get an efficient workflow either. Perhaps she's right, though. Maybe we work well together because we are friendly. It still doesn't change the fact that what she said affected me, and it took me by surprise.

John stalks down the hall, catching us how she didn't want him to.

"Here you are. . . and you're with your boss. Again." He stares at us with a curious flash in his eyes as I square my shoulders, unintimidated.

I'm only an inch taller than him, but he's built like a linebacker, all wide shoulders, thick neck, and muscular arms. His swollen biceps stretch the material of his short-sleeve white button-down shirt, showing ink on all his exposed skin—neck, biceps, forearms, and hands. One forearm has a large copper penny, and the other arm has a gnarly image of a geisha with a dagger exiting her mouth and blood spraying in various directions that transform into red rose petals.

"Babe," Penelope coos. "I think you're right. I shouldn't have had that champagne." She rubs her temples. "I'm ready to go home."

John extends his hand to mine as Penny walks away without saying goodnight. "It was nice meeting you," he says icily. His hand tightens around mine and I reciprocate until both of our knuckles turn to the color of snow.

John leans in closer, eyeing me from head to toe, and snickers. There's a charge between us, an unspoken animosity that appeared only after Penny walked away. He releases his grip and chases after Penny.

"What the fuck is his problem?"

CHAPTER FOURTEEN

I PULL UP to an abandoned property. A chain-linked fence lines the street, but the gate is wide open. I confirm the address Penny wrote again, making sure I'm in the right place.

The large, tattered warehouse shows years of neglect from the shattered windowpanes and the worn exterior. To the left of the building are three parked cars, all banged up and dusty, nothing like the ones in those Fast and the Furious movies. Upon spotting them, I'm positive this must be the correct location.

The vacant lot stretches further than my eyes can see, but I spot the bright orange safety cones off in the distance.

"You must be Jordan Stephens."

A brawny man with short, light brown hair approaches with his hand extended, eyes just as golden as Penny's. Even his smile reminds me of hers, big and authentic, welcoming and full of warmth. He's younger than I would have imagined her father would be, but there's no denying the family resemblance. It is woven in their DNA.

"I'm Patrick Matthews. Why don't you take a seat? We're starting soon." He ushers me to an open chair and leans into my ear, "If anyone asks, you're prepping for a car commercial." Penny's dad gives an affirming dip of his head and I take a seat facing a dry erase board, along with two other gentlemen.

Penny's father begins, giving us the basic safety precautions before we step foot near any of the assigned cars. Patrick pairs the other guys with two assistants. One was Officer Jackson Matthews, which I'm assuming was the same uncle Penny called on our way to lunch. Partnered together are Patrick and I. Perfect. Who better to learn about Penny than her father?

"So, how's she doing? Is she okay?" he asks as we walk to a beat-up white BMW M3 from the '90s.

"Penny? Yeah, she's great, the best assistant ever to work for me."

He takes a seat behind the wheel and starts the engine, flaring it to life. Where Penny's car purrs, this car roars, vibrating my whole body once the engine turns over, rumbling beneath us.

The supped-up car, although older, is equipped for fast speeds with harness seat belts and steel rods to handle accidental roll-overs. The fact that we'd need any of these safety features makes this experience even more intimidating, but awesome at the same time. Anticipation tickles my skin. The raised bumps on my arms are proof.

"We all found it odd when she approached my brother about getting you in on a lesson. Normally, she keeps us a secret."

"Penelope is on the mysterious side. Had we not taken her car to lunch one day, I would never know about her hidden driving talents. She drove like a speed demon, especially with that car."

"She has a death wish and I'm not only talking about her driving, but you can imagine how many speeding tickets we've gotten her out of."

As he speaks, he guns the gas, upshifting in seconds until he reaches a stretch of desolate land designated for our lesson. Now I understand where Penny gets her inherited need for speed.

For his first lesson, he shows me a basic J-turn. He explains that it's a 180-degree spin around a cone where you pull the emergency brake, locking the rear tires which cause the car to drift before gunning the gas again, bringing the car back in the direction you just came from.

During his first run, the thrill of the move distracted me from paying any attention to his instructions. After the second run, it became easier to focus on Mr. Matthews' timing. Like a mental checklist, I make note of when he yanks on the emergency brake and flicks the wheel. He executes the move a few more times and then orders me to switch seats, ready to let me try.

My heart races and I haven't even pressed on the gas yet. After a few quick breaths, I speed up and attempt the move, but mess up and hit the brake pedal instead of the gas after drifting in the turn.

"It's exciting, isn't it?" Mr. Matthews asks, eyes wide as if reliving his first-time rush.

With my heart beating in my throat, all I can muster is a flabbergasted nod.

"Start again," he orders.

With each attempt, my turns sharpen, and my timing improves, performing cleaner J-turns. Penelope's father gives me his seal of approval.

We switch seats again and the next move he shows me is a Rockford turn, which was named after the show The Rockford Files. Where the first trick started in drive, this maneuver starts in reverse, but by the time you've completed your 180-degree turn, you switch the car to drive.

"For maximum drift, you'll need to hit about twenty to twenty-five miles per hour in reverse before flicking the wheel as hard as you can. As the front of the car swings around, about halfway through the turn, you'll switch it into drive. It's easy once you get the hang of it. You can try this in any car, manual or automatic."

He runs through the move and describes each step as he's performing it. The detail in which he describes when each step is performed and why helps me feel as if I'm doing it myself. He repeats the Rockford turn a few times until I'm confident to try.

Before I attempt the maneuver, I gun the car in reverse to get comfortable with how quickly it picks up speed before driving back to the orange cone.

"Did Penny tell you she did some stunt work in a few movies?"

I slam on the breaks and a cloud of dust billows around the car. When I turn to him, he must've already known the answer to his question.

"Sadly, she left that tidbit of awesomeness off her resume."

He laughs, and my insides warm, noticing yet another similarity they share.

"A movie executive watched her horsing around on set, the liability alone," his palms cover his eyes, "should have gotten me fired, but Penny, she was a firecracker, worked a room like a professional salesperson. She could sell ice to an Eskimo. Penelope smooth-talked her way into a role. What normal sixteen-year-old can swindle that?" He laughs again. "After that, she landed a few jobs and one on-screen role, although minor. But everything changed in her senior year of high school. Penny made her choice." Mr. Matthews stares out of the window for a few seconds. His mood shifts, as does the beaming smile he had moments ago. "We hope she comes to her senses before it is too late." Before I can ask what he means, he adds, "Ready to try your first Rockford turn?"

I bow my head and gun the gas in reverse, holding the wheel steady before whipping the wheel to the left. Hard. Just as the front of the car swings right, I switch gears and throw the car into drive, righting the steering wheel and drive straight. If it weren't for my shaky nerves, the turn might've been smoother.

My heart races again. Adrenaline pumps through my veins. Fast. I can't wait to try again, and again. It's obvious why adrenaline junkies exist; the high is unlike anything I've ever experienced before, drugs included. Does Penny still get this intense rush while racing down the parkway, passing the world at lightning speed, or is the thrill of it gone now that she's done it a million times before? But with a high this surreal, I can't imagine I'll ever grow tired of it.

"Not bad," he commends. "Now, try again."

I run the trick a few times, and each time, my turn becomes less wide than the last until I get Patrick's two thumbs up.

"Don't go practicing this on side streets like Penelope used to do," he adds.

He teaches me a few other cool drifting maneuvers, nothing I can use in my daily driving, but the adrenaline rush is electrifying. And I owe this amazing experience all to Penny.

Just as my heart acclimates to beating a million miles per minute, the lesson ends, but Patrick asks to sit down and talk. All the questions about Penny run through my head. Why hasn't she seen her parents in years? Why does her father act as if she lives in another country? And what choice did she make? As simple as those questions are, they hold a heaviness that I'm not sure I want to stir up.

I keep the conversation light. As it is, whenever he speaks her name, his brows pull together, and his naturally pleasant disposition saddens. He goes on a Penny milestone montage, offering the highlights of her youth, moments he couldn't be prouder. I ask about her perfect bowling game, and he beams with pride over her achievement, just as Penny did when she shared the story with me.

"The entire alley came to a stop, and the crowd surrounded our lane. Everyone dropped their voice to a whisper. She threw a perfect hook, frame by frame," he says with immense pride. "Everyone started cheering, clapping, shouting. You couldn't hear the person beside you." His smile widens as he takes this trip down memory lane. "Even the local paper featured her. Then the alley hung a plaque with her name on it and gave her one to keep. She could do anything she put her mind to." Just as he finishes, sadness spreads over his face like a rolling frost.

The desire to dig further and ask the questions gnawing at my insides now seems far too personal. If Penelope wanted me to know, she'd have told me, right? The last thing I need is for her to punish me with silence, because upsetting her is the last thing I ever intend to do.

"We were so young when we had her, only seventeen. Kids ourselves. But she is a wonderful kid, always has been. After high school, though, things got bad. She chose, and now we all suffer from it." With his head hanging low, eyes fixated on his fidgety hands, he says, "I'm sorry, this is too hard." He rises from his seat and extends his hand to mine. "It was nice meeting you." Mr. Matthews proceeds to his car with his head slumped down. Once he turns over the ignition, he speeds away, leaving a trail of dust.

"What the hell happened after high school?" I mutter aloud.

As Penelope's uncle packs up the folding chairs and dry-erase board, I sit alone and do what I've been doing a lot. Think. My ass grows numb until I leave, driving slowly on the side streets with no clear destination in mind. Even after a day with her father, Penelope Matthews remains a vault of secrets.

Jordan's Penny

PART TWO: PENELOPE

CHAPTER FIFTEEN

THE TUNES BLARE from the speakers; the vibration shakes my insides. Music is my only salvation.

I slide the couch back in place, and pain seers through my shoulder, reminding me why the couch is out of place, to begin with. But like everything else, I grunt through the pain. As I walk through the house, I avoid every mirror we own, too ashamed of the other reminders.

I freeze when the door opens, expecting his yelling to echo through the halls instead of the dancing beats from the speakers. But there is no rage-filled screaming, only the stumbling of footsteps and then a loud crash of glass exploding on the hardwood floor in the foyer. I release a long, silent exhale. Guess who's cleaning that up.

"Alexa, turn the volume down," I request before he bitches.

"Dinner's not ready?" he scoffs, staggering in the hallway. His shirt has a long rip at the neckline and crusted blood stains his nose. John uses the walls for balance as he stumbles forward. If the glossy, drunken haze of his eyes didn't give it away, the alcohol wafting off his skin like a bonfire would. "Why isn't dinner ready?"

"What happened to you?"

John slams against me, bearing all his weight on me. I yelp in pain, loathing every inch of his muscular frame on my bruised shoulder as I struggle to keep us upright. He shifts his weight again and I slam my back into the wall behind us. He's like a boulder, bearing all his heft onto me, and his breath could set the house ablaze, burning my eyes with each hurried exhale.

His sloppy lips graze my neck until his teeth scrape against my skin.

"I let off some steam," he drawls.

He bites down on me, and I suck in a strained breath through gritted teeth. As his lips linger, I manage enough strength to push him off so I can help him to the bedroom.

The last time he used that excuse, he claimed he was going to the gym. When the police dropped him off two days later, they told me he started a fight at a strip club. They did not arrest him because an officer recognized John from his short-lived professional football career.

We stagger to the bedroom. Gravity and booze weigh his feet down, making every movement between us slow, jagged, and unsteady. John almost takes us both down when he falls onto the mattress with a thud. His drunken body goes limp, and for a moment I relax my spine.

"Come lay with me," he slurs.

"I need to check on your food." I turn to leave, but he grabs my wrist and pulls me onto him. The shooting pain between my wrist and shoulder is instant. My vision turns starry. His powerful arms wrap around me, caging me in a hug. It is tight. Too tight. "John, please. I can't breathe."

"Let me kiss you and make everything better," he slurs as his chilly hands travel under my shirt. His voice is full of longing and sadness, but his rushed movements are rough, too rough to be pleasurable. "Love me again and not that fucking boss of yours," he mumbles with disdain. John scrapes his nails down the length of my spine, and I dig my teeth into my lower lip to fight off my cries. "He couldn't possibly want you. Hell," John opens his eyes and searches for mine. "I don't even want you half the time, but only I can love you."

I wish I could show John what it's like to be loved by him. Oh, the pleasure I'd get from slapping, punching, and slamming him into walls or furniture every time his eyes wandered. Then I would run off and fuck anyone I desired as extra salt in the wound. But I learned fast what happens when I put my hands on him. That's a pain I never want to experience again, even though lately, I don't have to do anything to experience pain; he only needs to imagine I did.

His hands become rougher while his lips drag along the crook of my neck, sucking and biting my skin. The more I pull away, the harder he sucks or bites, so I grit through his drunken advances, just like everything else I suffer through with him. This is my life. This is the choice I made.

John.

I lay motionless and let him do as he pleases, hoping he passes out before any actual sex takes place.

"You will never be what I want," he moans against my skin. His hands burn as if dipped in fire, leaving a trail of heat in his wake. "But you'll always be the one I need, the one I always come back to."

He rolls me onto my back. In one swift motion, he removes my shirt and forces my bra down, caressing my breast in his mouth. I cover both eyes with my hands and rub away the tears with my palms. His constant reminders of how unattractive I am never dull in effect; the sting always bites. It's not long before his hands and mouth slow and his body goes limp next to mine. I wait. His heavy snoring has never been so appealing.

I slither out from under his arm, sliding off the bed and onto the floor.

The constant emotional abuse hits me like a high-speed train, knocking all air from my lungs. Sometimes, John's physical abuse pales compared to the emotional abuse he inflicts. The physical heals, but the emotional festers until it infects every aspect of my day.

I take in a few deep breaths, careful not to make too much noise. Waking him might mean he'll finish what he started, and I don't have the stomach for that.

I pluck my shirt from the floor, putting my sore and now discolored arm back in the sleeve. It's ironic how I'm always picking things or myself off the floor when it comes to John.

I stand in the foyer, admiring my favorite vase, now in a million shards scattered on the polished hardwood. The glass crunches beneath my shoes. I don't even have the energy to shed another tear tonight.

All I do is clean up after him while pretending my world is different. I put my music in my ears and turn off the house speakers as not to wake him any sooner than necessary; although when he's passed out like this, it buys me two hours of peace.

As I'm swept away by my tunes, I dream of a better life and pretend the happy lyrics are about me. Just like Cinderella, I get to work. She and I are similar in some respects. We both clean up after evil people who make an unescapable situation unbearable. But unlike Cinderella, no fairy godmother or Prince Charming was coming to rescue me. And I doubt Cinderella fantasized about gouging her stepmother's eyes out with shards of broken glass. She was too pure of heart to conjure up sadistic schemes, but here I am imagining them. There was a time I was full of love and happiness, but the longer I stay with John, the more the light inside me dies.

After sweeping the broken glass, I wash my hands in the bathroom and make the mistake of looking in the mirror.

"Oh. God."

My heart nearly flew out of my chest, startled by my reflection. How did I forget what I looked like? My swollen lip is split down the center, and the cut by my eye is a colorful mix of blues and purples with inflamed skin and dried blood crusting on the surface. The cut isn't as prominent with my glasses on, but I've got at least one week before my theater-quality makeup could even help disguise this. I've become a professional at covering up broken and discolored skin, but sometimes these things are impossible to hide.

As the music blares in my earbuds, no lyrics can erase this image. It's not like I haven't gone to work with injuries before. I dread the pitiful stares when they see the broken me, battered, no matter how many times it's happened at past jobs. But this will be the first time showing up at The Levaux Group with injuries this extreme.

I've never been strong, but working for Jordan has given me this perception of having strength. None of his prior assistants stayed his assistant as long as I have. No one. Yet, I've done the unthinkable. I've lasted. And no one has received the accolades from him as I have. No one.

But if I walk through the hallway with these battle wounds, they'll get a glimpse of who I truly am. They'll put two and two together and realize the interior wounds are just as vile and brutal as the exterior ones. My coworkers can't see this side of me. If they do, it won't end well for me. It never does.

Left to my own devices, I think about Jordan. Not the smartest move, I admit. After all, he's the reason for our most recent fight, but sometimes I can't help myself. His lesson was yesterday and as eager as I am to talk all about it, there's no way to conceal my lip. The wound is still too fresh, and the swelling hasn't gone down as much as I've iced it. Taking a personal day or two is my only choice, so I make the dreaded call.

With the table set for two, I eat alone while John snores like a chainsaw in the bedroom. I prefer it this way. The only time I enjoy an extra plate setting is when Jordan joins me, but John is wrong about him. There's no way he feels anything for me other than pity. I often remind myself about what he said to Alec the morning I gave him his present. Even though it hurt when he said I was gross, it's nothing new. I'm used to it. Hell, my fiancé says it, too. Jordan would never be into me. But, at least, he treats me like a friend. It's nice to eat a meal with someone that wants to talk and not hurl insults and threats my way.

And as hard as I keep my relationship with Jordan professional, its's as if he tries even harder to make it personal. He pities me, but maybe he needs a friend. Or since he's well-rounded at reading people, especially women, perhaps he sees through me, realizing I'm the one that needs a true friend. The concept isn't unfathomable. If he could see me, he'd be on a short list of friends I have outside of work: Josey and my dear friend, Alexa.

"Alexa, are you my friend?"

Her pleasant tone replies, "Sure, I'm always happy to make new friends."

My mind wanders while I plop down on the couch. No music blares in my ears or the speakers now, no television plays in the background, only silence and daydreams of work and Jordan.

A natural smile blooms when I reminisce about all the times he tried digging for information, either bothering me at my desk or calling me into his office. Just when I think he's about to give me another task to do, he asks a random question about me like he's writing my biography.

I mastered the art of being vague, only giving what's politely necessary and nothing more. For Jordan, it's a challenge to investigate further. Then, he puts on that look—puppy dog eyes, jutted lower lip with his head tilted to the right at a ten-degree angle. I don't like admitting it feels nice getting attention from him. Who would complain about that? He's gorgeous, successful, and sweet, even though he'd never classify himself as the latter to anyone. But he's out of my league, so I need to stop over-analyzing our interactions; I'm only making my life more difficult.

Ironically, it's those qualities that landed me in my current nightmare. And just like that, I'm brought back to my present reality when I see a picture of John and me at his friend's wedding. Pain always follows John's assumptions. He assumed I was flirting with the best man, so we left the reception early and he threw me to the ground in the parking lot. As he towered over me, I pleaded with him to stop. He couldn't have been more wrong about the situation, but John was never wrong. And good luck to anyone that tried telling him that. He spat in my face and then backhanded me.

I need not remember the pain of that night because the pain of last night is still too fresh—being thrown to the ground yet again, and landing on my shoulder and wrist wrong. When my head hit the floor, my glasses scraped my temple, narrowly missing my eye. As I tried to get up, he backhanded me, splitting my lip. Attractive men who are out of my league will be the death of me.

Most women drool over John. He's tall, at least five inches taller than me, with dark hair and eyes to match, and just enough scruff on his face to have that slept-in sexiness. He works out a lot. And it shows. His arms and chest are a solid mass of muscle. And John's body is like the perfect V, with wide shoulders with a slimmer waist, and olive skin decorated with perfectly placed ink. He's the type that women gawk at just as much as he gawks at women. And if women have a "spank bank," I'm positive John stars in many.

But through the years, I've stopped fawning over his looks. His character is all I need to know—he's a drunk, a cheater, a liar, and abusive, both physically and emotionally. None of those qualities are sexy, no matter how attractive his body is without a shirt. To me, he'll always be a monster.

When I was in high school, his charm blinded me, although not immediately. He was the outgoing football team captain, and I was the shy, overweight girl. When I became a tutor, hoping it would impress prospective colleges, the school paired me with John. He wasn't a quick learner, so we spent a lot of time together, more than I cared for. At one point, I swore he was the dumbest jock to have ever lived. A sloth might've been a quicker study.

But John wasn't mean back then, despite making up lies about me to his fellow teammates. None of it mattered because I had the upper hand. I didn't need a tutor, and he did, so I dangled that carrot in his face every time he pissed me off. As many times as I would quit, it never lasted long. No tutors volunteered to take him on and John told me how important football was to him. I would not give up on him like all his teachers had. He deserved a fighting chance at his dream. The only way to remain on the team was to pick up his grades, and I was the deciding field-goal kick. My determination made it happen.

Back then I didn't have a problem standing up for myself either—he'd push my buttons and I'd push his right back, only harder. It became our thing, our little game of who can piss the other off more, and I was the champion.

After a while, our pissing contest ended, and he became sweet, almost too sweet. I assumed he was pranking me like in the movies—lead the fat girl on and then BAM! Something embarrassing happens in front of the entire school and it shatters her heart. Well, I wasn't so foolish. I was no one's punch line.

John would show up at my job on the weekends, buying coffee even though he never drank one sip. He'd wait until I got a break so he could ask me a school-related question, one that would take more than a second to answer. In the mornings, he'd come to my house and walk with me to school. At first, I ignored him, but he persisted every morning. When he didn't have football practice, he'd wait by my locker, ready to walk me home. I couldn't get away from him and I tried. The more I pushed him away, the harder he tried to prove he was genuine until I gave in. That was my ultimate mistake.

Once we became official, he flipped a switch inside him. The sweet jock I fell for changed. If anyone talked about us, he'd start a fight. At first, it was nice to have someone defend me, someone to protect me and my heart; especially someone as swoon-worthy as John. To him, he was the lucky one, and he'd do anything for me or us. We were friends first, and that bond was solid, exceeding all else. He loved me for me, regardless of my weight. I felt safe with him, and he showered me with love.

After we graduated, he got worse. He became even more possessive. His temper was a short fuse. Not even a downpour could snuff him out. I worried constantly, making sure he couldn't misconstrue anything I did or said, even if it was innocent. The mounting stress took its toll. I put on more weight and became depressed, but I was still so hopelessly in love with him. He was my first love, and no one could tell me otherwise.

My parents tried to make me understand how bad he was for me, but when you're wearing rose-colored glasses, the obvious signs, even when they're right in front of you, were ignored. He cheated more times than I can count, and I'd always find out, crying for days, asking myself what I did wrong. Did I lack something other girls didn't? Self-doubt took over, but it wasn't enough for me to leave. He claimed he was no longer attracted to me with the added weight and found me gross. Even his outright evil comments weren't enough to get me to hate him, let alone leave.

I lost weight, hoping he'd love me again, hoping he'd remember the person he fell in love with, but the cheating never stopped. It never even slowed. He acted like a single man, adding notches to his belt. I wouldn't leave because John had an amazing way of making me believe no one could ever love me as he loved me. Even if he gave me half his heart, I was grateful. I took what little I could get and in time he'd find out none of those other girls would love him the way I did. And it'd be enough for him to stay and change for me.

I wasn't a total pushover or doormat. I confronted him about his cheating. After he admitted it, I slapped him so hard I sprained my wrist. He wasn't used to me fighting back, nor did he like me fighting back. John backhanded me.

"It was an accident," I told my parents, but I should've known it wouldn't stop there. All the red flags were blatant, flashing like neon signs.

By my third hospital visit, my parents told me I had to choose. As much as I loved my family, they couldn't give me the love John could. They didn't understand. When he behaved, things were great, mind-blowing, earth-shattering even. But my parents only harbored on the terrible moments because I didn't skip around every time things were perfect.

Dad tried pulling strings to get John arrested, but I always covered for him, so no charges stuck. I knew deep in my heart John was sorry afterward, and he always promised to get his temper under control. And once John's actions affected my little brother, they kicked me out of the house.

"Do you want him thinking this is normal, Penny?" Mom shouted as I threw my things in boxes and trash bags.

Her tear-streaked face still haunts my sleep. I miss them all so much.

Sitting here now, the silence has become too thick to breathe in. With my knees drawn to my chest and my tears running down my face, I fantasize about what life could be like if I left. The idea of being alone is more frightening than his fists, and that's why I stay. The physical pain always goes away, but being lonely can last forever. Living a loveless life isn't a life worth living, no matter how much abuse I endure to get what little love he provides.

Deep down, he loves me. I feel it. He shows it in endearing, subtle ways—pulling the sheets to my shoulders because I love waking up snuggled under the blanket or whispering in my ear how pretty I looked when he thinks I'm sleeping—it's when I'm not paying attention, his love shines the strongest.

Tears continue to trickle, wetting my cheeks as silence envelops me. Even his snoring has stopped. I glance at my left hand. The overrated ring sits back on my finger at his request. I never hated a ring so much in my life. It weighs me down and hurts my finger, just like everything else he gives me. I'm not dumb, it's all bribery to keep me here—the ring, the car, this house, the expensive handbags, and jewelry. He's given me everything I have, but if I leave, I'll have nothing.

CHAPTER
SIXTEEN

I PARK IN the farthest lot, walking across the connecting skyway. This is the first time coming to this job with extensive and very visible injuries, ones I can't cover with makeup or ugly accessories. Selling the lie isn't nerve-racking anymore, having told the same one many times at previous places of employment. The one thing making me nervous now is facing Jordan's invasive stares.

I've never cared about a job, not like this. After a big fight with John, I would resign and create some happy lie about John wishing I was a stay-at-home mom, barefoot and pregnant. I would leave one job and drive around the corner to apply for another. But I enjoy working here. I excel at being Jordan's assistant, and not only is the pay terrific, but aside from the few two-faced coworkers, mostly everyone else is great. Starting over isn't an option. Not again.

The office is empty, with nothing but vacant desks and the clicking of my shoes hitting the floor. It's peaceful, one of the best parts of my day, arriving early and getting a handful of things done before anyone else arrives. But today, I'm not alone. Tom is here before me, holed up in his office, cursing his assistant's name, because she messed something up the day before.

Arriving early also helps me avoid walking past too many faces. Nothing bothers me more than attention, and under the current circumstances, I'm in for my fair share today. But for now, sitting at my desk puts me at ease, and I doubt many people can say the same.

As expected, gossip flies around this office like an infestation, and once people trickle in, coworkers ask if I'm okay. On a normal day, most of the employees ignore me, but I suspect their concern is because Jordan is due in at any moment.

The elevator dings and my sixth sense kicks in. It's him. The inflect in Olyvia's tone is the only confirmation I need. He doesn't respond to her seductive greeting, only hurries his paces toward his office. Most likely he's pissed I took the past three days off.

He lifts his face from his phone and locks eyes on me. His scowl shifts into a half-grin. The expression is subtle, but it does big things for my mood.

"You're here today!" Jordan beams, sets his briefcase down as he takes a seat in his usual spot on my desk. Warmth radiates off his smile, swaddling me like a blanket until he narrows his sights on my lip. "What happened?" He leans in closer and the soft expression he wore moments ago shifts as he inspects my face. "Damn, Penny. Are you all right?"

"You should see the other guy," I joke, but Jordan doesn't laugh, he doesn't even crack a smile. I clear the lump in my throat. "We were in an accident. Nothing major—sprained wrist, bruised shoulder, and some cuts. I'll survive." As nonchalant as I make things appear, coupled with the way Jordan is surveying my face, the severity of the truth knocks the wind out of my lungs, and I spiral. Before my emotions run wild, I need to crack a joke or lighten the mood. I add, "Don't worry, the Jag is fine."

"Well, that's a relief," he deadpans. "Flashy ring, though." And like a magnet, my hand drops to my lap as I try to hide the gaudy accessory.

"I won't be able to type as fast." I hold up my wrapped wrist. The slow movement shoots bolts of lightning from the tips of my fingers to the base of my shoulder. "But I'll try to power through whatever you need by lunch."

His eyes spark with a curious intensity, focusing his half brown, half green eyes on mine again. My heart stammers in my chest. Has he seen bruises in the past, hidden under thick concealer or black and blue in the shape of fingerprints on my neck covered by ugly silk scarves? Maybe he assumes I enjoy dressing like a clown, with a hideous fashion sense.

"Do what you can. Don't exert yourself, though."

I nod, shove my earbuds in, and get back to my routine, the one task I'm confident in doing.

Jordan stays in his office most of the morning. Any tension I had coming into work eases as the day continues. As long as he stays out of my hair, I won't have any issues; he's the reason for everything—my daydreaming smiles, the extra pep in my step getting ready in the morning, and the laughter that comes too easy when we're together. Why is he so damn likable? It's my fault, though. I should know my lane by now and not feed into the questions. The more I do, the more ammunition I give John. I need to resort back to how I was, under-the-radar and quiet. Or maybe the simplest answer is one that's been demanded many times before.

Quit.

Jordan appears from his office and smiles as he heads toward the kitchen. When he comes back, two mugs fill his hands, and he places one on my desk.

"Thought you'd like some tea. Don't worry, I used honey, not sugar."

Whatever idea I just had vanished, replaced with the perfect image of Jordan serving me tea. If it didn't hurt to smile, I'd show him every tooth.

"Thank you."

"No problem. Don't worry if you can't get much done. I'm just glad you're back." He shoots me a sympathetic grin before trudging into his office, glancing over his shoulder one last time.

He won't make this easy, will he?

I change the play-list to nineties grunge. The edgy music might be what I need to get through today. The printer hums to life, spitting out page after page of the report I finished, organizing the file to Jordan's liking. Next, I tackle his calendar, rearranging a few conference calls and meetings, doing anything to avoid the sixty-seven emails left on unread.

"Excuse me, Jordan?" I ask, peeking my head into his office with a stack of papers in hand.

He tears his eyes away from his monitor and waves me in. "Everything okay?"

I take a seat in my usual chair across from his desk, tucking my pen behind my ear, and sift through the pages.

"Sorry," I mumble, unprepared.

Frustrated, I grunt to myself until I find the paper I'm looking for. I tick off a list of items in need of his attention, and he gives short, quick answers for each.

As I jot down my notes, I ask, "How did the lesson go?"

Like a bolt of lightning struck his ass, he jumps to his feet. The momentum sends his chair into a complete spin before he sits in the chair beside mine, scooting closer.

Jordan's face hums with energy, as does the rest of his posture, itching with excitement. "Do you ever tire of the rush?"

I bow my head, embarrassed, but smile as wide as I can without causing too much discomfort. "Not really."

"Pen, you gave me the most amazing gift ever." He unbuttons his sleeve and shows me the raised bumps of tanned and well-moisturized skin.

Jordan eases into his chair, tosses his head back as if coming down from the adrenaline high all over again, releasing a long, satisfied breath.

Jordan really is something else—perfect teeth, and a jawline sent from heaven, chiseled by cherubs, I'm certain, but for me, it's his eyes that dazzle.

"So," he starts before leaning forward, elbows on his knees. "I'm sorry you left the party early, but at least I got to meet your fiancé."

"Yeah," I stutter, not the topic I enjoy discussing. "Champagne does that to me sometimes."

"How long have you been engaged?"

I try to do the math in my head. Who can keep track considering all the times I ended the relationship causing him to propose again and again? But I'm pre-conditioned to lie when asked about my personal life, so that's what I do.

"A year."

"One year? High school sweethearts and he only asked you a year ago?"

Dammit. This is why I don't talk about my personal life. Why did Jordan remember that?

"Well… " I draw out, waiting for the perfect answer to present itself. "First, he needed to wrangle me away from my bosses. Don't worry," I rise from my chair and rest my bandaged hand on his shoulder. "My trifling days are over. You're safe from my grasp."

"Meh," he dismisses as he rises, too. "He probably needed a decade to save for the perfect ring."

With his words, I divert my attention to my hand as I hold it in front of me. It might appear as if I'm admiring the huge canary yellow emerald-cut diamond surrounded by many more flawless diamonds, but my bandaged wrist is the only accessory that stands out for me. As I take a deep breath, working through the discomfort that seers through my arm as it falls back to my side.

"Every piece of jewelry has a personality, and the key is to find a piece that pairs well with its future owner. That's when it's perfect."

There's no connection between me and this ring, it's a shackle on my finger, nothing more than a tether to John; the intention alone nauseates me.

"If a proposal took that long," Jordan mumbles, "I have a few years before your honeymoon."

With laughter on my lips, I interject, "Actually, we're getting married once my wounds heal, and jet-setting to Greece. I'll need three weeks off."

His mouth drops open. "What?" He gasps, the simple word is breathless on his tongue.

"Relax. I'm kidding."

He sucks in a relieved breath. "Almost gave me a heart attack. You can't leave me again. I started suffering from PTSD and you were only out for three days." Jordan makes his way back to his chair; his hand still clutches his heart. He's such a drama queen. "You got me good." He settles into his executive chair, adjusting his tie. "Now get back to work, Matthews. I am terribly busy researching contractors for the new office nursery, a preemptive measure for when you two start a family. Can't have you missing work if you know what I mean."

"Wouldn't want that, would we?"

Ugh.

Nauseous again. I would never start a family with John. Who brings a child into a toxic environment, scarring them for life? I know firsthand how it affects kids.

My little brother, Spencer, would sit at the edge of my bed and hold my hand while I sobbed myself to sleep. When he asked about the bruises, I lied; he idolized John and even dreamed of being a football player just like John when he got older. I couldn't tell Spencer the ugly truth, but it wasn't long before he figured it out on his own. And because I accepted the abuse, my brother assumed it was normal to treat others the same. The seed took root. Spencer kicked his classroom crush. After that, my parents had every right to kick me out of the house because I had no intention of leaving.

Staring at my brother's picture now, regret consumes me. Even though he's twenty-one now, he'll always be ten in my memories, just like he is in the photo that sits on my desk. God, I miss him. I loved spending time with my little brother; we were buddies. Even though there was a ten-year difference, our bond was solid. We hung out all the time and created a language only we understood. I don't blame my mom or dad for making me leave. They did what any parent would have done for their child. It's what I would have done.

Fatherhood might change John, soften him even. When he talks about having a son, the soft glint in his eyes dissolves all the harsh features on his face. He paints a heart-warming image of himself teaching our son football, and for a moment, I can imagine it too, a mini version of John running in the backyard as he tosses a foam football. But the instant a smile reaches my sore lip, the image disintegrates like one Thanos snap.

Deafening upbeat music vibrates through the speakers in the living room. Loud is how I prefer after a long couple of days of lying.

Josey stares at me through her thick lashes. "Most chicks go clubbing," she whines as the wine swirls in her glass. She's aware of the rules when he's out of town. "You're not allowed, I know."

She grabs the Cabernet off the counter and tops off her glass before dumping the rest in mine. The sun has set, and we've already polished off a bottle; it's going to be one of those nights.

Josey strains the pasta while I sprinkle fresh basil into the pink sauce. Every time I move my hand, this stupid ring rolls on my finger.

"Stupid fuckin—"

"He's making you wear that monstrosity again?"

If an engagement ring's sole purpose is to symbolize love, why does this one make me queasy?

"Yeah. Back to calling him my fiancé," I say, even-toned.

"Great." Josey rolls her eyes.

She sets the table and I bring in the bowl of pasta, making her a plate before my own. I miss nights like these with Josey. John hates having company over unless it's his idea and his friends. He makes me slave in the kitchen all day, orders me to fetch his beers and tend to his friends, and leaves me to clean up at the end. But when he's away, he allows me one friend over, which is okay, considering my only real friend is Josey. Alexa is cool, too. She brings the music and Josey brings the wine.

Josey updates me on boyfriend stuff while we eat, which takes up about three-quarters of the meal. With nothing positive to add on my end, especially in that category, we eat the rest of the meal in relative silence. The top-heavy ring falls to the side again and I throw my fork down, letting out a puff of frustration.

"Get the ring resized again; at least you won't have to wear it during that time."

I lift the second bottle of wine and drink straight from the bottle. Not one drop hits my taste buds. "I need something stronger."

"Now you're talking, Matthews." Josey claps once, scoots out of her chair and fetches two clean glasses. "Screw him and his no-drinking rule."

The stocked liquor cabinet overflows with top shelf finds and back-ups in case John over-indulges. I reach into the far back corner and pull out one I stashed months ago. "Got it."

"Mmm, cherry rum."

With our cups in a row, Josey pours the chaser into each glass while I pour the rum with a heavy hand. "Wanna do shots?"

"Don't threaten me with a good time." She rushes back to the cabinet, grabs matching Aruba shot glasses while I fetch the tequila.

We raise our glasses high. "To Penelope, the girl who does what she's told." My expression shifts from happy to annoyed in the blink of an eye. I hate that I do as I'm told, like some obedient dog. "But always gives him the proverbial finger," she adds, and the two of us throw a middle finger salute in the air.

The shot burns my throat, but I'm quick to snuff out the flames and chug my rum and coke.

"If I can't go to the club, I'll bring the club to me." I shout orders to Alexa, and she obliges, increasing the bass-heavy music. The pictures lining the wall vibrate until one fell. We giggle and leave the picture on the floor; I didn't like that photo, anyway. And like the walls, I want my organs to vibrate and my body to go numb. I'm sick of always feeling everything.

As the music blares, Josey flickers the lights. I dance around the couch, drink in hand, sipping, and laughing until my cheeks cramp. A little wobbly on my feet, I stub my toe on the coffee table, but it only slows me for a minute.

"Barkeep, I need another!" I shout, and Josey is swift with a refill. "Put it on my tab."

Shot after shot, drink after drink, the flickering lights, and the deafening music, which seemed like an outstanding idea before, now it may pose as a seizure risk. "Let's play a game," I suggest.

"Quarters?"

"N-nooo," I stutter. "You almost broke the coffee table last time."

"Checkers?"

With wide eyes, I fetch the box out of the closet. Unstable on my feet, I stumble back to the couch. Josey tends to our empty glasses while I set up, realizing the checkered pattern is dizzying. No amount of blinking is helping right the hypnotic movement of the black and red boxes.

Josey blinks at the board, leans in further, and backs away, disoriented. "Are your eyes playing tricks on you, too?"

I blink hard, trying to stop the board from spinning. It doesn't.

"Maybe we should sit for a few."

My body crashes onto the couch, and I sink into the cushions. Josey does, too, leaning her head on my shoulder. My eyes focus on all the bottles on the table—two empty bottles of Cabernet, an empty tequila bottle, and a bottle of rum that's waiting to be depleted. There's no use calculating our drink totals, but I make a mental note of what needs restocking before John returns from his trip.

My little songstress, Josey, sings at the top of her lungs, a made-up song about a chipmunk, until she pauses mid-sentence and jolts upright.

"We should make bourbon balls." She rolls off the couch and springs to her feet. Her agility impressed me until she slammed her shoulder on the doorframe and tripped into the kitchen.

"I saw that."

"Walls always move when I'm drunk," Josey shouts from the other room. "I have that effect on them."

A chaotic mixture of sounds comes from the kitchen as pots clank in the cabinet, and utensils fall to the floor. Josey curses each time something crashes to the floor. Before she breaks everything, I stumble in after her.

I can't contain my laugher when she lets out a tirade of curses. Josey stands, frozen in place, covered in powdered sugar.

"Did Homey da Clown whack you with his flour sock?"

She doesn't crack a smile. "So... the sugar canister opened on me."

It feels like a month of lifetimes since I've laughed this much. I'm not sure if it's the stream of alcohol coursing through my veins or if it's because John is away. Perhaps it's both.

We mix the ingredients, going a little heavy on the bourbon, and indulge. The kitchen looks as if a powdered sugar tornado ravaged through. A film of white sugary dust covers the countertop, floor, and Josey. If John was here, he'd lose his shit and demand we scrubbed the entire kitchen from top to bottom. But tonight, I'm free from his tyrannical hold and I intend to take advantage and let this mess wait until tomorrow.

My movement is sluggish, feet heavy like they're encased in cement. Josey isn't faring well herself as we extend our hands to the walls and trudge into my bedroom, slow and unsteady.

"I need to crawl." Josey drops on all fours and inches toward the California king-sized bed. She struggles to climb the tall mattress as if ascending Mt. Everest. Once she's reached the summit, she releases a triumphant exhale.

Josey might be the only girl in a fifty-mile radius that hasn't slept with John in my bed. Although the thought makes my body run hot, hands ball into fists, I burst into laughter instead. Josey laughs too, but I'm certain we aren't laughing at the same thing.

I follow Josey's eyes and balk at the sight—a picture of John and me.

"You deserve better." Josey tosses a decorative pillow on the nightstand and knocks almost everything off. "Yes! Three points for Josey."

"I know."

She raises herself on her elbows and eyes me. Or tries to, at least. My cheeks cramp from smiling all night, and my eyes must look like crescent moons. Thank goodness I didn't split my lip open again.

"You must be shit-faced. That's the first time you've agreed with me."

I've always agreed with her. I just never enjoyed saying it aloud because then it's real. Either these empty liquor bottles gave me the liquid courage

I needed, or I'm just getting close to my breaking point with John, no longer able to hide my unhappiness.

He treats me like yesterday's garbage, putting his hands on me and calling me every derogatory name in the book. But whenever it gets terrible, good times were always right around the corner. A long stretch of happier moments. But lately, it's only shitty days. No matter how well I treat him, putting all his wants and needs before my own, he returns the gesture by treating me like I'm nothing. I don't deserve to be treated that cruelly. It's been going on for so long. Genuine love is foreign to me now. I forgot what it's like to show love and respect. All my wants and needs have been left in the cold, unattended, and malnourished.

Staying with John is dumb. He's beaten me down for so long that I don't trust I'll find better; a lack of self-esteem and self-worth has that effect on a person. One terrifying reason I stay is that I fear his wrath when he inevitably finds me. He always finds me.

As if he senses we're talking about him, my phone shrills his ringtone. He will be livid if he finds out I've been drinking. I clear my throat and try composing myself, even though with every blink, the room spins like a record.

"Hey, babe."

"Just making sure you are home," he yells. The music in the background drowns out his voice.

What's good for the goose isn't always good for the gander.

Josey rolls her eyes, despising the authority he has over me. Deep down, a bubble of a laugh rises, tickling its way to the surface. "No, sir." I salute the air, even though he can't see me. "I wouldn't dare."

The laughter I try suppressing reaches the surface and becomes uncontrollable, as if the headliner just told one hell of a zinger at Giggle-Fest. This happens when you're a happy drunk. Josey tries to cover my mouth, but it doesn't muffle the laughter.

"Are you fucking drunk?" he asks through gritted teeth.

"NO!"

Once I spoke—the defensive yet arrogant tone—I messed up. The laughter disintegrated like mist on a scorching day. But it's already done.

"Don't lie to me, Penelope Matthews," he growls.

"J-just wine. That's all."

He groans into the receiver, shy of a snarl. "I'll be home in a few days."

And with that, the call disconnects. Even when I was living in my parent's house, they never spoke to me like that. But he controls me now—what I wear, what I say, who I say it to, where I go, and what I do.

"Why can't it be Monday?" I roll to my side, away from Josey's stares. "The weekend sucks."

Josey spoons me, draping her slender arm over mine. Her even breaths hit my back, and we lay in silence for a while until I match my breathing to hers.

"It's that boss of yours, innit?"

I roll onto my back and Josey rests her cheek on my shoulder.

Jordan is handsome, but he's more than that, too. When I first started as his assistant, he tried everything to get me to transfer. Jordan preferred good-looking ladies that never learned the alphabet. He got me instead. He tried to be a dick, accusing me of nonsense, but dealing with John prepared me for a boss like Jordan. Jordan yelled, and I didn't falter. I'm accustomed to John's constant berating that I switch to autopilot, throw on a tiny smile, nod, and tune it all out. It's effective for both men. Once Jordan got his head out of his ass, he stopped trying to break me. That's when his true personality appeared.

"He's nice, and kinda sweet, too."

Thoughts of Jordan and John cloud my head in a draining, jumbled mess. Filaments of memories pull me in opposing directions, torn by which direction I should run. Choose Jordan and the smile will come too easy. It'll only be a temporary fulfillment, digging myself deeper into a fictional yet emotional connection to an unattainable man. Choose memories of John, and I suffer through all the times he's hurt me. No matter which man I choose, the endgame is the same. What I need to do is put a restraining order on myself and think about neither. Hurt will surround me no matter who I choose.

I'm brought back to reality when Josey's steady eyes pierce through me.

"What were you thinking about?" Josey asks.

I unleash a deep-barreling laugh. "I don't know...I don't remember." Man, I love alcohol.

Her unwavering smile forces me to beam just as wide. The glint in her eyes sparkles under my bedroom light, and she rubs her palms together. She's crafty.

With a smile as wide as the Cheshire cat, she says, "I have an idea."

CHAPTER
SEVENTEEN

THE BEAUTIFUL MORNING sang to me, but this pleasant day has a limited shelf-life. With the weekend over, John's return is imminent. I bottled up all the splendid things—the silence of the house, the cheery mood from waking up without John's heavy snores and getting dressed without John critiquing my every choice—and I hold on to this jovial sensation for as long as possible.

I make the most of my day at work, appreciating every minute I'm here and John is off wherever. Even though I've restocked the liquor, he will reprimand me for drinking, it's only a matter of how. I don't fear punishments anymore, too numb, both inside and out, to let it sour my day.

"Morning, Penny." Jordan walks in, briefcase in hand, and disappears into his office.

My day just got better. I switch on my music and get cracking on my daily reports.

Laughter. His laughter. Jordan's joyous laughter fills his office. As hard as I try to disregard that beautiful and yet curious sound, my eyes betray me, and I turn to his door, intrigued. With a smile, he rests his back against the frame, eyes locked on his phone and then on me.

Like a hunky model, he poses on the door frame, whether or not intentional. He has a way of always posing like he's being photographed. Soft sunlight from his office glows behind him as he perches one heel on the doorframe. Jordan tilts his head back as his smile grows. That delicious Adam's apple pops out. I've never liked apples until this very moment. Even my lady parts have become hungry. Too bad I don't have a camera to capture Jordan in all his Greek god-like glory. But I'm almost positive Greek gods didn't wear Tom Ford.

What's that look about?

"So," he drops his 'America's Next Top Model' audition routine and walks toward me with his work phone in hand. He takes his usual seat and flashes me a delicious grin. "I left my work phone here over the weekend."

He pinches his chin between his thumb and index finger. The smirk shifts into something naughty, yet playful. Although subtle, it does big things to my curiosity. His eyes are vibrant today, but they haven't decided if they want to be green or brown in the well-lit office. Either way, they play off the rich red of his tie that fits snug against his neck in contrast to his stark black vest and white shirt. It should be a felony to look that fine in a vest. He's the best-dressed man in this entire building and he revels in it. Jordan could walk for Dior. All his features are sculpted for the runway.

"How did you manage all weekend without it?"

He waves away my question without answering, only shifting his stare back to his phone. That grin of his grows again as if hopped up on growth hormones. He shares an intimate chuckle with no one but himself.

"I missed an odd text."

Whatever shenanigans he's up to, I refuse to let it distract me and divert my attention back to the email I'm replying to, letting my fingers flirt with every letter on the keyboard. I sense he's watching me. The heart of the stare turns my body warm. When I can't take the pressure of his eyes on me anymore, I give in. That steroid-filled smile is just shy of being too big for his face.

"Okay. And?"

"From you," he amuses.

"What?"

My brows pull together in a state of disbelief. Too distracted by his eyes to conjure up any coherent memory, I turn away and replay the weekend's events. All I did was laundry, hang out with Josey, and clean up the drunken mess the next day.

"Did I butt text you?"

He laughs and shakes his head. The grin may have dimmed, but I sense he's fighting hard not to burst from the seams. "Unless you have another hidden talent, butts rarely form clear sentences."

My head drops again, digging deeper into the depths of my memory from my drunken night. Everything is hazy still. And then it hits me, like a dream I had days ago. The way his hand rests on my desk, fingers sprawled in front of my trinket box, the memory presents itself.

After John called, Josey begged me to tell her why I loved work. She and I agreed, courtesy of the alcohol, that we were geniuses, up there with Gates, Musk, and Einstein. The plan was brilliant. As I whizzed through my contact list, first seeing John's name and balking at it, but resting on the name of the man staring into my soul right now. It took forever to spell the words correctly; I remember that much. My fingers and eyes didn't work as a team while I typed: I miss you.

Holy shit.

Jordan must see the terror stitched on my expression. How could he not? The laughter he's been trying to suppress must tickle his throat. I don't need a mirror to sense my skin shift into a wonderful rainbow of red. At this rate, my entire body burns like I'm being roasted on a spit.

Two options play out in my head: slap my forehead with my palm or beat my head against the desk. Both options might appear as an admission of guilt. A fun bonus, he'll assume I've lost my marbles and have me carted off to the storage room where I can spend the rest of my days regretting this exact moment.

Think, Penelope. Think.

"Um. . . Josey, my friend, and I got drunk that night." My heart stammers like it's trying to break free from my chest as I rushed my off-the-fly excuse from my mouth. "I missed John because he went away, and your name must be near his. Yeah, John and Jordan. You guys are contact neighbors, so I m-must've sent that to you by accident, which is pretty funny, and thank goodness you left your phone here because that would've been awkward if you got that and didn't have me to explain things in a sober state like I am now." After a few indrawn breaths and a lot of blinking and indirect eye contact, I sneak a peek at him.

Good going, Penny. That was about as smooth as a three-month-old bikini wax.

His smile doesn't fade, it doesn't budge. "Penelope drunk texting. Interesting." He ponders for a beat, then stands, shoves his hands in his pockets, and fiddles with some loose change with an air of cool confidence only he can pull off. "Imagine if I texted back?"

No. God, no. I can't imagine that. I can't. My imagination would be far too nice compared to what reality is. His playful expression wears away the tension like waves on a rock, but where that erosion takes time, years, in fact, Jordan has the power to sculpt me in one swift sweep.

"One time, I sent a private picture to my friend's wife by accident. She shared names with a female I was seeing. To this day she winks at me at parties." He shakes his head, but deep down, he loves the attention. He bathes in it. Hell, everyone in this building knows he does.

The moment Jordan retreats to his office, I scroll through my phone and delete the message. John would kill me and dump my carcass on the side of the freeway if he ever read something like that on my phone. He'd knock my teeth from my mouth, and cut off the tips of my fingers, careful not to leave any trace of evidence to who I am.

The rest of the day flies by, and I do everything in my power to avoid Jordan at all costs. Embarrassment sits at my desk like an annoying intern, bothering me throughout the day. Every time Jordan would leave his office, I'd duck my head down or turn my chair, pretending to file something. The cat-and-mouse game had me on edge all day long.

On my drive home, I prepare for the onslaught of verbal and physical assaults aimed at me when he returns in a few hours. No amount of yoga will namaste me to a calm place; not in this relationship, and maybe never.

My stomach plummets when I pull up to the house. John's car sits in the driveway. He's home early.

With my nerves on shaky edge, I tip-toe into the foyer as if trespassing in my home. The music plays in the living room, soothing R&B echoes through the speakers while John hovers near the stove, cooking, of all things.

Did I walk into the wrong house?

"Hey, sweetheart. I'm making your favorite. You know, that chicken and pasta dish with the spicy pesto sauce. The dish won't be anywhere near as good as yours, but I'm trying."

Seriously, did I enter the Twilight Zone? I remain cautious, waiting for his expression to morph into a ferocious beast while he slings a barrage of insults and flashes his red rage my way. But nothing happens. He's as pleasant as ever as he tends to the food on the stove.

He advances toward me, removes my handbag from my shoulder, and places my purse on the black, circular table in the vestibule. A chill settles in my spine when he helps me out of my coat and hooks the loop on the hanger.

Again, I wait. Any minute now, he'll throw me against the wall, grip my throat in his hand, and unleash.

"How was your day?"

Who is this person? And what has he done with John?

"Fine."

"Terrific." He returns to the stove and tosses the chicken and pesto concoction. "Go change, dinner will be ready soon."

I tread lightly, as if he were a bear, careful to not make any sudden movements.

The last time he wore that impervious calm, his mask dropped in minutes. He went from Jekyll to Hyde with Usain Bolt-like speed. I close the door to the bedroom and strip out of my work clothes; the business attire has no give, not like a tee shirt and leggings do.

When I emerge, he's set the table, lit candles, and put one of my favorite soundtrack scores on in the background, ditching the R&B radio station. Everything is picture-perfect, even him. He pulls out my chair and I half expect him to sweep it out from under me as retaliation for my insubordination, but he doesn't. John gives my shoulders a quick massage.

"You're so tight, Pen. If work is stressing you, quit."

If he were anyone else, relaxing could come easy. But every muscle in my body is as stiff as a corpse. His hands travel to my neck, and I suck in a quick breath, holding it as he kneads my skin. Here it comes. Instead, he drops his hands and returns to the table with a bowl of diced chicken and thin spaghetti, tossed in a light, spicy pesto sauce.

"What's with all of this?" I ask with trepidation.

He stares back as if I asked why his neck sprouted three heads. "What? I can't be glad to be home with my future wife?"

The way he says "future wife" is funny to me. For one, he doesn't want to marry me. He reminds me all the time. John has always squashed any plans to get married, but he likes to pretend I'm the one dragging my feet to the altar; at least, that's what he tells his friends and family. He only proposed because I was ready to leave him after one of the many times I caught him cheating. It was a last-ditch effort to make me stay.

When I wanted to marry him, he claimed he wasn't ready. And now, I'll never be ready even if he is.

After dinner, John clears the table and loads the dishwasher while I remain frozen in my chair, nursing the wine he poured me. Considering how much he loathes me drinking, I'm surprised he gave me any. John hums as I observe, turning to me and offering a kind smile. He has an extra bounce to his step, and his face lacks his usual scowl; he appears happy. I remain silent, fearing this mythical creature will take off running once I make a peep.

"Did you want to do anything tonight? Movie? Stay home and cuddle on the couch? We can watch one of your favorite movies."

These questions are rhetorical. I never have a choice. He likes to pretend to give me one, but we always end up doing what he decides, anyway.

In my usual mono-toned voice, I answer. "Whatever is fine."

"As long as you're with me, I don't care." His phone shrills. I can tell when a woman calls. His mouth turns into a wicked grin, but nothing happens this time. All he does is silence the ringer and shove the phone back in his pocket. "Come here," he summons. "I've missed you."

I've missed a lot of things about John, too. But the qualities I used to hold close to my heart have been absent for far too long. I'm not even sure if I can know what they are anymore. Nights like tonight might help jog my memory, but how long will it last? Four nights? Two weeks? A month or the next three hours?

I tell him what he wants for my own sanity. "I've missed you, too." They are only words. A robot might have repeated them with more conviction.

John stands, arms stretched in front of him, pulling me to my feet. He wraps his bulging muscles around me, pressing each one of his hardened arms around my middle as he leans in and kisses me with care. His eyes remain closed while mine stay wide open, readying for the unknown.

But his lips are gentle, same as his hands around my waist as if I'm a delicate flower and he's too afraid of bruising my petals. He smells sweet, too, like the cologne I bought him years ago that he swore he'd wear but never did. Not until today. This John owned my heart.

With his lips against mine and his eyes still shut, he says, "Remember when we used to kiss for hours outside in the cold under your kitchen window?"

Memories flood to the surface of him and I locked in an embrace that ignited fires. His warmth stole the chill out of my body. And his kisses, man, those kisses. The heat between us burned hot, able to melt icecaps. We were all each other needed, filled with such passion, nothing else mattered in the universe when we were together. And when our smooching session ended, our swollen lips formed giddy grins.

When John was near, my heart was complete. Then he became a loose cannon, ready to explode over silly assumptions. Memories of good times are few now, painted over with anger, aggression, lies, and deception.

"Yes."

He takes my hand and places tiny kisses on my knuckles before leading me to the couch. John presses the remote, and a movie awaits in the cue as if expecting we'd retreat to the living room after dinner. What would he have done if I opted for a night on the town? See. I never had a choice.

For a moment, John disappears into the bedroom while I sit on the couch, watching the opening credits.

The living room isn't any different from how I left this morning, but this strange energy makes everything out of place, including John. How twisted has my life become that my home only seems weird when John's being nice? Normal behavior is him screaming, punching, or pushing me into walls or walking in three hours late for dinner, demanding I scrub the table a third and fourth time, but not this. Not this attentive, pleasant, and nurturing John.

He returns after a few minutes and sits beside me, draping his arm over my shoulder as he pulls me toward him. My tension returns, building with each passing moment. I glance at my watch, placing my bet at how much longer he'll keep up with this charade before the facade crumbles.

We watch the movie together and he interrupts to ask how the book differs, asking question after question as if interested in each answer until the credits roll.

"Ready for bed?"

I stretch my body, loosening my limbs from staying pressed against his hardened frame for the whole two hours and ten minutes. "Yeah."

He grabs my hand again, leading me to the open doors of our bedroom. On the black and white Damask printed bedspread are red rose petals in the shape of a heart. Ashton Kutcher must be hiding in my armoire, riddled with cramps from being trapped all evening.

John stands behind me and wraps his arms around my rounded middle as he presses his body against my back, sweeping my hair to one side. Delicate kisses fall on my neck while I take in the sights. Things have gotten far too weird.

"John, what's going on?"

He says nothing, only hugs me tighter. We sway into a slow dance until he grips my chin with his large hand, tilting my face upward. His lips continue to shower me with kisses from above. As much as I want to fight him off, I miss all the sensations that come along with being loved. I yearn for it now. If only for now.

I lean my head against his chest and enjoy his sensual touch. I revel in this touch. John turns me around, and with deep intensity, stares into my eyes. For once, his warm and welcoming gaze isn't hardened by disdain.

"Hi," he says, carefree.

He's beautiful when he's like this—loving, sweet, and compassionate. I lace my hands around the nape of his neck as he rests his forehead on mine.

"I love you so much, Penelope. I can't lose you," he whispers as his lips brush against my ear.

The words are nice and endearing. Though I stand in front of him, I checked out a long time ago. Nevertheless, I press my lips to his, hoping my actions convince him since the power behind my words could never. His moans echo in my mouth as his hold on me tightens, but not with pain, with passion.

We side-step toward the bed, but he stops me from disrobing.

"No," he whispers through gentle and loving kisses. "Let me take care of you."

I turn the lights off, too ashamed of my body to be naked in front of him anymore; the full moon offers enough illumination for the room. He lifts my shirt over my head, unclasps my bra, and removes the straps from my shoulders with the tips of his delicate touch. The hair on the back of my neck stands on end as his tongue runs along the delicate skin below my ear, moving lower at a snail's pace.

I run my fingers through his dark hair with my eyes closed, trying to enjoy his sweetness. John's saying and doing all the right things, so I give him what he wants—my heart—but only for tonight.

I pull his face to mine, eyes as soft as before.

"John, I love you."

Unshed tears rim my eyes, but his large hands cup my cheeks, and he kisses me with a deep yearning before they fall.

He lays me on the bed and places himself between my legs. His hands travel up my body as a wake of desire consumes all my senses. As our hurried hands explore one another, each kiss becomes deeper, hungrier, as if we've starved ourselves far too long. Riddled with sweat in a sea of kisses, I give him another part of me—my body. I bury my face into the crook of his neck, filling the room with sounds of pleasure and not pain, for once.

It's as perfect as it is beautiful, and we move, united, holding one another as if our lives depended on each other's next breath. I melt against his body, and my defenses weaken. A raw flare of desire sprang into John's eyes as his masterful seduction sent my body spiraling until we both descended the heights of ecstasy.

John spoons his body against mine, and we stay connected as the tides of euphoria recede. Gathering me in his protective arms, he held me. As pockets of fatigue settle under my eyes, John caresses my hair and continues covering my bare skin with whispers of kisses.

My brain drifts. Could I be happy again?

Shimmery facets of hope flicker behind my closed lids. It's the first positive emotion regarding John that I've had in a long while.

Are we on the right path? Or am I a fool to still believe John can change?

Just as my eyes become heavy with content, on the cusp of sleep, his lips brush near my earlobe.

"You still awake?" he asks with a soft tone fading into a hushed stillness.

But I don't answer. My mind withdraws into a vague half-sleep, too filled with bliss to let my tired, raspy voice ruin this renewed sense of promise. His kisses don't stop, and his thumb strokes my arm, back and forth, soothing me to unconsciousness.

Jordan's Penny

"I made Jessica get an abortion. No one is having my babies but you," he whispers.

The sharp pang throbs under my breast as the terrifying realization ripples through me. Everything makes sense now.

CHAPTER EIGHTEEN

D AY AFTER DAY I keep to myself. Or try to, at least. Before Jordan insists I join him for lunch or distract me with his presence, I rush to busy myself with something else. Whenever he's got that glint in his eyes, the one that means, "let me ask you a few hundred random questions," I pretend I'm on a call. As much as I hate these evasive maneuvers, I can't stand to look any man in the eye anymore; especially not after the beautiful night with John, turned to shit from his confession. All the men in my life lie to my face after reeling me in their kindness.

With all the attention Jordan gave me, the lines between boss and assistant blurred. We became friends, and even worse, I started liking him. There's no one to blame but myself. I'm no better than all his previous assistants. I allowed this to happen, just as I allowed myself to think John changed.

Why am I such a fool?

Thank fucking God John can't read my mind. He'd know why I care about this job so much. It'd be as if I signed my death certificate. Cause of death: Murder. How would he do it, though? Blunt force trauma to the head? Toss me down a tall flight of stairs? Cut my brake line? Or maybe hit me with a car?

Not only would John classify Jordan as a threat, but every coworker I befriended would be one, too. If I like a job, that means I dedicate time and energy to it, away from home where I'm not under his thumb, bending to his will. Having friends at the workplace means talking and confiding in coworkers, even if it only occurs within office walls. John can't risk me divulging our relationship's darkest secrets.

Jordan's Penny

I remind myself daily how Jordan pities me and nothing more, replaying his conversation with Alec on loop until I ingrain the word that broke my heart into my DNA—gross. Sure, I've been told that before, but the word lives in my bones with a colder bite when coming from someone I respect.

And then there's John. He assumed I was sleeping when he admitted his secret, but for days he's sent loving texts, cute gifs, and relationship memes confessing his undying love. Naturally, I assumed they were for someone else, but no, they kept coming. With promises of more romantic evenings together, I didn't need a nose to sense how full of shit he was. It was all bullshit coming from a man incapable of loving anyone but himself. And then he threw in, "Don't wait up, working late." See. Bullshit.

I hate no matter how far removed my heart is from that man, he still makes me sick to my stomach. For the better part of the week, I could not keep food down. His lies were making me ill.

But with nausea at bay, the one emotion that floods my veins now is anger. I wake up angry. I go to bed angry. And I'm angry all the hours in between. It's throwing off my focus at work. I've read the same God damn email four times already. Nothing computes.

"Ugh," I groan aloud and storm into the bathroom.

With palms press onto the cool countertop, I stare at myself in the mirror.

"Get yourself together, Matthews," I chant as my body burns from within.

Angry tears pool, but I refuse to let them fall. I let the heat of my body burn them away. I need this rage to fuel my next move. If only I could wrap my head around what the fuck my next move is, I'd feel a hell of a lot better. The stress on my face is clear—lines of worry travel along my forehead, and the bags under my eyes are so big, a TSA agent might classify them as luggage. And not the carry-on kind.

I contort my facial features, widen my eyes, and wear an unnatural grin. On the surface, I could appear happy and awake, I suppose. Approachable and friendly, maybe? But deep down, my cheeks are already sore from the lie. My entire body aches from lying. It's all I do. It's all I ever do. I fix my blouse. The hideous floral pattern screams retired grandmother of twelve, the top John bought, so I'd always know humiliation even when he wasn't

153

doing the humiliation. I adjust my necklace, re-adjust my smile, and head back to my desk.

Just get through one more day, Penelope. You can do it.

Jordan hovers near my cluttered area, waiting, while he slips into his suit jacket. "Are you okay? You seem off."

"Just busy," I snap. The friendly disposition I practiced seconds ago drops the moment I took it for a test drive.

Get your shit together, Matthews.

He watches as I shuffle papers that didn't need shuffling and shove pens in my penholder. Half don't even make it in, only fall through my fingers. It only makes me angrier. When I turn my attention back to him, giving him my best, "can I fucking help you" face, his eyes go unmoved until I clear my throat aggressively. Something needed to break him out of whatever comatose state he's in.

"Sorry." He shakes his head as if to right himself. "I need to run out. If you need me, call my cell."

With him gone, the tension in my shoulders ease, not completely, but enough that I no longer need to stay on alert to appear busy. Instead of listening to music, the mundane tunes of typing, phones ringing, the hum of the printer, and the billowing of the copy machine will fill my ears. I find my rhythm again. My chair moves on the carpet as I push myself to the filing cabinet nearby, clearing some of the clutter off my desk.

The phone rings.

"Jordan Stephens's office. How can I assist you today?"

"Penny," Jordan rushes. "I need you to meet me at 3094 Montgomery Drive. Now." The phone disconnects abruptly.

Without hesitating, I grab my things and rush out the door, notifying the receptionist that I'm meeting up with Jordan for some unknown emergency.

When I pull up to the address, I'm left dumbfounded. No wonder the address sounded familiar.

"Emergency, my ass. He's got to be fucking kidding me."

A guard swings open the door for me. Although the store has been through many renovations, that long-time family-owned aura of wealth and abundance still lingers. The air inside is distinct, too. Converted from a gentlemen's cigar lounge, the room has tobacco-scented remnants in the air from years of men polishing off cigars. Now, the only things getting polished are various shades of gold and diamonds.

For decades, this jewelry store has thrived through every major recession. If this establishment were suffering or in need of a re-brand, newspapers would report it. So why am I here?

Lit display cases fill the space, and inside each glass display is an array of custom-made pieces, either created in-house or by private designers. John bought my custom-made ring here. I roll the gaudy bauble over on my finger. If they spotted the ring, they'd recognize their work. I'm in no mood to pretend I'm still in love with it. Pretending once was enough.

Jordan waves me over. Behind the counter stands an attractive woman—flowing hair the color of wheat, crystal blue eyes, and a slim body with slender limbs—hoping to make a sizable commission. She's got as much self-esteem as she does cleavage, overflowing and hanging out of her white silk blouse.

"Knew you'd make record time," he boasts.

I stare in disbelief. "A pompous-looking poodle was almost collateral damage, too. Tell me I left work to help you shop. I dare you to say those words." Boss or not, I couldn't hide my frustration even if I tried.

He stands silent. Jordan watches with what appears to be amusement on his perfectly sculpted face. He must sense my mounting aggravation because he holds his hands up, as if to surrender, but not quite. "This is an emergency. My mother's birthday is coming up." The corners of his eyes crinkle as he smirks, still amused. Both his hands sit in his pockets, rocking on his heels with an expression that could light a match.

My defeat is imminent. I won't win any battle, not against him. Now annoyed, I survey the glass display where the sales lady has placed a strip of black velvet fabric on the countertop. Many white gold necklaces sit on the dark velvet as she and Jordan await my opinion. Her watchful eyes are familiar; she's assessing us, determining our affiliation.

While she plays with the pendant around her neck, she canvases Jordan's landscape with eyes only meant for the bedroom. She's undressing him in the middle of the fucking jewelry store. I can't say I blame her. I stop myself from doing the same thing almost every day. But when her sights fall on me, her face contorts a little, lips curl, wrinkles her nose, and cringes as she turns away. I'm hoping she's cringing at my shirt, and not because she thinks I'm the Hunchback of Notre Dame. Jordan stands oblivious, per usual, entertained by his phone, but I catch everything. Her expression, full of disgust, is one I'm too familiar with. Once she catches me watching her, she shoots me a fake smirk.

"You said it yourself. I'm useless without you," he mumbles, still half distracted by some childish game on his phone. "And you're right, but you also mentioned something about jewelry and personality. That's why you're here." He places his hand on my shoulder. The gesture is innocent, but the way the tips of his fingers rest on me, my body reacts instantly. My insides turn warm. "If you didn't make valid points, you'd be at work still." His smile is like Thor's hammer, pounding against the wall I've built to keep him away, or vice versa. Is there any actual difference anymore? He holds up one necklace. "This is like something you own, right?"

No. I own that exact diamond-encrusted heart pendant and the fact that he's mentioned it means his eyes wandered near my chest; the pendant falls half an inch above my full cleavage. My pulse thrums in my ears.

Is this what a-fib feels like?

As hard as I try to ignore his comment, I peruse the selected pieces of jewelry in front of me.

I think back to the day I met his mother in Tom's office a few days ago. I tried to avoid Jordan all day, but once I caught wind she was in the building, I lingered around to glimpse what beauty created the man I collate copies for. There was no reason for me to talk to Tom's secretary, but I went over there to shoot the breeze and sneak a peek at Jordan's mom. She didn't disappoint.

Jordan's mom and Tom go way back. It was fun hearing Tom drop his professional voice and have playful banter with someone. There's always more than meets the eye with people. We often only see them in one light, but there are so many layers that we miss until we get to know a person.

Jordan's back pressed against the window with his head in his hands. Mrs. Stephens shared an embarrassing story from Jordan's youth, something about him getting hit in the face playing dodgeball, and then as he was walking out of the gymnasium, he walked right into the double doors. Oof. They laughed at his expense, but Jordan took it in stride. After the laughter subsided, she doted on him, fixing his tie and asking if he ate. At that moment, Jordan eyed me near Tom's door and summoned me inside for an introduction.

The woman was beautiful. I have never been nervous to meet someone's mother before. Until that moment. Most moms adore me. And forget about grandmas; I've got the grandma circuit on lock-down. They all love pinching my full cheeks. But once he introduced us, her eyes lit up with recognition. I'm not sure why. I've never met the woman before, but her welcoming smile oozed warmth and enthusiasm. When she shook my hand, we shared a gaze. There was so much life behind her eyes, it took me by surprise. Thinking back on it now, nothing is surprising about it. She's the proud mother of a successful son.

But unlike her son, she didn't dress in high-end clothing or flaunt expensive jewelry like I assumed everyone in his family did. Her attire was classic. Timeless. If she rolled out of bed in fifty years, she would still be fashion-forward. Unlike Jordan, who wears clothes and accessories for other people, her style is simpler and her own, donning what she chooses, regardless of what anyone else thinks. And nailing it.

One thing that spoke to me about her style was her wedding band—yellow gold. The woman didn't wear an ounce of white gold or platinum on her.

"You could have sent me a picture," I snap with a huff. "She won't like any of these. Who picked these?" I hold up a white gold chain with a Yorkshire Terrier pendant attached. The tips of my fingers give my temples a workout. "You're shopping for your mother, Jordan. Does she even have a dog?"

I'd classify all these necklaces as cute, nothing appropriate for his mother. If he was shopping for one of his many bedroom trollops, sure, they might work. These are for younger recipients flaunting their new highlighter on Instagram, nothing an older woman who dons classic pieces would wear. She would never turn her nose at any gift, but she would also never pick these either.

"I picked them," the blonde associate answers. With a bit of snark might I add, but I tune her out like the white noise she is even as her glare darkens.

I glide my hand over the clean displays, trolling from one case to another on the hunt for the perfect gift. Something fitting for his mature mother.

This store is well-known for its one-of-a-kind pieces, but none of these remind me of her, or at least the quick impression I got upon meeting her.

"Can you give us a minute?" Jordan asks, and the sales associate nods, retreating to chat with a coworker nearby. "Why are you giving her an attitude? She's just trying to do her job."

Me? Giving her an attitude? My hands fly to my chest. That stung. He would take her side, wouldn't he? She's beautiful and I'm... not.

"I was trying to do my job too, but someone called me away from that. I can't be here."

My ears prickle from the low chatter coming between the saleswoman and her brunette coworker. The two women share a private conversation that isn't as private as they planned. Their volume is obvious, with Jordan and I being the center of the conversation. Smart people, like Jordan, don't concern themselves with other people's opinions. Then again, good luck finding a flaw in him to gossip about. But I have many and I care too much about what others think, so I hear everything.

"They're not together," the blonde whispers. "She couldn't land someone like that." With zero subtly, they don't even take turns. They narrow their sights on me, and again, their lips scrunch in the corners, but their expression shifts with dramatic awe when admiring Jordan. "She must be a relative."

The brunette feigns a smile at me. For someone with lips that resemble pulled-back curtains, an obvious botched lip job, she should tone down her judgment.

Classical music plays in the speakers, and I hum along to the Debussy tune, hoping to mask their hate. It doesn't.

When I'm with John, the whispers don't bother me at all anymore because I know who he really is. But today, I'm seconds from pulling my hair out, or better yet, theirs, and scream until my vocal cords bleed. Their hurtful words drill into my head, infecting me with their poison. Nothing like a constant reminder of how inferior I am to them, how inferior I am to Jordan. Why do I feel so ugly and fat walking into a store that doesn't have a designated plus-size department?

I point to a necklace and pendant in the display case. "This one."

The yellow gold chain is a beautiful diamond cut link with a solid gold rectangular bar pendant. Three beautiful black diamonds sit in a line, along the elongated brick-shaped gold right at the top.

I spin on my heel with my duties fulfilled.

"Where are you going?" He grabs my arm, pulling me back, but I jerk away out of habit, too used to John's rough grip, leaving black and blues on my skin. "Talk to me, Pen. What's the matter?"

"How can you be so oblivious? I won't be the subject of anyone's conversation anymore. I'm out." The frustration spills so thick, it drips.

I turn to leave again, but his hands held my arms, making it clear I wasn't slipping away from this conversation. When our eyes meet, I must turn away; perfect eyes like his are dangerous. Staring too long is bad for my health. Instead, my sights fall to his hold on me, delicate yet firm.

As to not make it obvious, Jordan glances toward the two associates and back at me. "Why do you care what those half-wits say?"

Tears claw their way to freedom, but I don't dare give them the satisfaction. "You wouldn't understand. I'm going back to work."

"Just wait a minute, please," he begs. The powerful softness behind his gaze keeps my feet planted where I stand.

Like two beautiful hazel pools, his eyes search mine. He is the most handsome man I ever met, from his strong jawline to the perfect curvature of his lips. I've stared at those lips enough times to memorize the left side curls up when he's deep in thought, and he nibbles on his top lip when something bothers him like he's doing right now.

I lean into him, dropping my voice. "They're talking about us, but mainly me. Listen, you're just my boss, and I shouldn't even be concerning you with this, but I'm fucking sick of others judging my worth based on my size. And today…" I tug my hair back and fidget with my hands, too wound up to stand still. I want to run, run far away from these mean girls, run away from Jordan. From everyone. "Today, that shit bothers me, okay? I can't even find the strength to cry about it anymore, too tired from being the butt of every joke." I gulp air, it's the only thing calming me down. That, and Jordan's cologne. It's enough to calm my racing heart. "Can I go back to work now?" This time, I beg.

"No."

He calls the girl over again, points to the piece I picked, and requests the manager.

The manager strolls over, donning a paisley bowtie and a grin. The men shake hands with familiarity between them. If I'm not mistaken, his name is Wilbur Henry III. To think, three people named their son Wilbur. Someone in the family must've been a huge "Charlotte's Web" fan. This hipster dipshit would rather eat the pork than read about it. Coincidentally, he's the asshat that talked John into buying my ring.

"All ladies love diamonds," he told John. "The bigger, the better."

I beg to differ.

"Ah, yes. Mr. Stephens, how can I help you today?"

Jordan holds the necklace I picked, admiring the pendant once more. "I came in today for a gift. And this necklace," he raises the yellow gold diamond-cut chain high in the air, eyeing the piece in awe, "is exquisite."

"Yes. Jean Baptiste designed this. It's a part of his Symphonique Collection; he's quite popular right now. I'm confident we can work out a fair price. I always take care of my favorite customers," the manager boasts.

Who else has Jordan jewelry for at this store? The unsettling discomfort in my gut puts all curiosity on pause.

Jordan's smile travels to his eyes. "You might, but your employees don't. This sales associate has made some rather rude comments about my fiancé." Jordan grabs my hand, interlocking our fingers together, and tugs me closer. "She's unprofessional and rude." His thumb strokes my knuckles as he speaks, an unnecessary gesture as our woven fingers are not in anyone's line of sight.

He turns on his heel and hurries toward the exit, dragging me behind him.

"Mr. Stephens, please wait. There's been a misunderstanding," the manager calls out.

Jordan doesn't stop. He doesn't even slow. Once my feet hit the pavement, I break our contact and regain possession of my hand. This lie only hurts me. His hazel pools drift to his empty hand for a moment before he puts both back into his pants pockets, wearing that smug grin.

Man, what I wouldn't do to kiss that grin off him.

My heart thumps fast and loud as I dig into my bag. For what? I'm not sure. I just need the distraction until the wonderful sensation of Jordan's enormous, yet warm and soft hand in mine disappears. It was as if he had electricity humming in his blood.

"You didn't need to do that."

His presence still tingles on my skin as if I stuck my entire hand in a socket. The way he held my hand in his, strong, soft yet firm and perfect...

Jesus Christ, you need to stop, Penelope Matthews.

As the seconds tick by, the sensation fades and my hand turns cold and lonely, an exact reflection of the internal struggle I face daily.

"Yes, I did," he chimes. "I'm offended though, Ms. Matthews."

Now I'm offended. Ms. Matthews? I don't like the formal connotation, not coming from him.

"Oh yeah? Why is that?"

Jordan walks me to my side of the car. "I may be your boss, but we are friends, too."

There it is again. A-fib.

He opens my car door as the rude saleswoman exits the store with her Chanel purse slung over her shoulder. Her handbag isn't the only accessory she's donning now. A menacing scowl straddles her face, but even with nostrils flaring like a dragon, she's still quite attractive. Ugh.

She turns to us and says, "Fat bitch."

"Enjoy the walk to the unemployment line," Jordan retorts as she stomps down the street.

Words are a crazy thing. After John put his hand on me the first time, he showered me with sorries, and I was naïve enough to believe them. Over time, the more he apologized, the less the word meant. "Sorry" became as common as "and" in my house. But no matter how many times someone says what she did, the sting never dulls. Its potency is as strong as ever. I doubt the power of that phrase will ever lessen.

Jordan turns toward me. The show of emotions playing out on my face must be clear. "Ignore her, Pen. She needs glasses."

My insolent eye-rolling is becoming an automated reflex. "She said what she saw, what everyone sees. Although," I pause, realizing something, too. "You were the bitch because you got her fired, yet I'm the one that got cussed out. Hmph, go figure."

"It's not what I see."

He had no reason to say that, yet he chose to lie, anyway. Again. I cannot trust anyone. But I'd be fooling myself if I said his fib didn't help me find my smile again.

Jordan's head tilts to one side. "Wait. . . did you just call me a bitch?"

I wave him away as if all this is yesterday's headlines. "And you still don't have a gift for your mother." I point to the jewelry store entrance and then Jordan. "He fired her, so you can go back in and buy that necklace."

Jordan clicks his tongue and rocks in place. "Nope. It's the principle of the matter."

I sigh loudly. "Let me do some research. Maybe this Jean Baptiste guy showcases his work elsewhere."

"I'll race you."

After one lesson with my dad, does he believe he can win against me? Game on.

I'll amuse him. "I'll even give you a five-minute head start."

He starts toward his car parked fifteen feet away. "Wait." Jordan runs back toward me. Watching him run toward me is a lot better than watching him run away. "What are we betting?" His smile, all teeth, and confidence are as beautiful as a sunset.

Damn. I'm doing it again.

"If I win," I tap my index finger to my chin a few times, "you have to make me a playlist of your favorite songs."

"Like a mixtape? That's very 1990s of you, Penelope Matthews."

"What if you win?"

"Pfft," he mocks. "You mean when I win? When I win, you'll make me dinner for a week and a three-game bowling match. Winner gets to gloat for a month."

"That's two things," I shout, but he ignores me and speeds away from the curb. I glance at my watch and give him what I promised. It won't matter. Either way, I'm getting that play-list.

CHAPTER NINETEEN

I SIT AT Jordan's desk—hands folded in front of me, feet rooted into the floor, back as straight as a rail—and I wait. When he turns the corner, he'll eye my empty desk and assume victory. But once he steps foot inside his office doors, that victorious elation will disintegrate, and I'll be one play-list happier.

"Yes!" He shouts in the distance. His pace hurries, as do his strides. It's difficult keeping my blank expression. The urge to gloat tickles my nerves.

Jordan saunters into his office, a smile so bright it could light Earth for centuries to come. And then it changes. His expression falls. For a moment, guilt smacks me square in my jaw, but it doesn't last long as the corners of his lip inch up a hair.

"How the hell?" He collapses onto the edge of his desk and pokes my shoulder. "Just making sure you're not one of those holograms like they did for Tupac at Coachella."

I rise from his executive chair and shove a folder of documents George needed him to review. Jordan crashes into his seat, reclaiming his throne, raking his hands through his thick, light brown hair while groaning. My insides erupt, but I don't gloat. Not yet at least, but dammit if I didn't want to.

Either way, win or lose, I wouldn't have minded. Cooking and bowling aren't terrible punishments. But making him create a list of his favorite songs has the power to erase my shitty mood and the many shitty moods to come.

You can tell a lot about a person through the lyrics they connect with. Jordan's always teasing me about my choice of tunes, so I'm eager to listen to his go-to song list, whether he's trying to get through a workout or setting a mood for one of his many conquests. Well, maybe I don't want the latter.

For the rest of the afternoon, I troll the web in search of that necklace or one similar. After a few calls and a lot of pleading to the heavens, I hit the jackpot.

I hightail my fat ass into his office with a smirk spread from ear to ear. This time, I gloat.

"I'm amazing. What if I told you, I found the necklace?" I drop my ass into the chair in front of his desk, relieved. I needed this win, today of all days.

Without turning to me, he responds, "I'd say you were heaven-sent, but only demons need speed as you do." He finishes jotting down a note before leaning back in his chair, hands stretched behind his head. The vast city landscape sits behind him as if he's their mighty ruler. His enormous presence makes everything below him puny by comparison. Jordan oozes more confidence and authority than any one person should possess. And for a person who just lost a bet, he should dial it down a notch. "Just tell me one thing. How the hell did you beat me?"

"Well," I hold out the paper with the jewelry store's information. The tips of his fingers graze over my skin with a delicate flair all his own.

You're reading too much into this, Pens. Get yourself together.

"They're holding the necklace for you."

As hard as I fight this feeling, because it's wrong on so many levels, he's the best part of my day; especially during moments like this, watching his face transition between unknown thoughts.

As I leave, I add, "I'll be expecting that play-list sooner rather than later." I spin on my heel and exit with a little extra victorious swagger to my stride.

"I'm being serious," he shouts after me. "Which way did you take? How did you beat me?"

Wearing my most flirtatious smirk, I pop my head back into the doorway. "I'm just better than you." With a quick flip of my hair, I burst into laughter as I sit back at my desk.

"I'd disagree, but facts speak for themselves."

Right as my ass hits my seat, Jordan waltzes through his doorway with his key fob in hand. "Forward my calls."

I salute him, and he chuckles, racing toward the elevators. With Jordan gone, I'm left to my own devices and take advantage, having done most of the work needed for the day despite lacking focus earlier. I whip out my notepad and do the research I can't do at home, too fearful John will become tech-savvy overnight and discover my intentions. My chances are slim considering he hasn't learned to delete his searches of single, local women in our area; unless he intends to make me aware that I'm replaceable for an evening, I'm not testing fate.

Too enthralled by my research, the work phone startles me. I jump off the seat for a split second, much like I would have if John caught me.

"Hello?"

"Ms. Matthews. Can you come into my office for a second?" Tom requests and I oblige.

I grab a notepad, shoving the one I was just using in my drawer, and hurried to Tom's office. His assistant is not at her desk, per usual. I peek my head into the door and Tom is quick to usher me in.

"Ms. Matthews," he says with a broad smile. "Please, come in. Also, can you close the door behind you?"

I do as I'm told. I hope he's not mad I've been using the internet for personal use. His assistant trolls Instagram, Twitter, Neiman Marcus, Saks, Nordstrom, Michael Kors, and who the hell knows what else. Not that it justifies anything, but at least I get my work done. She can't say the same. I take an apprehensive seat across from his desk, the chair Jordan sits in the most.

Tom's desk is such a disaster, I may call FEMA. I stop myself from moving him aside to organize the clutter; although I doubt he'd mind.

As if reading my mind, he says, "As you can see," as he gestures to his mess and smooths his hand over his balding head. "I've had better weeks." His usual pleasant expression fades as he moves one folder to the opposite side of his desk, only shifting the mess, not organizing it.

Tom has always been nice to me, sometimes to a fault. I've never seen him stressed, but stress lines are set deep in his skin now that Grace has retired. He flings his glasses onto his desk and pinches the bridge of his nose, and huffs out a tired breath.

Where Jordan wouldn't have a problem scolding me or anyone for being disorganized, Tom deals with the problem in silence. In my opinion, he's being too kind; his assistant deserves to be reprimanded.

On the corner of his desk, a stack of folders teeters on the edge, inches away from being knocked onto the floor. I can't help myself, and grab the files, and make a neat pile on my lap.

"Oh, no, Penelope. Please," he insists, rising from his chair as if to stop me, but doesn't. "This is my problem. You mustn't."

"My OCD is flaring up," I joke, and lift myself off the chair to grab another stack, fixing that one, too. I alphabetize both stacks together.

He chuckles to himself, a pleasant laugh I haven't witnessed since Grace's departure. "I didn't call you in here to rearrange my desk, as much as it needs it," he starts, as I continue to sort. "You're an asset to the company. We all agree you have a lot of potentials."

Jordan compliments my work, too, but when Tom dishes out the praise, it hits differently. He reminds me of my grandfather, and his generous words fill me with pride.

"Thank you, Mr. Peters."

Content with the few subtle adjustments I made, his desk is fifty percent improved, so I refrain from doing anything more.

"We've all noticed," he continues. "The work you two did with Oakfeld... outstanding. For the first time, Jordan gave you most of the credit after his presentation. Not all," he jokes, "but most."

My cheeks warm further, grinning from lobe to lobe.

"We all agreed you deserve a raise. You've more than earned it. That boss of yours will jump through hoops to make sure you're happy and here to stay."

"I enjoy working here," I admit. Starting somewhere else gives me agita. And a day without Jordan isn't a day I'm ready to face.

"As of next week, there will be a nice bump in your paycheck, a much-deserved bump. We appreciate your hard work. And the way you wrangle that tyrant of yours... commendable. He gushes about you constantly. Brags actually, and we're sort of jealous." He chuckles to himself. "Safe to say, this is a first for us all."

"Thank you so much. Tyrant is a pretty strong term, but I have many years of experience dealing with strong-willed men."

"Well, whatever you're doing, keep it up." He peers down at his less disheveled desk and offers a grateful nod.

"Thank you, again." I rise and head to the door. "Open or closed?"

"Ugh," he mutters, the exhaustion in his eyes returns. "Closed, please. The clicking of her nails is driving me insane. I can't afford to lose any more of whatever's left of my mind. How do you ladies type with those talons?"

She can't type period, with or without. I close the door behind me and turn on my heel and become startled. Hovering outside Tom's door is Jordan, damn near scaring me half to death.

"What were you and Tom talking about?" He folds his arms in front of him, mouth slack-jawed and head cocked to the side as he weighs his evidence.

He follows me back to my desk, trailing behind, almost stepping on the back of my shoes.

"I swear, Jordan. You don't listen when I talk." I'm amazed I've managed the words straight-faced.

"I listen to everything."

The words themselves didn't make me pause. It was the conviction behind his voice that made me do a double-take.

"I have to update my resume."

"What?"

He walks faster, coming up to my side, matching my strides, and leans in close. His cologne, a robust mixture of cedar and sandalwood with vanilla and a hint of something floral. Whatever it is, I swear it's what Heaven smells like. "What the hell are you talking about?"

I pull out my chair and take a seat. The earbuds are a mere inch away from my ear when he puts his hand on mine, stopping me.

Why are his hands always the perfect temperature, able to warm my entire body?

"Penelope?" The way he says my name freezes me. That warning tone is all-too-familiar. I remind myself that he's not John.

"Jesus, Jordan, relax." I ease back into my chair and move my hand out from under his. "I was going to say, 'I reverted to my old ways again, having a love affair with my boss,' but you got all weird on me."

"Tom isn't your boss."

I roll my eyes. "You're missing the joke."

His stern expression dims, just a hair. "Well, if you're going to have an affair with your boss, at least be aware of who your actual boss is, is all

I'm saying." His sarcasm is weaved so thick, I'm surprised it didn't drip onto the floor.

"Ugh, whatever, Jordan. You ruined a great joke," I exhaust, defeated. "Did you get the necklace?"

"Yup," he shouts from his office and emerges with a big white bag. "And I got something else." He places the unmarked bag on my desk. "For you."

I eye him first and then the bag. "Jordan, what did you do?"

"Open it."

I peek inside. When I remove the item from the cloth storage bag, the monogram, YSL, shines in gold against the black quilted leather. The price tag with one too many digits in front of the decimal, remains attached. Jesus Christ.

"Jordan," I gasp, unable to utter another word.

"You were admiring Olyvia's bag the other day, so I bought you one. Yours is a little better." He winks. "Open it, there's more." With his watchful eyes on me, I obey. Inside the luxury handbag is a plaque, similar to the one I received after bowling my perfect game. "You looked heartbroken when you told me yours got destroyed, so I replaced it. See," he points to my engraved name. "I pay attention," he boasts with his chest puffed out. Just when the prickle hits my eyes, he points to the bag again.

Inside is another gift. As if two weren't enough, there's an envelope with cold, hard cash inside.

"My mom always said it was bad luck to give a purse without throwing money inside." He retreats to his office with a triumphant exhale.

I waltz my enormous ass right after him, and set the expensive purse on his desk, holding the plaque close to my chest. "Your mom is right, but she meant a dollar or some pocket change, not," I flip through the envelope, "not over two thousand dollars. Jesus, Jordan."

He shrugs. "In all fairness, you left the holiday party early, so you missed out on some giveaways. Also, you didn't take the gift I left you, and it ended up getting stolen by some pimple-faced server, which I had fired, by the way. You're welcome."

"I can't accept any of this. The raise is enough."

Jordan sucks his teeth. "I told Tom we'd tell you together. Unbelievable."

He acknowledges nothing I've said. "Um, hello? I can't accept this. I'll take the plaque, though," I exclaim, fawning over the thoughtful gift, holding the cool marble against my warming heart. It's not as if you can walk into any trophy store and get one on the spot. This took time and planning. How did he know what the original looked like?

He relaxes back into his chair with his hands folded in front of him and his heels resting on his desk. "Nope." His exuding authority makes my pulse skitter. Definitely A-fib. He shakes his head. "Remember who your boss is the next time." He laughs and lowers his feet back to the ground. "Now get out," he orders with a playful tone. "I have to yell at Tom for having that meeting without me."

I head for the door, and he coughs as if beckoning me to turn around.

"You're forgetting something." He points to the bag of never-ending goodies with his chiseled chin.

Reluctantly, I snatch the bag from his desk. My cheeks warm, and I'm sure they've shifted through a variety of red shades. Maybe that's why he's wearing that goofy smirk.

When John destroyed my plaque, my most prized possession, he destroyed me, too. He didn't care. Of all the things on the shelf—photos, a trinket box, and a framed award I won—John chose the plaque, the one that meant the most.

Now, the plaque Jordan gave me is more special than anything before that. It is an exact duplicate to the first—black marbled-finish with a bowling ball and pin inside a gold ring at the top. At the bottom sits another gold plate, engraved with my name and the date of my infamous game. The energy and effort behind this gift overwhelms me; the tears that prickle my eyes are proof.

Nothing John has ever given me took this much thought or care. He walks into a store, picks whatever high-priced item the pretty sales associate is selling, flashes his wad of cash, and leaves. He leaves seven digits happier, too.

The rest of the day is a blur as I rush home, needing to hide Jordan's expensive gifts. Awash of relief spreads over my surface when John's car isn't in the driveway. With Jordan's bag slung over my shoulder, I hurry inside, contemplating where to hide the gifts for safekeeping. Without further delay, I head into the bedroom and drop to the floor in front of the closet.

A moan startles me from where I kneel. Any breath I would release sits tight in my chest as my heart palpitates in my chest.

John sprawls himself on the bed with his arm draped over his eyes, shifting in a slow motion. I'm not sure how I missed it until now, but the bedroom reeks like the cushioned mats behind a busy bar—stale beer and booze. I cover my mouth, muffling the faint gasp that escapes.

"Hey, babe," he groans, groggily, most likely hungover, as he elongates his bulky body with one long and loud stretch. "How was work?" He removes his arm from his eyes. A drunken smile plays on his lips.

I try gliding the purse into the closet without him noticing, but the heavy chained strap scratches along the hardwood floor.

"What's that?" The question had the effect of a record scratch.

"Nothing. Just rearranging the clutter. You're home early. Where's the car?"

He sits up on the bed and narrows his glare. "What's that?" he asks, pointing with his chin.

"Oh, th-this…" I fumble the word as they catch in my throat. "Nothing. Just a gift from the company."

"Show me."

Without delaying the unavoidable, I raise the bag for him. No good can come from hiding it.

"All the assistants got one," I lie, but his eyes confirm otherwise.

"Bullshit, Penelope." He hovers over me in an instant. His eyes shift from me, then to the bag. John's jaw flexes, his eyes turn sharp like daggers only meant for me. "What the fuck did you do to deserve this?"

"I work, John. And I didn't do whatever you're assuming I did." I bite back, unable to hold my tongue. Who does he think I am? Him?

My pulse quickens as I try swallowing, but my mouth is as dry as the Sahara. The nauseating sinking of despair spreads inside me as I watch his hands ball into a fist. The heat of his gaze burns like it was an actual physical touch. I flinch.

John looms above and his enormous frame casts a grim shadow on me. My panic riots as he works his fist, opening and closing it. With my eyes distracted by his right hand, his left grabs a chunk of my hair and yanks me to my feet. I try prying him away, but his hold is impeccable. John pushes me against the wall, and a framed photo falls and shatters on the floor. With the black leather purse still clutched in my grasp, he snatches the gift and shoves the fresh leather in my face, rubbing my nose in it.

"No boss would buy you this." He leans in close. Foam sits in the corners of his mouth. "Not unless you're spreading something or sucking something," he growls as spit sprays my cheek. "Which one is it?"

Tears fall, but he doesn't care. "John. Please s-stop. You're hurting me." He doesn't care about that, either. He never cares about that anymore, blinded by rage.

John slams the purse to the floor as if spiking a football. While I claw at his left hand, his right whips across my cheek. It starts as a warming sensation until the sting intensifies. His hand flew at hyper-speed. I couldn't prepare myself for the impact.

John yanks my head forward, then forces it back, slamming my skull into the wall. I bite back the bile as the pain lances through my head.

"I never pegged him for a chubby chaser," he spits. Literally. "You're quitting that fucking job."

He glowers at me and then storms out, slamming the front door behind him.

I sink to the floor. Hard. Drawing my knees to my chest, I sob with one hand holding the back of my throbbing head. When I pull my hand away, loose hairs tangle between my fingers. My cheek radiates heat, and my skin vibrates as if stung by a hundred bees.

I crawl to the bag and remove the plaque. Luckily, it's unharmed. If John found this, there's no telling what he'd do. With the engraved plaque in my hand and tears pouring down my cheeks, I stash the gift, along with the money-filled envelope under a loose floorboard in the dark corner of the closet.

After a good icing, my reddened cheek dulls in color, but my reflection is still a lie. Under all this cover-up lies the true Penelope Matthews—beaten, inside and out.

Carefully, I wash my face, watching the mask I wear every day muddy the water and spiral down the drain. I stare at my reflection again. The skin around my eye is still healing, but yellow remnants remain. I shrug off my cardigan and admire the faint fingerprints of his too rough grasp on my upper arms lingering on my paler complexion. My hand massages my tender scalp. A lump has already formed.

Stefanie Stratton

The longer I stare, the more I hate myself. My stomach churns and the bile rises. My food wants out.

I need out. No matter how carefully I tread, I live in constant fear. Even if he's not given a reason to be mad, John finds one. But this is who I've become. And I hate it. I sacrificed too much for this shitty life.

"This is the real you," I say aloud. "This will always be you. Are you happy now?"

The only person who should witness this unaltered version, bruised and battered, is the man who created these wounds. He should soak in each cut, each bruise, each handprint, and scratch he gives during one of his fits of rage, fueled by alcohol or assumptions. Or both.

Hours pass as I wait for John to return home. I stir the simmering chili with one hand while alternating the ice between my cheek and scalp. Maybe he won't come back.

John spends less and less time here, anyway. With any luck, he's started a future with someone else and this house is now his part-time one. As much as it's unsettling, I contemplate his demand.

Quitting is like slapping a band-aid on a gunshot wound. It solves nothing. If it's not Jordan, it'll be my next boss or a coworker. He always finds something to bitch about. With the mere thought of leaving yet another job, the hot, salty tears start all over again.

The door opens, and my prayers go unanswered as he nears the kitchen. Any appetite I had disappears, yet again. I pat away the tears.

"You hungry?" I ask.

Chapter Twenty

"YOU OKAY?" JORDAN asks as he stands in front of my desk with his mug of peppermint tea in hand and takes a judgmental sip.

I tip my head forward, assuring Jordan, but we have spent too much time together for me to convince him that easily.

My heart aches to sit in his office, shoot the breeze, and ask and answer a million and one questions, but the more I enjoy working here, the more John senses it.

I need to take a step back and rebuild my wall. The days of me laughing and joking should end. Work needs to be my number one priority again, and not building a friendship with my boss.

As much as Jordan keeps staring in my direction, I pull at no stops to avoid him. I'm sure he didn't ask for a bipolar assistant, cracking jokes one day and shunning him the next, but I can't keep putting myself in a position John can misread.

"Who the hell are those for?" Jordan asks, aloud.

While he stands near my desk, fiddling with something in his pocket, I scroll through my play-list in search of loud, angry music. Music about destruction. I need a bass line loud enough to burst my eardrums or with guitar riffs that could shatter glass. If another sappy love song comes on, I'll throw my stapler through the window myself.

With his mouth ajar, I follow his gaze. In an instant, a painful knot forms in my throat as sharp as if I swallowed a ball of jagged shards.

Josey moseys through the long corridor, carrying four dozen long-stemmed red roses arranged with white baby's breath in a crystal vase.

She lugs the heavy vase, blowing a pink bubble with her gum. My coworkers gawk at the extravagant arrangement, one most people only see in movies, but this isn't a Fifty Shades kind of love. It's a million shades of fucked up.

Josey grins a meek grin but is beautiful still. She knows more than anyone what these flowers signify. The shop should name this arrangement, "I'm Sorry I'm the Biggest Asshole Bouquet." One dozen is to say sorry. Two dozen shows he's sorry for being sorry. Tack on another dozen for the slap, and an added dozen for yanking out a chunk of hair. Josey sees John almost as much as I do, working in her parent's florist shop, the only shop he buys from.

And I'm not the only recipient of his purchases. Josey told me of a few occasions he's bought bouquets in the shop, but when she asked if I liked her arrangement, half the time I had no clue what she was talking about.

"Hey, Pens. He never gets off that shit-list, huh?"

Jordan eyes the arrangement, counting the flowers with his mouth. "Must be an extensive shit-list," he mumbles.

"You have no—" Josephine starts.

"My favorite vase broke a while ago... by accident. This must be his way of replacing it," I blurt, giving Josey her cue to keep her mouth shut.

Josey nods in agreement and rocks on her heels with her hands tucked behind her back.

Jordan is still counting. I don't need to count anymore; I've gotten my fair share of apology arrangements. They are as useless as tits on a turtle.

"Must've been a special vase," Jordan comments.

The moment the rose scent travels to my nose, I can't fake it anymore. "Ugh, I hate roses." Contempt wafts off me.

Josey pops another bubble. "Oh, he knows. I tried suggesting something else, but John is always right. Wanna see a fun, fresh twist he added?" She lifts her sleeve over her shoulder, exposing her tanned and now torn skin. "Thorns stay on."

A God-awful sound flies past my lips. It was a cross between a gasp and a groan. "Of course. He always finding new ways to injure me." I lift a single rose and tap on the pointed spikes on the stem.

"Pen..." Josey warns. Her scolding tone is almost as frightening as John's loving one. I'm wary of both. She's never liked when I make light of what he does.

"Injure?" Jordan hesitates.

Fuck. I forgot Jordan was still standing here.

"Josephine, this is my boss, Jordan Stephens."

They shake hands and I don't blame Jordan for gawking, as if he's photographing her with his eyes. Josey is more his type to begin with—soft, feminine features, ample curves in the right places with that Latina flare—she's the starring role in every straight man's X-rated fantasies.

"You can call me Josey."

"She's my best friend," I add.

"Wait." He holds his chin in his hand. "Josey? The Josey you drunk-texted me with?" His posture loosens, and his face becomes less crunched.

I cover my face, careful to hide the heat in my cheeks as Josey bursts into laughter.

"Yeah, that was a fun night," she wheezes and nudges my side until I come out of hiding.

What if he responded?

"Well, nice meeting you, Josey. Enjoy the flowers, Penny." Jordan retreats to his office and closes the door behind him, something he never does.

Maybe he hates the smell of roses, too.

"Damn, Pens. He's way hotter than I imagined," she whispers. "That explains why John is spazzing out more than usual." She glances at her watch. "I need to get back. No need to tip." She hands me a literal wad of twenties. "I overcharged him for the vase and flowers. Told him they were the Juliet Rose, some rare rose from England, and that dumbass paid. Add it to your secret checking account." She turns toward the closed door. "Be careful. Can't have a repeat of job number 10. Or 15?"

"That makes two of us."

Josey disappears toward the elevators while I pull the stems out of the vase and discard them, one by one. A thorn catches on my skin and my breath hitches. God, I hate John.

He's singlehandedly made me loathe beautiful flowers. Unless I just detest when they come from him. The only time he buys them for me is when he's inflicted physical pain, never out of love or care. And now, with these thorns, he continues to inflict pain even when he's not here.

I had dinner ready an hour ago, and he's still not home. Instead of waiting on the uncomfortable kitchen chair, I lounge on the couch with a book in my lap, drifting off to a world of demons and magical beings. Man, do I wish I could escape into the pages of a book. Even this one. Their world isn't entirely different. I, too, live in a world full of demons, one in particular, except I don't have magical powers to destroy him.

The unsettling torment grows like an infection, and I can't ignore what needs to be done, nor do I want to. This mental glass cage John has trapped me in is suffocating me. If I don't escape soon, I'll lose my sanity forever. This is all I've ever known, but this isn't normal.

None of Josey's boyfriends degraded or laid a hand on her, no matter how often she drove them crazy.

I can't live like this anymore.

How much further down the rabbit hole must I go? Unless buried six feet under taking a dirt nap for eternity is the epitome of rock bottom, that will be the ultimate punishment if I don't get out while I'm still breathing. I must've hit rock bottom. As scary as separating myself from John is, the overwhelming fear that tethers me to stay isn't so powerful anymore. The threat outside this relationship isn't as scary as the threat within.

Attempts to leave in the past never worked. I'd rush out of the house with no game plan; I never planned to come back, but I never expected myself to stay away either.

Things are different now. I've set money aside in a secret checking account, building a safety net until I found the courage to pull the trigger once and for all.

John's car pulls into the garage and all thoughts come to a halt. I place his supper in the microwave and press the buttons harder than necessary. I shouldn't need to warm his food; he should have been home when he said he would.

"Your food is being reheated," I shout as he enters the door.

"Thanks." He kisses my neck and, like an automatic reflex, my teeth clench tight.

Jordan's Penny

Before he's down the hall, I swat at my skin, wiping the wet stain left behind, but it's too late. His saliva burns like acid.

He doesn't even care I've waited for him. Again. He strolls in as if nothing's wrong and he's not three hours late for dinner. I reheat my food, too. God forbid I eat without him.

John strolls into the kitchen, taking his normal seat, and dives into his food without waiting for me. Asshole. The sound of his fork and knife against the ceramic plate is like nails on a chalkboard running right through me. I watch as he chews the steak, half hoping he chokes on the meat as he shovels chunks in his mouth.

I sit down, but not without difficulty. My movements are stiff as my rage multiplies with each passing breath. I've never been one who got angry easily, but being with John as long as I have, the change in my behavior was inevitable. I despise him for that.

"You get my flowers?" His voice grates on my very last nerve.

"Yes." My eyes shift to all the spots on my hand where the thorns pricked my skin. They still hurt. "Beautiful, as always."

"I'm going away on business tomorrow and returning next Thursday."

He launches into a one-sided conversation about recruiting some college kid, offering so many unnecessary details, none of it could be true. I have zero interest in anything he's saying, so I pick at my food, nod sometimes, and slowly realize he will be gone, and I will be free.

"We'll celebrate your birthday when I come back." His voice is void of any emotion, only a rehearsed mono-toned inflection as if forcing himself to say the words. But no matter how he says it, it is music to my ears, and my mood soars.

I take a relaxed breath and hide my elation. Even as the corners of my mouth spring to life, it draws no attention, which isn't abnormal. He rarely pays attention to me anyhow. If he's not on the couch hypnotized by ESPN+, he's glued to his phone, texting God knows who. I could hang myself right in the living room, and he'd assume I was a new hanging plant until he ran out of clean boxers. Maybe then he'd question it. Who am I kidding? He'd just buy more.

"Okay," I respond with ease.

Relief washes over my shores, rushing in like a high tide on a full moon. All nausea that's plagued me for days subsides.

"I'll take you someplace nice. You'll wear that black dress I bought you, straighten your hair, you'll cover up all your... you know." He gestures to all the mixed-matched colored skin.

Yes. I know. I'll slather myself in concealer to hide all the places where you struck me with your bare hands so no one suspects you to be a monster.

Oddly enough, one boss, a lawyer, who might've been a worse human being than John, approached me about my bruises. The lies and foundation didn't fool him. He had a set of steel balls in the courtroom and outside of it, too. Mr. Ingrams confronted John. He didn't fear anyone. John forced me to quit the next day. No two-week notice. Nothing.

"You'll do your makeup real nice. It'll be fun, just the two of us. You'd like that, right?"

"Mm-hmm."

"And you're quitting that job. We were fine until you started working there."

Lies. More lies. Our relationship has been plagued with problems, and John creates them all. His abuse never stopped no matter where I worked, only varied in intensity depending on whatever imaginative issue he concocts. Hell, even when I didn't have a job, he complained, calling me a lazy, freeloading bitch. There's no winning with him.

"John, please." I tread with caution, keeping my voice calm and light, anything but defensive. "There's nothing between us. He's nice because he pities me. He told those exact words to another partner." Nothing I've said is a lie, but despite my carefree shrug, every tendon in my heart aches as I repeat the devastating truth aloud.

He throws his fork down. The metal clanks on the ceramic and I flinch.

"What's the big fucking deal? Unless you're the one that's into him."

John's jaw clenches. If I don't snuff out his fire, the entire room will become engulfed.

"Baby," I coo, and my stomach retches, using that endearing term for him. "The job is easy money."

"Penelope, I'm not arguing with you. Not tonight. I make enough to support us both."

"Baby…" Feeding his ego, laying on the sweetness thick like honey is the only way to skate through this. "I enjoy helping with the bills. It gives me purpose and I enjoy helping. How about this? I'll keep working, but I'll be on the lookout for another position somewhere else."

I breathe easier once he picks up his fork again. He smiles, a crooked smile, but nothing is ever that easy with John. He shoves a forkful of mashed potatoes into his mouth.

"We'll continue this conversation when I get back. You've been different since they transferred you to that guy," he answers. His voice, a low vibration that sends a shiver down my spine.

All these years I've always been torn between leaving and staying as if each foot was in two different boats. Day by day, I struggle to keep the boats together, hoping John will decide for me and leave. But the only thing that happens is my legs stretch further apart. My only chance for survival is to pick a boat, once and for all.

I rise from the table and place my plate in the sink. With John gone for a week, it'll be the perfect opportunity to do what's needed.

I move behind him and drape my arms around his muscular shoulders. The sheer width of him is immense. He can be so handsome when his anger stays locked inside.

"I thought no one would love me and until you showed up at my locker, sweaty from the gym with your oversized red jersey on." John rests his hands over mine, holding my embrace as I whisper near in his ear. He reeks of a woman's perfume, not a scent I own. "We became friends, and we grew into something… more. I'll never forget how much you've changed me."

And I'll be damned if I ever let a man change me again.

John chuckles to himself. "You gave me a run for my money back then. You'll never understand the lengths I'd go for you, to prove how much I need you to stay." I'm awfully familiar with his love language and how he proves that love, but I don't deserve it. Any of it. He lowers his head and kisses the back of my hand. "When everyone else swore I'd amount to nothing, just a dumb jock, you loved me and supported me. Through the good times, getting signed to the NFL, and then sticking by my side after my injury, and all those surgeries. You nursed me back to health and helped me get stronger." Now I'm regretting helping him get stronger. "You chose me in the beginning and have been loyal ever since. Loyalty is rare."

Yes. He's right. Loyalty is rare. Honestly, I'm surprised he's heard the word before, having never practiced it for the ninety-eight percent of our relationship. But I have to a fault. No matter how many times he cheated, I didn't get revenge. I forgave.

John spins in his chair to face me. "You're the only woman who knows me through and through. No one else."

For a man that says a lot of wrong things, he's spot on tonight. I know John better than everyone. From his little quirks, like how he sucks his teeth for forty-five seconds after he flosses, to how he rolls his shoulders seven rotations counter-clockwise before doing his evening pull-ups. Or his annoying habit of moaning like he's in ecstasy when he pees first thing in the morning or when he leaves his toenail clippings on the bed. And then I can tell you how badly the hardened ridges of his bare knuckles hurt when they hit my jaw or arm or thigh. I know exactly how many days it'll take for the bruises he's left behind to heal. I know the power of his words, the strength of his hands, and the devastation those two things combined have had on me for the past thirteen years. None of his side pieces have had the pleasure of knowing John through and through like I do.

"I'm always scared of losing you," he adds.

A normal person might swoon over the endearing compliment, but for someone afraid of losing me, he does all these things that make me want to run, not walk to the nearest exit.

"I'll never leave you for another man." I lean in close and press my lips to his, just a gentle peck.

Nothing I said is a lie. My heart warms with its truth. He was my everything, and these tears are proof. I'm not leaving for another man. I'm leaving for myself.

CHAPTER
TWENTY-ONE

W HEN I OPENED my eyes this morning, the sun peaked over the horizon, returning from its slumber. The soft amber glow gave little light through the blinds, but the birds started their morning song and Mr. Woodpecker hammered away a few trees down the block.

John's arm drapes over me, although drapes might not be the right verb. His arm is like a cage, holding me prisoner with nowhere to go, but he can't keep me forever.

He stirs beside me, unwrapping his powerful, well-muscled arm, and rolls onto his back. I can breathe again as I put a healthy amount of space between us. John yawns and stretches his limbs. His elbow slams into my shoulder. If I wasn't awake before, the elbow jab would have done the trick.

"Morning," he greets groggily. "I just had the best dream," he starts, still stretching his massive body in place, elongating each limb again. "We started a family—a boy and a little girl. We posed for a family picture. Your hair was almost black, and you weren't heavy, either. Plus, you looked as if you sun-bathed for a week, with dark, tanned skin. Everyone smiled and laughed for the picture like one big, happy family. Sounds nice, right?"

Sounds like he was dreaming about someone else entirely.

Ass. And. Hole.

John sits on the edge of the bed, combing his rough hands through his thick, dark hair. With his bare back towards me, the vertical lines—lines of ecstasy—claw down the length of it.

Many years ago, he demanded I kept my nails short because he hated clicking when I tapped on surfaces. I eye my stumpy nail nubs. He doesn't even try to hide his infidelities anymore.

John disappears behind the bathroom door and turns on the shower. His annoying moan echoes off the bathroom tiles. While he hums in the shower, I throw on a robe and make our morning coffee.

As the dark beans perk, I stare at his travel suitcase sitting by the front door and relax into a soft smile because of his upcoming trip. I don't even question or concern myself with where he's headed once he exits the front door. Too many possibilities come to mind, and none of them are work-related. The only concern I have is where I'm headed. For the first time in a long time, I'm not a shell of myself. My body is alert, full of energy, and ready to start anew. Whatever fear that crept to the surface in the past didn't appear now. A future without John is no longer terrifying. I'll be able to do what I want when I want. I can wear whatever I choose and answer to no one but myself. The days of making an excuse for other people's behavior are gone and I can say goodbye to my theater-quality cover-up and horrendous clothing.

It isn't long before John joins me in the kitchen. I pour him a steaming mug. Grateful, he takes it.

"You seem different." He eyes me through his lashes before taking a sip.

I shift in place, changing whatever expression I wore moments ago. "Do I?"

He gives me a complete once-over. "I'm not sure. Maybe I'm still tired."

"You all packed? Got your ticket?"

John glances at his wrist and lets out a huff. "Yeah." He pats the back pockets of his dark blue skinny jeans, checking for his wallet. John always balked at the idea of wearing skinny jeans; his latest fling must have talked him into wearing them. He must grow tired of juggling all these variations of himself.

I give limited versions of myself, too, but Josey is the only person who gets me, the real unfiltered me. Maintaining this lie is draining me dry, and I'm relieved it'll be one less task I'm responsible for.

For years, John groomed me into believing no one would desire an overweight woman. Hell, if the man that claimed to love me hated the sight of me, what chance did I stand with someone else? He needed me weak, so I'd always be his hostage, relying on the limited love he would afford me until I believed that's all I deserved. His physical abuse kept me in line. The mental abuse kept me here. He didn't need to say the words to make me stay; he made me accept I had no other choice. John weaponized my hang-ups, using my low self-esteem against me. All that mental abuse I endured secured my position at home, cooking, cleaning, and picking up all his messes.

That's over now.

John swings open the front door, rolling the suitcase behind him in one hand with my hand tucked in his other. I cling to his arm, much like I've clung onto our blossoming love and the overwhelming emotions that warmed my soul because of the old John, not the man beside me now. I've been holding onto something that no longer exists.

"It's only for a week, babe."

With our fingers laced, the smile behind his eyes is undeniable. We both wear grins, but the happiness that fills us is for differing reasons. I breathe in his scent, catching whiffs of dark musk and fig trees with Mediterranean zest. With closed eyes, I tattoo that scent in my brain and not the varying female fragrances he's been wearing as of late.

Before he heads to the airport, hotel, or wherever he's going, I throw my arms around his neck and stare into his cocoa-colored eyes. The sudden desire to press my lips to his takes over.

I haven't kissed John willingly, not like this, in months. He wraps his hardened muscles around my waist, pulling me closer as I part my lips, allowing him his last taste. His hand presses on my lower back, deepening our embrace.

As teens, this is how we kissed for hours, locked in each other's arms and we never tired. Our kissing styles matched then, and nothing's changed now. My tongue strokes his and he moans in my mouth, tightening his grip on my body. The flight of butterflies I used to get is a thing of the past. They died of starvation from a lack of love and lust over a decade ago. Nothing can resuscitate those emotions back to life now. Nothing.

As I end our kiss, I say, "I'll miss this."

He chuckles, a low and husky laugh as his hands stay wrapped loosely around me. I need him to let me go.

"Aww, babe. Don't worry. I'll be back in a week." He bites his bottom lip and searches my face as I give him my smile. He places another kiss on my lips, a quick peck, and then releases me.

With my imminent freedom approaching, my mouth carries a beaming grin. I welcome the unknown with open arms and let this sensation envelop me in its mysterious wonder.

"Safe trip." As I turn on my heel, he slaps my ass, and I jump, startled, but I giggle just the same. "Get outta here before you miss your flight," I shout as I stroll back to the front door.

He smiles, one filled with mischief, and says, "Oh, it's not until… yeah, you're right. I'll call you tonight. Behave yourself, Penelope."

And there it is. My orders.

From the doorway, I watch him back out of the driveway as he waves one last time, and I do the same. The tires screech and smoke billows from the friction, speeding off to the unknown.

The weight that's been living on my chest for years lifts. Even breathing becomes easier. I remain in the doorway, staring at nothing in particular, but seeing everything with a fresh pair of eyes. I pull the phone from my robe pocket and send Jordan a text. He responds in an instant, as if waiting for me.

"Alexa, play dance list."

In moments, my play-list kicks on at the loudest volume possible. I hop in the shower, singing at the top of my lungs, something I would never do with John home. Dancing in my towel, I sort through my closet and pick an outfit that's been calling my name for months, but John would never allow me to wear it. I take my time getting ready, perfecting my hair, and tending to my makeup.

Ready to start my day, hell, ready to start my life, I swing open the front door. Opportunity fills the air, and my lungs take in as much as they can hold. With time to spare, I drive to my appointment.

The complex has gates surrounding all sides, with a guard sitting in a booth near the entrance.

"Hi. I'm meeting with Angelique."

The guard, a stocky man in his forties, greets me with a pleasant, welcoming grin and makes a call. Nerves run through my veins like electricity as I tap on my steering wheel and wait. The gate soon swings open as he leans toward my car. Although friendly-looking, he also might toss a man clear across the street. That might come in handy.

"The Leasing Office is straight ahead. Park to the left of the turnaround."

Whenever I passed this apartment complex on my way to work, I admired the gated entrance—thick, black steel with spikes at the top—it gives an unwelcoming vibe. I enjoy the aesthetic of one person who isn't welcome. All the other amenities they advertised online only add to the listing like icing and sprinkles on an already heavily decorated cake.

The landscape is well-groomed, and at the center of the turnaround sits an enormous fountain with a tiered bird-bath basin that trickles water in the center. The sound is soothing. It'd be a shame if people didn't come to the fountain for the tranquil sounds of water dripping after a stressful day. I would.

As I open the office door, a beautiful woman approaches with her hand extended.

"You must be Angelique," I say.

"Yes. Welcome. Nice to meet you, Ms. Matthews." Her face-splitting grin is as lively as her hair. A fiery red. "I can show you the apartment we discussed and show you the property."

A flood of emotions overwhelms me as my hands tremble. I'm doing this. I'm really doing this.

"No." The sting in my eyes starts, no matter how hard I fight back the tears. "I'm here to sign a lease, but I need to move in today. Give me an apartment, any apartment, a closet, I don't care. I'll take it," I beg. "First, last, security, an entire year, just say how much. I'll pay whatever it takes." With nothing left to hide, I allow the tears to wash away my mask. "I need to get away from my abusive fiancé. I fear this might be my only chance."

Just as I settle at my desk, Jordan bustles around the office, whizzing past me, and heads straight through his door. I inhale, dragging his lingering cologne deep into my lungs. His scent, some expensive outdoorsy-inspired cologne, reminds me of our late nights trapped in the Conference

Room. I taste him in the air like fire burning in winter. My mouth salivated then, and I'm salivating now.

"Penny!" Jordan shouts, then cusses. "Where did I put my mother's gift?"

I laugh to myself, shaking my head. "Bottom left drawer." Even his voice sounds expensive, too. How did I not notice that before?

"I knew that." He slams the drawer closed, steamrolls out of his office, and brings that cologne-scented breeze with him.

"Everything okay?"

He gives me a quick once-over while I stare back. "Yeah…uh, running behind schedule." The tone, neither pleasant nor scolding. I arranged most of his morning to be free of stress because his true brain potential doesn't come alive until noon. Jordan gives his head a good shake and his eyes soften a smidgen. "No music today?"

I soak him in, like really soak him in. Until now, I tried to be impervious to Sexy Stephens, his questions, and random glances, doing everything in my power not to over-analyze them, even though I did anyway. With nothing holding me back, I let myself indulge, even if only for my fantasy.

Today, he's donning a gray suit, designer, no doubt, with a navy printed tie. The silver tie tack is a nice accent without being flashy, which is surprising considering he loves to be flashy.

A natural smile plays on my lips. I'm an idiot. This is how his assistants got distracted. They stared too long.

"The office will be my soundtrack today."

He tosses the wrapped box from one hand to the other. "You're awfully smiley today, too. What's the occasion?" The question comes across as rather dickish, but I don't blame him. For the past couple of weeks, I've taken him on a bipolar rollercoaster. Fun one minute and stand-offish the next.

Everything inside me aches to confess and tell him the truth. My chest pulsates like a beacon from all the lies. But it's bad enough he pitied me before. Once I spew the news about my psychotic, abusive boyfriend who brainwashed me for years, he'd replace me in a heartbeat. Jordan is a businessman. The last thing he cares about is other people's problems and feelings. Neither is conducive to the workplace.

"Woke up on the right side of the bed is all."

His features become more animated. "You can't fool me, Matthews. Stayed in bed a little longer." He winks. "You got that afterglow."

The rise in my body heat is instantaneous. This deodorant better be strong enough for this man-like sweat that happening under both pits.

I refuse to have a sex talk with my boss.

"No. Besides, he left on a business trip," I mention. "I had an early appointment that went well. So there." I stick my tongue at him.

I grab papers from the printer and catch Jordan scanning my outfit from head to toe. My hair is pulled into a high bun, and I'm wearing a black semi-sheer top with tiny white polka dots, and a black skirt that complements my fuller curves. His eyes fall to the floor as he spots my black patent leather pumps, the ones that give me another four inches. I might be taller than him with these puppies on.

"If I find out you went on a job interview, Penelope." He narrows his eyes, a gaze that makes my body tingle in a foreign and wicked way.

"Never," I confess as I approach him and make one final adjustment to his appearance. He watches me with a calmness set in his eyes, a characteristic John always lacked. A strange surge of unease whirls in my belly as I straightened his tie, but I ignore it. "Now you're presentable."

He glances at his wrist, staring at the large-faced Rolex, and then back at me. His eyes sparked an indefinable glint as we shared air. Jordan clears his throat and takes one pace away from me. "Thank you, Penelope. Call if you need me."

He races toward the elevators, and as I figured, I prefer when he's running toward me, not away. I don't blame him. I'd run away from me, too.

Why did I get that close to fix his tie? Stupid Penelope. Stupid.

I ease back into my chair and breathe, the first real breath I've taken since I signed my lease. While Jordan is off to lunch with his mother, I take advantage of his absence and make the dreaded call to Josey, one I've made several times in the past, only to backtrack days or hours later.

"This is different, Jo," I say with finality. "I'm talking clean slate, only taking what's mine. In some weird and possessive way, he's the one that has always needed me, but I'm done, Jo. Done."

"Are you prepared for the aftermath? He'll lose his shit. I'm talking Chernobyl-level scary."

"I've parked in the wrong lot since I started here. Besides, he has more than enough women to keep him busy. He'll replace me in a day and forget me in two."

She sighs on the other end, supportive but apprehensive. "He won't stop fighting for you. And I've seen what he does when he finds you. Hello?" she says in a pointed tone. "New Year's Eve, circa 2009?"

The goosebumps are instant, and every hair stands on end.

A day before New Year's Eve, I told John I needed a break. He didn't argue. He agreed. That should have been my first clue something bad was on the horizon. Josey convinced me to go to a hotel party for New Year's, and I looked forward to bringing in the year as a single girl. I didn't care about kissing someone at the stroke of midnight. Hell, half the time John disappeared five minutes before the clock struck twelve, only to return fifteen minutes later with lipstick stains on his mouth. I wanted to enjoy the countdown with my friends, drink a little, and bring in the new year dancing.

To this day, I'm unsure how he tracked me down. John caused a commotion and dragged me out by my arm. And when Josey's boyfriend tried stopping him, John's right hook knocked the man out cold. After that, everyone else stood back, except for Josey. She climbed on his back as fearless as a rabid orangutan, fighting until he let me go.

While she fought him from above, I fought for my freedom below. His fingers dug so deep, the police could use the marks left behind as fingerprints. Punch after punch, nothing helped. Our effort... futile. Booze wasn't the only thing in his system that night. His strength was magnified, fueled by rage and some illegal substance. Josey clawed at his face, but his grip on me only tightened. After he tossed me in his car like a rag doll, I woke up on New Year's Day in the hospital.

The only person waiting when I awoke was the doctor, not John. The nurses advised me of our accident, saying our brakes failed and we crashed into the corner of a brick building. I broke my nose, arm, had bruised ribs, and both eyes were black-and-blue, but one swelled shut. A deep gash with twenty-eight stitches curved along my hairline. My body was a roadmap of bruises, some old and some new.

I was lucky to be alive while John escaped unscathed. Apparently, he was the only one wearing a seatbelt even though I buckled mine despite how frantic I'd been. A lot of memories are fuzzy from that night, but I was certain I was wearing my seatbelt. When he showed up, the doctors signed my release paperwork three days later.

While I healed, he took care of me, fulfilling my every need, waiting on me hand and foot. He showered me with love and affection until I could take care of myself. I ignored Josey when she told me her theory about unbuckling my belt and crashing the car on purpose. He loved that car. He loved me.

Thinking about it now, he might have done anything to stop me from leaving him for good. Even sacrificing his pride and joy, Cami—a 1973 Chevrolet Camaro Z28, lime green body with black racing stripes on the hood.

Would he destroy her to make me need him?

No matter how bad the threats get this time, his mind games won't work.

"He's got that psychotic thing that makes him bonkers with you." Neither of us speaks because she's right. "Okay, Pens. Whatever you need me to do, I'm with you." Even though she isn't in front of me, she's thankful I'm leaving. "Does this mean we can celebrate your birthday like normal girlfriends?"

"Took you long enough to ask. Loud music, dancing, and enough alcohol to make my lips tingle." I gush, elated, and daydream about the perfect birthday celebration.

"Okay, Pen. I'll meet you at the house after work."

After I hang up, I glance around. Eyes take in my usual sights, but with a fresh perspective. Things I forced myself to ignore, people I forced myself to exclude, are no longer off-limits. Even my peppermint tea tastes sweeter and more refreshing. My mood is undeniably chipper and if my coworkers paid any attention, they would assume I've lost all my marbles.

With all I can muster, I get to work and tick items off my checklist, pushing aside the tsunami of tasks that need my attention at home.

After getting caught up, Jordan whizzes past me, whooshing papers off my desk. His door slams behind him, knocking the abstract painting off the wall. Thank God the frame wasn't glass. I'm done getting a million tiny cuts cleaning up shards.

Two ladies from the Billing Department stop in their tracks and eye the scene as I shrug, bewildered. They continue toward the kitchen as I pick up the unharmed canvas, propping the painting back onto the wall.

What crawled up his butt?

His mom doesn't give off the impression she'd balk at a gift, and not one from her only son. With my ear pressed against his door, I wait for any grumblings coming from inside. The sound of a crash and then glass splintering behind the door makes me jump.

I didn't leave one destructive man only to find out my boss is one, too. My mind wanders for a moment.

Do I ask what's wrong or mind my business?

I do what Jordan would do. Tap-tap-tap.

"Come in."

Scared something will come flying my way, I peek my head in. Jordan slumps at his desk, face in his hands. With my shoulders back and head high, I adjust my skirt and top and walk inside, fearless.

He raises his eyes and watches me walk to my usual chair, surveying me again, from my toes to my nose. John would never allow me to leave the house, not dressed like this; the only attention he wanted me to get was humiliation. Oddly enough, I'm comfortable wearing things fitted for my curvy figure as opposed to the boxy pieces John approved of, but with Jordan staring at me now, my insecurity builds.

I spot the crime scene in the room's corner. Remnants of the mug he uses every day lay on the black carpeting. That'll be easier to clean than a crystal vase.

"Bad lunch?" I whisper.

He works the skin on the back of his neck. "You can say that."

I rub my damp hands down the length of my full thighs. "Did she hate the gift?"

"No." His stare drifts over me, never staying in one place too long, like staring at me hurts his eyes.

Maybe I shouldn't wear these types of clothes.

"She loves the necklace, Penny." The way he says my name, with such endearment, hurts my heart.

Then why does he look so upset with me?

"She said the necklace reminded her of a piano key."

She noticed that too.

"The necklace made sense coming from you," I add.

He stays quiet, jaw clenching under his skin while he nods in agreement, thumbing something, a coin perhaps, between his fingers.

Jordan's Penny

"So, what's wrong then?" I ask again.

He jerks his eyes to me now, putting whatever he was playing with back into his pocket. Jordan sits up in his executive chair and straightens his posture, shaking the stress off his face.

"Oh, sorry. I didn't mean to scare you." Jordan picks up some folders and levels them on his desk. "I just have a lot going on. Personal stuff."

"Pfft," I mutter. "You do not scare me; I have a thick crust."

He chuckles, and it helps ease the lingering tension in the room. "Crust? That's different."

I shrug but match my grin to his. "Because I'm doughy."

He rolls his eyes. "So, Penny," he starts, before pausing. When he watches me now, his eyes stay fixed on mine. "A friend gave me passes to this couple's spa." He pauses again, and picks up a file, opens it, and reads my notes on the inside.

Is he pretending to read notes right now?

He's stalling.

"But you mentioned earlier that your fiancé is out of town?"

On any normal day, I'd entertain Jordan on these little fishing for information expeditions, but talking about John is never my preferred conversation topic. And I sure as hell would never go anywhere with him. All I want is to shout from the rooftop that he's not my fiancé anymore. He's not my anything. I'll lose my voice with no regrets. Instead, I pretend nothing's changed.

"Yes. He left early this morning."

"I never asked, what does he do?"

If I could run, I would, but I stand from the chair, hoping Jordan follows my cue. "Football recruiter. Coercing impressionable young men into signing onto whatever team he's being overpaid from now."

"He looks like he's played some ball himself."

"Yes." I shuffle closer to the exit. I've been down this road before. Talking about John's quick stint in the NFL always wins people over, and having Jordan be on Team John Hill would devastate me. John already has enough cheerleaders. "Um, you've got a lot going on right now and I don't want to add to your stress, but would you mind if I left a little early today? I'll come in early tomorrow and work through lunch."

He watches as I swipe my palms against my hips. My nerve-sweats are in full swing. Jordan says nothing. He just watches me with his intense focus, like he's searching for something he's not even sure exists. I clear my throat, waiting.

Jordan snaps back to reality. "Oh, sorry. That's fine." I'm halfway to the door when he speaks again. "Pen, can I borrow your music? I need something because…"

"Say no more." I rush to his side and pull his keyboard toward me. He watches as I type my Spotify login, but glances away when I enter my password. I'm a thousand percent sure he would make fun of me—Need4Speed!2.

While he's inches away, I refrain from inhaling too deep. They designed his scent to make a female's body salivate. Or perhaps his pheromone chemistry is what does the trick. Either way, I don't have a change of clothes.

I scroll through my lists, showing him all his options, but his eyes are elsewhere—my ring. Ugh. "Here." I remove my hand from his mouse and throw it behind my back. "Just don't make fun of my music. It's all I have left."

He lends a grateful nod. "Close the door and hold all calls."

I do as I'm told and leave him to the music, hoping it'll soothe his worries as it does mine. As I sit back at my desk, the ring that weighs me down stares back, taunting me with its glittering facets. If this ring had ears, I would tell it how much I hated every minute it sat on my finger. I yank it off and chuck it into my purse, glad to have that shackle off me.

My mind races over what might have put him in such a foul mood. I can't even imagine how much work would suck if he became a grumpy nightmare that kept to himself while I'm in a talkative mood. That's irony at its finest.

CHAPTER
TWENTY-TWO

"**W**HO'S BETTER THAN you?"

Josey smiles wide, popping a pink bubble. She lugs in flat boxes and drops them to the floor with a thud. "Please tell me we're drinking while we pack. The two go hand in hand."

I hold up two bottles of wine without a word, pick up my phone, and cue our soundtrack for the night's events. We tackle each room together, starting with the bedroom. She sorts through the armoire, and I take the closet. The pile of clothes tossed on the bed form one giant mountain. I sort through the pile and separate the hideous garments John forced me to wear versus the ones I prefer, bagging the former for donation. I won't need the ill-fitted tops, shapeless pants, and hideous sweaters anymore. If I never see another scarf again, I'll be the happiest girl in the world.

"Who's are these?" With a scrunched face, Josey lifts a red thong with the point of a pen. It must be seven sizes too small for me.

My shoulders lift to my ear. "Anyone within a thirty-mile radius is my best guess."

She finds another, and another, ranging in sizes, styles, and colors.

"He swore those belonged to me when I found them in the laundry bin." I roll my eyes, a wicked somersault, but I'm numb inside. There isn't anything left John can do to hurt me.

While I shove my belongings into boxes, Josey seals them and loads up her car. Once we fill her truck, we drop the boxes off at the new apartment and start all over again.

The fresh-paint odor still lingers inside. They just painted all the rooms with a fresh coat of pristine white. All the appliances are brand new, too. Every inch of this apartment screams a fresh start for me. I dreamt of having walls with character, rather than the pale hues John preferred. And now I can. There won't be anyone to bitch and moan about a bright accent wall or chair. Or I can go dark and make it my goth apartment, fill the walls with oddities from Etsy. Whatever I choose, it'll be all mine.

On our way back to the house, I chew the inside of my cheek, and blood hits my taste buds. Josey must sense my unease, too.

"We can get paint swatches when we're done. Pick up some magazines for ideas?"

I nod, but my mind wanders, surprised by my emotions. A deep sadness fills me now, but not because I'll miss him or that it's over. I'm sad because I wasted my life on John and his bullshit. I missed countless family birthdays and anniversaries, missed the chance of watching my little brother grow up. Regret. That's what hit me hardest now.

I own my past and I live in it all the time. Why didn't I just brush off his advances in school? I should have known after that lie he told his teammates back in school, the one that painted me with an unflattering image, John shouldn't be trusted.

"Pen." She reaches her hand across the middle console, laying her palm on mine. "You're doing the right thing. And you're not alone."

I place my hand on hers, thankful she's in my life and staying by my side.

When we arrive back at the house, Josey rummages through the bathroom while I sift through the living room. Nothing in here is mine. Through the years he's destroyed most of my knickknacks, finding new ways to hurt me without his words or fists.

I sip my wine and peruse the pictures hung in a pattern too pleasing to the eye to be accidental when the idea comes to me. I clear the walls and shelves of all our pictures, stacking the frames on the couch. One by one, I rip myself out of each picture before placing the torn half with John back into the frame. I redecorate the walls and admire my work. I may not own much in this house, but I'm taking me. All of me.

The kitchen is unchanged. Again, nothing is mine. I stand in the doorway with my glass of wine and survey the room, hoping to spot something I might've forgotten to reclaim just as Josey squeezes by me and makes a beeline for the blender.

"I bought this." She hugs the appliance to her body, cradling it like a newborn. "We can make margaritas later." Josey ditches the blender in the truck and comes back inside to get another box.

Jordan's Penny

The bathroom appears unchanged except for my missing makeup and toiletries. Only the bedroom closet shows an actual void. All that remains are his clothes on one side and bare hangers on the other. I double-check the floor to make sure we packed all my shoes when a spark hits me. The most important things—the plaque.

I lift the loose floorboard in the closet's corner and reach into the space below. The happiness is almost instant once my hand connects to the cool marble. I run my fingers over the etched plate with my name and a droplet hits the bowling pin on the plaque—a happy tear.

I dig my hand back into the hole and take out the envelope I stashed inside. Another nest egg. With my plaque and envelope in hand, I turn the bedroom light off and close the door. Without a deeper inspection, the house looks untouched, like I never left, and was never here.

How sad is that?

Even without my belongings, the house is still full and lived in. Then again, it was never mine. Every inch of this house was John's ruling from the wall colors to the furniture. Christ, even the selection and placement of photos and artwork were chosen by him and him alone. My say never mattered.

"Ready?" Josey stands in the doorway, holding a shoebox filled with little trinkets I stashed through the years so he couldn't destroy them as revenge.

"Yup."

I stand in the foyer vestibule with my back against the boring beige wall and inspect the crystal vase he sent with the prickly roses. A zillion emotions run through my head, but I don't dwell on any in particular. I set the house key beside the Jaguar fob, but my eyes keep drifting back toward the vase.

The crystal is so pretty when the sunlight shines through the window. The vase sparkles like a diamond, sending rainbow prisms on the walls. I pick up the heavy vase and get lost in the intricate cuts. As if in slow motion, I open my hand and let the crystal drop to the floor. Josey gasps, but I don't flinch when the vase explodes before our eyes. Millions of glittering shards blanket the hardwood floor. It's his turn to clean this up.

I reach into my back pocket and pull out the engagement ring, the worst shackle of all.

"That ring would've been amazing if someone amazing proposed," Josey says, as she stares at me.

She's wrong. Even if the most amazing man gave this to me, it still wouldn't have been right. This ring never fit my personality or style and the man of my dreams would know that. All I ever wanted was unconditional love, a love that transcends expensive gifts.

"Not even then."

I drop the ring and step away, surveying the room for a final time.

John's violence—the screaming and yelling, the slaps and punches, every time he tossed me to the wall or floor—will forever haunt these walls. I should've been safe here; this was my home, my haven, too, but as hard as I try to remember better days, only pain and tears flood my memory now. To rid me of those memories, I must rid myself of John.

"Goodbye, John."

Waking up alone in bed is nothing new. John has spent more time away than he spent home as of late. But waking up in my very own place is unlike anything I've experienced before. I'll take the hum of the fridge and occasional drops of ice cubes over waking up to chirping birds if it meant being as far away from John as possible.

The futon we bought is a rough change. My stiff neck and aching back are proof, but I refuse to let that dampen my spirits. Even with the bare apartment, save for my boxed belongings, nothing can remove the smile that sits on my face. I can't wait to put my interior decorating skills to work once I finish buying the essentials—a bed, TV, a real couch and chairs, dinnerware, and silverware. In time, this will feel like a home, but until then all I need is my futon and my coffee table. A place to sit, eat, and sleep.

Josey and I sat here until midnight, celebrating my departure. I was sad when she left for the night, afraid I'd be too lonely, but the loneliness never surfaced.

I stretch in place and start my day with some light music, nothing upbeat, but nothing sad either, only soothing music to set my mood. It took a moment to figure out the shower. A smidgen too far to the left and fire shoots out, but too far to the right and I'll turn to an ice-pop. The steaming water, pressured to perfection, is like a baptism, cleansing my soul.

I prance around the apartment in a towel, and sift through my box of clothes, thankful for Josey's packing skills. Most are wrinkle-free. Like yesterday, I wear what I choose, flaunting the new Penelope Matthews— the girl that lives without limits, and answers to no one.

Looking in the mirror, my confidence flows, a new characteristic I rarely experienced before because of John. He's always knocked the wind from my sails right as I caught a swift breeze. I put the wine glasses in the sink and locked the door behind me, wearing the best accessory I own— my smile. My apartment isn't the only new thing in my life now. I walk to my new ride, one that suits me better—a used, bright cobalt blue Honda Civic. The pickup is out of this world.

My lips turn up when I greet my coworkers on my way to my desk.

What's not to smile about?

Jordan's tea seeps, ready for his arrival, as am I. He stalks past without taking the mug from my extended hands. My lungs deflate. Without a word, he reverses, grabs the cup, and continues to his office.

While the phones are dead, I call Melissa. She's always treated me with genuine kindness, extending invitations to hang out, or inviting me to lunch. I declined every time at John's demand. He never allowed me to become friends with anyone at work. He even tried telling me to cut Josey loose one time. That never happened.

After a while, he got used to Josey. He never approved of her, per se. He let me keep her, but that is where he drew the imaginary line in the sand. Friends share feelings, memories, experiences, things he wouldn't want to be divulged. Our truth was too dark to extend further than needed. The only other acquaintances allowed were his friends, where he orchestrated the storyline, told his tales, and turned me into the villain each time.

"Hey, Mel. Did you, by any chance, want to go to Maverick's with me and my friend on Friday. We're going straight from work."

"Count me in. Do you mind if I invite a few other girls?"

"The more the merrier."

Goosebumps roll over my arms. It's been forever since I've celebrated my birthday, let alone celebrated the day as a single woman with friends.

My phone dances, vibrating on my desk. The excitement that tingled seconds ago plummets into my belly.

John.

I send him to voicemail and after a minute, my phone chimes with a new voicemail.

Against better judgment, I check the message.

"Penelope Matthews, answer your fucking phone. What the fuck did you do? I came home early for you, and this is how you fucking repay me?" he said in a harsh, raw voice. Early is an understatement; he only left for the night. I thank my lucky stars I didn't wait until the weekend. "I've given you every fucking thing." He releases a booming growl. "You know what? Fuck you, bitch. I'm sick of your fat ass, anyway. Good luck finding someone to touch you drunk, let alone sober. Good riddance."

Where the call ends, the tears begin. He inflicts greater wounds with words than his fists could ever accomplish. With one voicemail, John sucked all air from my lungs. His words penetrate my brain, burrowing in deep to release their poison. I hoped to be stronger this time around. I was wrong.

"Penny, can you run these to Tom for me? I'm on a call, and he needs this right away."

I raise my eyes, forgetting to wipe the streaming tears that run down my cheeks. "Sure thing." I extend my hand to retrieve the documents.

"Are you crying?"

"I'm fine." The words sound cracked on my lips. Jordan's expression reeks of concern, or impatience, or maybe a bit of both. Many of Jordan's assistants have cried, but he was the one to cause the tears.

"Penelope," he calls out with authority.

He's right. Work is no place for my tears. I stand up straight and hold my head high, swiping my index finger under my eyes. I won't let John's words hurt me, not anymore. He's nothing to me, but this job is everything.

"I'm fine," I repeat with more confidence.

"Pen, what's the matter?"

"If you won't let the papers go, I can drag you to Tom's office, but then everyone will think I'm taking you for a walk." The skin on his knuckles is still as tight as ever until he releases and then storms back to his office. A loud slam of his door follows.

Jordan's Penny

I knock on Tom's door, and he waves me in. "Jennifer isn't at her desk, is she?" Tom asks his rhetorical question. "Can we clone you?" My cheeks warm from the compliment. I needed that. "I'm not sure technology is where we need it to be for that just yet, but I'll keep my eyes and ears open for anyone looking for work."

"Please do." He removes his glasses and tosses them onto his desk. "I'll trust anyone you recommend. You're the boss-whisperer."

The only reason Jordan is easy for me to manage is that I've dealt with John for over a decade. But when you're good at your job, your boss has nothing to complain about.

"Assistants are like relationships, not everyone is compatible."

"Then you two are soul-mates." Tom rests his elbows on his disorganized desk and leans toward me. "But if you ever wish to leave that dead-beat tyrant," a sly grin plays on his mouth, "and come work for me, I wouldn't disapprove." A warm and gentle grin forms on his thin lips. "Or find me my perfect match. Oh god, if my wife overheard parts of this conversation, she'd contact our lawyer."

Now I laugh. "You'll be the first to know when I jump ship. In the meantime, I'll keep my eyes and ears open." I give a quick nod and head back to my command station, with my mood lifted.

When I return to my desk, my cellphone chimes again. Seven new voicemails. All from John.

My stomach isn't strong enough to listen to his messages; I'm not sure my stomach will ever be strong enough.

As the day ticks by, I can't tell if I avoided Jordan or if he avoided me. Every conversation only comprised of a few words. My diversions worked until he caught me waiting by the elevator, leaving for the day.

"You shouldn't walk to your car alone. Let me walk you. It's dark out."

My eyes roll to the back of my head. "The garage is always dark, Jordan. It doesn't matter what time of the day it is." I test the frozen waters with a little jab. Those always get his attention. As I hoped, the sly grin forms on his sexy lips, but he stares at his shoes.

We share the elevator, just the two of us, and I'm encapsulated by his heavenly-scented cologne, light and sweet, not overbearing like the one Alec bathes in. I might die of suffocation if I get trapped in the elevator with Alec again. My lungs will refuse air. The last time I got stuck with him, I could taste his cologne for the rest of the day.

Jordan reaches across me and presses the button for the floor with the sky bridge while I press the button for this building's garage.

"You didn't park in the other one?"

"Nope."

The elevator ascends.

We continue to ignore each other in stony silence as I breathe in his expensive scent. Damn, he smells divine. John wore nothing as pleasant as Jordan's scent. If he didn't have other female's perfume lingering on his skin or clothes, he reeked of sweat, sex, or booze, or a fun mixture of all the above.

The elevator drops to the garage, and he waits for me to exit before matching his pace to mine.

"How's my play-list coming? I'll never make another bet with you if you don't pay up."

"Relax." He eases into our usual banter. "I'm working on it. It's more difficult than I expected."

I walk toward my car, beeping the alarm when I'm nearby. Even in the dimly lit garage, my car stands out. In a sea of basic white or black luxury cars, my bright and sporty ride is the oddball of the mix.

"What happened to the Jag?"

"Uh…" I freeze for a moment and run a line from my past. "She's in the shop."

He opens my door, says goodnight, before he heads to his more expensive Benz parked in the assigned partner's spot, closer to the elevators.

"This car suits you better," he yells back.

I couldn't agree more.

I drive to my apartment. As the gate swings open, welcoming me to my haven, a relaxed grin settles on my lips. As soon as I lock my apartment door behind me, I kick my shoes off, toss myself onto the futon and lean my head back, basking in the silence. I won't need to rush dinner only to have to reheat the food hours later, and I won't need to clean anything to his liking, only my liking. This new life is amazing.

For a while, I stare at the bowling plaque, the only decoration on my wall at the moment. It might remain that way, too. With my lids closed,

Jordan's expression when I pulled the plaque from the purse is the first thing I see. He was eager with wait, and his smile, blessing me with his pearly whites, grew to the smile of the Cheshire cat. The memory still tickles my insides. John was never that eager to watch me open anything. He'd toss the bag to me and say, "Here." Half the time he'd leave me to go watch TV or go into another room to text.

My phone vibrates in my bag again.

John.

He's filled my voicemail in-box to maximum capacity and flooded me with texts.

New message: "Penelope, you get your fucking ass home now. I'm done with your bullshit. This isn't funny. Am I supposed to clean this fucking mess?"

New message: "You fucking bitch. You didn't have the balls to tell me face-to-face. Only cowards leave as you did. Rot in Hell, Penelope."

New message: "Penelope Matthews, if you think you can leave me and disappear, you're mistaken. No one leaves me, you understand? No one," he snarls, and I flinch as if he said it to my face.

New message: "Okay, listen to me, Penelope. I fucked up, but you've fucked up, too. If you would've found another fucking job, it would have solved all our problems. You slept with him, didn't you? The way he was gawking at you at the party, undressing you with his eyes. Deny it all you want; the truth is obvious."

He's being irrational and delusional. Jordan did no such thing. John is a master manipulator, shifting the truth to fit his narrative and create illusions only he believes. He's done it a thousand times before. He'll continue tearing me down until I need him to put me back together. Those methods won't work now, and he doesn't own glue strong enough to piece us back together.

New message: "I'm sorry, Penny." He changes tactics and his Tourette-filled voicemails turn to apologetic ones. "Whatever I did, whatever I've done, I'm sorry. Okay? Baby, I'm sorry."

New message: "Penny, please, don't do this. I love you. I'll change. You can work wherever. Just let me love you," he begs. "I'm nothing without you. I only said those things because I'm hurting. Penny, please."

Next message: "Penny, if you need time, I'll give you whatever you need. Just don't say you're done with me forever. I can't live without you. I can't live without you."

Next message: "I'll go to anger management classes. I'll do anything you need me to do. Please call me. I need to hear your voice. I'm dying over here. Please come home."

New message: "Penny," he cries. "Penny... please. I love you so much. I've loved you since you sat at the table in the library, trying to teach me ratios. I've loved no one like I love you. No other girl has my heart. You're the only one." Silence ticks away on the call timer. Only his hysterical breaths are audible. "Please don't break my heart. Please."

New message: "Remember our vacation in Puerto Rico. I fell in love with you all over again. We can go back. Maybe you'll fall back in love with me. I'll take you wherever you want to go, just say the word."

New message: "I'm done with other women, Penny. You're the only one I want. You're the only one I'll ever want. Are you happy? I've learned my lesson. But please, baby, I need to hear your voice, sweetheart. This house isn't a home unless you're here with me in it." He pauses, but his rushed breaths continue. "I'll buy you a bigger house, and we can fill it with kids. You always wanted kids, right?"

New message: "Penny, this is fucking ridiculous. Answer your God damn phone. I'm pouring my fucking heart out to you, and you don't even give a shit. Do you? You're willing to throw away everything and for what? A job? I can't believe you're doing this to me. You really are something else. I should've left years ago," his vicious words resurface. "I wish you died when I crashed Cami."

For a moment, my heart stops. Josey was right. Deep down, I must've known, but reconciling that information would have been far too painful to accept.

New message: "I didn't mean that, Penny. I'm sorry. This is driving me crazy. I need to speak to you. This can't be the end."

I disconnect the call without bothering to listen to the last voicemail. No guilt or apprehension surfaces as I take in a much-needed breath. This is where I belong—alone and far from him.

Chapter Twenty-Three

THE WEEK DIDN'T drag like I assumed it would; especially with Friday night's plans anxiously awaiting. And it's finally here. Even though John's calls don't stop, the threats and promises, and the promise of threats no longer affect me. By now, I expected to regret my decision, but none of those emotions surface. If anything, I've never been surer.

And in this time, Jordan's mood has remained iffy, on a good day. Since lunch with his mother, only on rare occasions has he emerged from his office talking to me like before. But most times, he avoids all conversation, and on some days, he avoids me altogether.

This is all my fault.

I stepped over that imaginary line and John was right; I grew to care about him in ways an assistant shouldn't.

"Hey, Pens." Josey strolls through the hallway that leads to my desk. With her change of clothes slung in a bag over her shoulder, she walks with a bounce, and her ponytail swings from left to right. "Where can I change?"

"Bathroom by the elevators. I'll meet you in a minute."

I make the finishing touches on Jordan's report, color-coding it to his liking, and grab my change of clothes from my desk drawer.

When I bought the new top, nothing could have prepared me for how one piece of clothing could change my mood. For once in a long time, insecurity didn't rear its ugly head. I felt beautiful, confident, and so sexy. The black draped-neck top shows a lot of cleavage, more than I've ever shown before. John would beat me into oblivion if he caught me wearing this. The rest of my day's outfit goes unchanged, leaving on my black skirt and platform pumps. I add a suicide roll to the front of my hair and thicken my winged liner. I dig into my make-up bag and pull out a liquid matte lipstick in the hottest red I own. My final touch.

"That retro style suits you, Pen."

I stare at my reflection and admire myself. She may be right. One thing is certain, the tattooed smile on my reddened lips is here to stay tonight. Add the fact that I'm celebrating my birthday with girlfriends, and I will gladly welcome smiling cramps in my cheeks. Living without restrictions reinvigorates my excitement all over.

"He came by the shop yesterday. Tried to throw his weight around, but he can't intimidate me." She leans into the mirror and applies her mascara, opening her mouth in the embarrassing way most women do. While I look ridiculous making that face, Josey still oozes sex appeal.

"Be careful, Joes. He might follow you."

She scoffs. "Since you left, I'm always looking in my rear-view. I've seen enough movies to spot when I'm being tailed."

I touch up my foundation, the little I wear now, and leave Josey to finish. With a last glance in the mirror, I'm more than satisfied with my outcome. I can get used to this, getting dolled up to hang out with my girlfriends every Friday night.

As I approach my desk, Melissa sits in my chair with her heels resting on the corner, relaxing and laughing with Jordan.

"There you are," Melissa says as I approach. Her chestnut brown hair is curled, full of volume and bounce. She, too, changed out of her work clothes and replaced them with a black bustier cami, sleek black sateen pants, and strappy heels to match. "Ooh… Penny. Sexy mama."

Jordan steals a glance and shifts his focus to his phone. His moodiness hasn't changed, even after work hours. I'd be lying if I said his lack of interest didn't drop my confidence level a notch.

What were you expecting, Penelope?

He shifts his weight to a different leg as he surveys me again, diverting his eyes every time I catch him staring. I fold my arms across my chest, self-conscious, hoping to cover some of my cleavage. All that ends up doing is pushing my boobs closer together, so I drop my arms and fiddle with my fingers instead.

"Thanks," I mumble, turning to Melissa. "Josey is still getting ready. Is anyone else coming?"

"Olyvia bailed. She forgot today was her anniversary," Melissa shrugs. "But two of my girlfriends will meet us there."

Josey saunters, swaying her hips down the hallway as if it was her runway, dressed to the nines—short black skirt, a nude-hued sweetheart neckline crop-top that shows off Josey's endowed bust with black lacing down the center, cinching the material together and pushing her boobs to record-breaking cleavage goals. Her voluminous brown tresses, along with her sky-high heels, add inches to her height. Never one to need much, she wears just enough makeup to enhance her already flawless features, adding some mascara, a smudge of liner along her lashes, a swipe of highlighter on peaks of her cheeks, and Vaseline for her plump lips.

Jordan lifts his head as she approaches, openly studying her. Who wouldn't? She's smoking hot. Even I'm attracted to her on most days that end with Y.

"Jordan, you remember Josey?" I ask, and Josey gives a quick wave while he nods.

"So, what's the special occasion?"

Josey blurts, "Pen's birthday."

As a reflex, I smack my palm to my forehead. I was so close to making it out of there, with no one finding out.

"We're going to Mavericks. Penny hasn't been out since, well," Josey eyes the ceiling to count the years or ceiling tiles. Either way, the total number is high. "Forever."

"Just another day to me," I mutter.

"Oh my God. I'm slipping on my HR duties. How did I miss that?"

Jordan glares at Melissa, giving her a dark scowl. "Yes. Yes, you are."

Josey turns to Jordan, and a sharp pang shoots through my gut as a sensuous light passes between them. She's more his cup of tea, so I'm not surprised he would gaze at her with such intent, but it didn't make his appeal for her less devastating for me.

He's your boss, Matthews.

"You coming?" Josey asks, pointing her head at him. She basks in her power, an innate ability to get what she wants.

"Don't be silly, Joes," I balk. "He can't be bothered associating with us." If only I said what I meant: He doesn't want to associate with me. "He has plans tonight with that lady... what's her name?" I rush, fumbling to remember the name of the lady with the high-pitched voice.

"Suzie... Sarah... Sandy, Sandy... Sadie! Sadie. Tonight. Dinner plans with Sadie," I point to Jordan. "He has more important people to do, things... I mean things to do." With renewed humiliation, I turn away and gather my bags, ready to leave, and throw myself in front of a moving vehicle.

"Don't be silly. I'd love to come and celebrate my Penny's birthday. And I canceled that date a day after you put it on the calendar." His face brightens like he swallowed a light bulb as he shifts his eyes to the three of us. "Count me in. This will be fun." He directs his attention toward me, disarming me with his dashing smile as he rocks on his heels. "I need to finish something first, but I'll meet you in a few."

"Great. You can be the first guy to buy Penny a drink as a singl—"

I jab my elbow square in her ribs. "Great. We'll see you in a few," I chime, careful to mask my sarcasm. I hook my arm with Josey's and drag her to the elevators, with Melissa following close behind. Melissa and Josey talk amongst themselves while I breathe through the sudden panic jittering through my nerves. So much for a fun girl's night out.

"I'll meet you at Mavericks." Melissa heads toward her car as we exit the elevator.

Once Josey turns on the ignition, I lean my head against her seat. "You invited him? What were you thinking? And don't you dare mention anything about me being single. I didn't tell anyone." A cold lick of dread settles in my gut.

"Relax, Pens. Jordan seems cool. He said 'my Penny'." She flirts with the words and gushes as if he said them about her, but I remind myself of his actual feelings—pity.

He could've easily said, "my assistant" and nothing would change in his sentence.

The three of us skip the line, courtesy of Josey's perched-up boobs, and walk past the tall, beefed-up bouncers. Once inside, I whizz past the dancefloor and rush the bar as if my life depended on it.

"Six shots of your best tequila, please," I shout to the bartender.

Loud music echoes off the walls. The bass resonates in my body as the overhead disco lights project on the crowd, shooting beams of green and red streaks onto the sea of people below. The club is jumping, bodies grind into respective bodies and the alcohol is flowing. There isn't one unhappy soul in this place.

"To the birthday girl," Melissa toasts over the blaring music. "And the nicest person in the office. May this be the best birthday ever."

After shot number two, dancing is in my immediate future. I may not be as trim as the other girls, but I can dance for hours without stopping. I love it, and it's a great workout.

Melissa dips out of our dance circle in search of her other friends, while Josey grinds her butt on my hip. As much as I spank her away, she doesn't stop. We've only been here ten minutes and already my cheeks cramp from laughing so hard.

"Found you," the low, husky voice shouts over the loud, pumping music.

I spin on my heel as my heart pulsates in my stomach.

Relief spreads as I spot Jordan weave his way through the dense crowd of club-goers, waving to get my attention. For a moment, the blaring music distorted Jordan's voice. I feared it was John.

Jordan unbuttons his collar, loosens his tie, and rolls up his sleeves, boogying to the music. It's weird seeing him in this setting, like a model off the page of a magazine, selling cologne or watches or high-priced vodka, and not in the office asking me to run a ledger for some random company. Either way, I'll buy three of whatever he's selling. Hell, I'll buy it all.

Jordan leans into the crook of my neck. He brushes my hair over my shoulder. The innocent gesture causes an instant reaction. My entire body tingles, keenly aware.

"Can I get you a drink?" His warm breath kisses my neck, and for a split second, his mouth brushed against my skin.

Someone must've bumped into him. He didn't mean to do that.

His presences make my stuttering pulse impossible to calm. The shots simmering in the pit of my belly don't help. Unsure if the alcohol is making me weak or if it's the way his hand cups the crook of my neck is what's causing this wobble in my knees. I might have licked my lips at him.

"Sure. Surprise me."

He asks Josey and gets swallowed by the crowd after he leaves.

"We will find you a man tonight, Pens," Josey shouts. She dances to the fast beat of the song blaring through the speakers. The lights swirl in a dizzying effect. The rays of blues, greens, and purples beam all around as the fog machine fills the room with a cloudy haze. "You need a plumber," she adds before twirling me. "You need a real man to clean your pipes."

Josey twerks on my leg as I burst into laughter. This is life—friends, music, drinks. The uncontrollable burst of joy enraptures me. My hips sway to the beat, and my jovial mood burns brighter when I get a tap on my shoulder. I spin with a grin, eager to see what drink Jordan brought for me, hoping he introduces me to something different. Something he likes.

"Hey, Penny."

If I could gasp, I would, but my throat constricts. My lungs shrivel up like a raisin. Hell, my entire body deflates, and my legs are on the verge of giving out underneath me.

John.

He licks his lips and traces his eyes over me, head to toe. "Damn, Penny. You look…" A small moan hums in his throat. "Nice outfit. Can we talk?"

Josey twirls. Her cheerful expression evaporates like water on a sweltering day. Josey is quick and moves into position, placing herself between us, ready for war. The animosity hums between them as they wear competing scowls.

"Get away from her," Josey orders.

"Mind your business, Nosey Josey. This is between me and my," he holds my engagement ring up, expecting me to take the handcuff back, "fiancé." The title stabs my ears, and the flinching tick is automatic. He tries to nudge Josey aside, but she holds her ground.

In a sea of moving bodies, we are the only three at a standstill, getting bumped from every which direction. Josey and I lose our footing, but not John. Anger roots his feet into the dancefloor, unmoved as dancers bump into him. He ignores the guy who spilled twenty dollars' worth of booze on his shoes. If he didn't reek of alcohol before, he does now.

Usually, John would flip out, maybe toss the guy across the room, but he didn't flinch. His eyes remain on me, shrinking me down to the tempo of the music until I'm small enough for him to squash like a bug.

I replay the past week in my head, and how happy I've been without him. After listening to his anger-filled voicemails and enduring through the morose ones, never once did I allow his words to change my decision.

I swallow the lump in my throat and find my courage, the courage I always had.

"She's right," I command. "You need to leave. I have nothing left to say to you."

I suspect he won't go, so I will. I hook Josey's arm with mine and pull her in the opposite direction, expanding the space between us and John.

John weaves through the other dancers and reaches for me. Like a vise, his fingers curl around my wrist. "You've had your fun. Now you need to come back home."

I yank my arm, but his hold is strong. "Get off of me, John." I swing around, trying to rip my arm from his grasp and almost knock out a girl wearing a fuzzy bachelorette sash. With another powerful tug, I free myself, but the spot where he gripped throbs now.

"Penny, I got your drink."

John eyes Jordan and Jordan watches John. Either the lights in the club are making me light-headed or all the tequila is hitting me at once. Now's not the time to lose my senses. John's expression darkens like a bottomless pit, void of any light or life. He turns back to me with a knowing glare, clenched teeth, and trembling fists.

"I knew it." He jerks his head toward Jordan.

John gets a hold of me again at the same time Josey grabs my other wrist. With both clinging onto me, I'm stretched like a rag doll, pulled in different directions, but Josey is just as determined to not let me go.

"She's coming back home," he snarls.

"Get off me!"

Josey's grip slips on my dampened skin, and I'm catapulted toward John. His fingertips dig into my shoulders like an eagle to his prey before shifting his grasp onto my upper arm. I push against his middle, trying to get away, but my efforts are futile. When I peek over my shoulder, Josey stands with both drinks in her hands as Jordan rushes toward us. I fight harder, flailing my arms and dragging my feet.

"She's not going with you," Jordan commands.

John sucks his teeth and scoffs. "You fucking told her, didn't you?"

With one good shove, John releases me. I wobble in my heels, almost losing my balance before righting myself. John narrows the space between him and Jordan, their chests almost touch.

"What's the coincidence that Penelope moves out of our house right after you saw me?"

He stalks closer, eyes locked on his target, ready to fire at will, but Jordan doesn't back down. They stand face-to-face, squaring their shoulders at each other. John's eyes said he didn't just want to bloody Jordan; he wanted to kill him.

I force my way between them. This isn't Jordan's fight, it's mine.

"I left because you're an asshole and I deserve better," I shout over the window-rattling music, which gets quieter the louder I scream. "This is about you and only you." I slam the palms of my hands into his hardened chest, one good shove powered with enough force to send him back a pace. "You're the reason I left. I left because I hate you," I hiss. Despite my better judgment, I continue. "I loathe you."

John leans in close, close enough for only me, and says, "I fucked hundreds of women in our bed. How does that make you feel?"

Before I can stop myself, I swing my right fist and with a vicious blow to his nose. The bone gave way with a grinding sensation beneath my knuckles. The front of his too-tight white shirt turns red. Quickly. With my adrenaline skyrocketing, the pain I assumed I'd have doesn't register, only a wave of shock flows through my hand, ending with a riff of satisfaction. Josey wraps her arms around my waist, pulling me from behind, pulling me away from him.

"I fucking hate you!" I scream through the tears.

"You broke my nose, you fat fucking bitch."

My brain must've known he would react, but my body didn't process the data quick enough. His knuckles flew so fast even Mohammad Ali might not have been able to dodge this blow. The powerful punch knocks me out of my heels, and I crash to the floor as the surrounding dancers realize what's going on. Everyone scatters like roaches; high-pitched screams of girls overpower the volume of the music. Pure chaos.

Josey and Jordan rush to my side and kneel over me while John appears to snap his nose back into place. My jaw and cheek throb. The adrenaline isn't enough to dull all the pain, but I'm grateful it's masking eighty percent of it. I blink a few times, surprised I'm still conscious. The only way to flee to safety is to pass him.

"You'll come crawling back. You always do." He spits, narrowly missing me before pointing a warning finger. "You're mine. Never forget that, pig."

With Josey's help, I rise to my feet, unsteady. When I graze the back of my hand against my lip, blood stains my hand. My mouth fills with it too. All I can do is swallow it down.

"Did he break your jaw again?" she asks.

Before I can answer, Jordan says, "Again?"

In the blink of an eye, Jordan's eyes turned to slits and rushes John, slamming his shoulder into John's stomach. John falls backward from the impact and the two men crash onto the dancefloor. With the strobe lights flickering overtime, it is impossible to tell who's hitting who, but both men snarl and growl, their alpha instincts kick in. I'm aware of John's truth strengths; especially when he's filled with black rage. Even though Jordan hadn't started this fight, he damn well looks like he wants to finish it.

"No!"

I try to rush toward the mass of tussling bodies, but Josey pulls me back and yanks me toward the exit.

"Come on. We need to get you out of here," she shouts as the chaos continues behind us.

"But John will kill him."

She points toward three large bouncers advancing to the center of the dancefloor. Josey pushes us through the crowd, dragging me behind her with both of my shoes in her other hand. Breaths as hot as fire race out of my lungs as I turn back to see if Jordan is okay, but all I see are flashing lights and unrecognizable silhouettes.

This isn't the celebration I planned.

"What's going on?" Melissa asks as we shuffle past. She turns to the commotion in the distance. "Why are you bleeding, Penny?"

"I've gotta get her out of here." Josey does not explain further, only drags me outside.

The fresh air fills my lungs, but the cooler air does nothing to snuff out my burning breaths. I don't remember running to the car, but my lungs can't keep up with the demand they need. She peels out of the parking lot, speeding to the office garage. My jaw aches, a tooth moves as I press my tongue against it, and blood stains my swollen, throbbing hand.

She pounds her hand against the steering wheel, hard, shouting colorful curses to herself. "You've gotta get home before he drives around."

I rest my hand on my cheek. Somehow, the pressure helps ease the pulsating under my skin.

"He's never seen my car, but he knows yours," I mumble.

My hands tremble as I rock back and forth, watching the streetlights turn green as if some higher force must sense my urgency to flee to safety. He split my bottom lip, and my swollen cheek is pushing my eye closed. And that God-awful metallic taste continues to trickle down my throat.

"Happy birthday to me."

She speeds into the garage and parks next to my car, putting my swollen hand in hers. "Can you move your fingers? Maybe it's broken. Penny."

Careful not to hurt me, she inspects my hand as I attempt to move them. It's not broken, but I can forget about holding a pen for the foreseeable future. The tears start again, and she pulls me into a hug, careful not to squeeze too tight.

"You should get going," I urge. "If he left after us, he'll be searching for your truck. I'll sit here for a while."

The loud shriek of tires burning the pavement echoes in the garage, and I freeze on the sudden verge of hyperventilating.

Jordan's Benz pulls in next to us and comes to a screeching halt. He jumps out and rushes to my side as I get out of Josey's truck.

I gasped, seeing the damage John did, even though it's nothing compared to what he's capable of. His eye is reddened with a cut on his cheekbone right under his eye, but other than his tussled hair and untucked shirt, Jordan looks fine, still Dior worthy. Relief fills me like a pool.

"Josey, go. I'll call you when I get home."

She nods as I head to my car with Jordan close behind.

"Are you okay, Penny? Let me look at you."

I nod. My cheeks were still wet with tears. I clutch onto my jaw and toss my bag into my car. The sudden motion reminds me of the punch I threw. Pain makes my eyes whirl.

Jordan must sense it too and places his palms under my elbows for support. He stands in before me, waiting for an explanation, but all I can muster is, "I never meant to get you involved."

The cut near his eye looks worse the closer he gets; it's deep. "You might need stitches. Does it hurt?"

He does not swat my hand away when I reach to inspect it closer, rather he leans into me.

"I'm fine." His fingers graze my lip as gently as if brushing it with a feather. "He's hit you before, hasn't he?"

I exhale, almost like a laugh. "That's one of his ways of showing me he cares. His other way was the expensive gifts. There was a tracking device in the Jag. He was always watching my every move, that's why I parked in the other lot, so he'd assume I worked in the other building." Everything that happened replays in my mind, but something makes little sense. "John said you saw him. What was he talking about?"

Jordan eyes the ground, much like how he has been doing as of late, teeth biting his lower lip as he tosses his right hand in his pocket.

"When I went to lunch with my mother, he was in the restaurant with… another woman. It wasn't innocent."

Nothing surprises me anymore; he's been a cheater for the better part of our relationship. "Is that why you've been avoiding me all week?"

He nods. "I debated telling you, but you were in such a great mood the past few days. I didn't know if it was my place, and I didn't want to upset you. Damn. I'm sorry, I should've told you." He peers down at me, his eyelashes shadow over his greenish-brown eyes, but a twitch of a smirk spreads on his lips. "Let me guess. Your pleasant mood was because you left him?"

I nod. "It took me a long time, but I finally realized I deserve better. Better late than never, I suppose."

"No one deserves to be treated like that, Pen. No one. You're beautiful, let no one tell you differently."

"Thanks. Coming from my boss, who just got into a fistfight with my ex-fiancé, that means a lot," I joke, even though my voice doesn't express any humor as I fidget with my car keys.

My legs wobble as if they might give out. Whatever adrenaline I had steamrolling me through all this starts dissipating. I'm ready to lock myself in my apartment until the end of time.

Jordan inches toward me, backing me against my car while his eyes soak me in. Our bodies are so close, we inhale the same air. With the shift of a breeze, a mix of his exotic cologne and sweat envelops me. The mere scent of him sends bolts of electricity to every nerve-ending.

"I'm your friend, too. And none of what he said was true, you can't believe any of it."

My heart hums in my ears as he narrows the space further. If I inhale too deeply, my ample bosom will brush against his firm chest. His eyes never fall from mine, begging me to listen to his words, but coming from his mouth after that conversation with Alec, it's wrong. I force myself to meet his gaze.

Jordan's pheromones float around, hypnotizing my senses. My limbs tremble. A massive amount of butterflies flutter their wings in my stomach. They aren't dead after all. As if time has stopped and I'm dreaming all this, Jordan continues inching closer and closer, but I'm powerless to stop him.

He cups my cheek in his hand. His skin is as warm and gentle as the day his fingers entwined with mine at the jewelry store. His thumb grazes over my cut lip again and for a moment, the throbbing stops.

What the hell is happening right now?

I can almost taste Jordan's sweet breath as he brings his lips closer to mine until they touch.

Jordan's lips, velvety soft like a petal of the most beautiful flower known to man, caresses mine with care. He breathes in deeper, crushing his toned, lean body into my soft one. As his hips press into mine, my lips part for him.

I've never been kissed with such care and tenderness. All light and air, not heavy and rushed like John's drunken assaults. He holds my face in his hands, keeping us connected in this special moment, a moment I've only assumed happens in books.

Until now.

Jordan takes my breath away.

Goosebumps explode over my skin. I was both hot and cold all at once. Jordan's tongue glides with mine and traces the soft fullness of my lips. His breathing, along with the uncontrollable movements in his body, quickens, too. I reach up, wrapping my arms around his neck, twining my fingers into his already tousled hair. As if I don't need air anymore, Jordan gives me all the sustenance I need to survive, making me complete again.

I was flying and yet somehow anchored to this moment by his arms, his body, his lips.

As if I already knew how the fabric of his crisp white shirt would feel on his warming body, I bring my arms down, resting my palms on his biceps. His chest muscle twitches. His body heat is desperate to escape, and I'd love nothing more than to free him of this unnecessary garment, but none of this is right.

Locked in his embrace, I'm safe from the outside world, but once this kiss ends, I'm on my own again. My hands cup his cheeks, and I pull away from the perfect kiss.

He's taken aback and out of breath, but as he opens his eyes, he hides behind a quiet grin.

"Thank you, Jordan."

While I have some remnants of my pride still left intact, I slide into my car and race out of the garage before he sees any more of my tears.

CHAPTER TWENTY-FOUR

THE LONELINESS IS real. As much as Josey's company would comfort me, we agreed it'd be safer if she stayed away until the dust settles. She's already caught John following her to the grocery store. We can't risk him following her here.

I've scrubbed my already clean apartment from top to bottom to keep myself busy. My closet is now organized and arranged in color order. Man, do I own a lot of black clothes. I've put away all my boxed-up belongings, flattened the boxes, and stored them in the back of my closet. It wasn't like that would take me forever; I had little to begin with. It took a good hour, but I arranged my books by genre and sub-categorized them by author and release date. With little left to do around here, I sit on the couch and think.

When I left John, I assumed I left behind the cuts and bruises, but whenever I move my face or see my reflection, I'm reminded how the past never stays where you want it. Everything hurts. My hand is wrapped and sore, my lip is split and bruised, and my eye is semi-shut. Smiling is off the table for a week. I'm not sure how long it'll take before I can type normally again. And with that, I picture Jordan in my head. The guilt of him sticking up for me eats me whole. How will he explain that to the partners?

And then, like a moth to a flame, that kiss surfaces again. I don't blame my lady bits for bursting into an angelic chorus, as I recall every single time he's touched me in vivid detail.

Oh. My. God.

He was so gentle, lips caressing mine with care, and it's as if I can still sense them on mine now. I graze the tips of my finger across my mouth with my eyes closed, reliving the moment our lips touched. A new spiral of ecstasy flows through me. My body erupts into this wonderful sensation, almost unbearable in its tenderness.

But while the vivid memory of that kiss sends me to the clouds, there was also a sadness in it, too. Perhaps he regretted the kiss halfway through, or maybe it was my sadness consuming me because I knew his true feelings. Through all the years I've been with John, I've never experienced this level of heartbreak before.

The worlds I've kept separate for so long have now become one, entwining my professional heaven with my personal hell. It's my fault. No one hangs out with their boss as much as I have. I gave John every reason to question my actions. My first mistake was caring about the job. And then I got close, too close, to Jordan, another man out of my league. Falling for men a million times better looking than me has never ended well.

Now that intimate moment will hang between us, and nothing will be the same again. His name alone lingers on the cusp of every thought, but being in his presence, memories will always filter back to that kiss. That magical kiss. It meant something different to each of us. While his intentions were pure, trying to take me out of a place of chaos, it was a moment I'll never experience again and, for that reason alone, it was unintentionally cruel.

Even with little in my apartment, I can't breathe. The walls feel like they are caving in on me. I need fresh air and a distraction from myself, an escape only a book can provide, one page at a time. There's only one place that'll give me the refuge I seek.

I travel up and down the aisles, plucking books from the shelves, sci-fi ones, nothing that involves love or heartbreak. There's something magical in the aroma of a physical book. It has the power to uplift my spirits. As I continue on my literary journey, dread coils in my stomach like a writhing snake for Monday morning. That's a first.

With the terrible images of Jordan and John's fight playing on repeat in the depths of my mind, John's scent lingers in my nostrils. My mind must be playing tricks on me, but my body reacts like Pavlov's dog with the bell. The jittery nerves build, shaking my hands. And my stomach turns to knots all over again. Fearful if I breathe in his acrid scent too much, terror will live in my veins forever. Nothing soothes me now.

I turn the corner into another aisle of fantasy novels and scope out my options before I head to the checkout counter. I reach a dead-end in the aisle. When I turn around, my trembling hands make sense.

John stands in the aisle, hands hang loose at his sides. He wears his ragged expression, but that's not the only thing about him that's rough. Never one to leave the house less than perfect, John is a mess—his hair is unbrushed, wears uncoordinated clothes as if he dressed in the dark with a slept-in wrinkle to them. He doesn't hide his blackened eyes behind a pair of sunglasses like I do, showing off his battle wounds like a badge of honor.

My insides grow cold, but my knuckles ache again as I back away from him, placing myself back in the dead end. The shelf digs into my shoulders. My only exit is on the opposite side of John.

"I knew you'd come here." He holds his hands up and takes a mini step back. "I didn't come to fight. I'm sorry, Penelope. Are you okay? I never meant to hurt you." His head falls. "I never *mean* to hurt you."

Am I okay? Which does he mean? Physically or emotionally? The question is laughable, but any exaggerated expression will split my lip again if I do. Either way, the answer will always be an astounding and definitive no. I'm scarred in more ways than one, but he never gets it. He always acts as if he's pinched me too hard, instead of throwing a full-force sucker punch.

"Please," I beg. "Leave me alone." My voice cracks with every spoken word as my fear escalates. "I need some t-time. Y-you know… to-to think things over. Give me that, John. Pl-please?" I stutter.

The lies are easy as blinking. I've been saying them for years. He needs to believe that time is all I need before I'll come crawling back. I do need time, just enough to get past him and back into my apartment where the gates and three deadbolt locks keep me safe.

My pounding heart thumps in my ears as he slithers closer in one fluid motion. Each of my limbs shakes as if caught in an earthquake. My world tumbles around me.

"No need to be afraid, Penelope." His soft tone means nothing with his fists opening and closing like that.

I find my voice and hold up a shaky palm. "If you don't want to scare me, st-stay where you are."

But he doesn't stop. He presses his body against mine. The chill of the shelf cools the low burn of my body. I wish these pages could transport me away, bring me anywhere else but here. John cages me in with his arms on either side as he leans his face in towards me, pushing his mouth on mine. John's kiss is frantic and crude. I don't move, instead choosing only to whimper in his mouth. His hand travels up my arm and ensnaring my neck and growling into my mouth when I don't kiss him back. The tightened grip threatens my air, but I still refuse him.

He breathes in my face, breath reeking of alcohol. "Kiss me," he orders, gripping tighter. "Now."

I try with all my energy to push him away, to pry his hand off my neck, but it is no use. I'm not strong enough. I'm never strong enough.

"John, please," I mouth as he squeezes tighter, cutting off all chances of breathing.

"Say you'll come home."

He sees it in my eyes and a fuming rumble resonates in his gullet.

Even if I say the words, I won't follow through with them. A single tear falls down his cheek while my eyes flood. I gasp, dropping my books and flailing my arms. I claw at his face while I put pressure on his still-tender nose. Anything to get him to let me go. My sights turn to TV static. I need air. John releases me and I choke on the much-needed oxygen. He grips a fist-full of hair on the side of my head and forces me down with all his might.

A beautiful burst of color sprays behind my lids, like the Macy's fireworks display, as my temple hits the sharp metal shelf. I crumble to the carpeted floor, choking on air as my vision flashes on and off until my vision turns gray.

Dreams of John attacking me run on an infinite loop, like a montage of terrifying memories. And there's an incessant beeping in the background that sounds very familiar. I fight him off, but it's pointless. I never succeed. The beeping gets louder, along with some distant chatter.

I blink, peeling my eyes open. Instantly, I squint, not only from the pain but from the bright light pouring through a nearby window. And the throbbing, damn that throbbing. It is as if someone is banging a gong inside my brain over and over and over again. The pain turns my stomach.

Once I survey my surroundings, the beeping in my nightmares finally makes sense. I'm back in the hospital.

"Pen?"

With trepidation, I turn my head. Josey sits bedside. Her deep, relieved breath doesn't go unnoticed. My eyes fall to the intravenous drip in my arm and various machines around the bed.

"Joes?"

The moment my hoarse voice vibrates in my throat, I regret speaking. I touch my tender neck and bite through the pain a simple swallow makes. My brain turns fuzzy, like static, unable to recall anything.

"What happened?"

"John attacked you at the bookstore. Since you dialed me last, the police contacted me."

I remember very little. Of course, various incidents of John's abuse come to mind, but it's difficult to decipher if it's an old memory or a new one. I'm trapped in a thick fog.

Why can't I remember? What can't I remember?

As the day progresses, nurses check my vitals, explaining my newest list of injuries, and what my instructions are for my release. I've been down this road more times than I can count, but each time, there's always something new added to the list.

Little by little, memories of what happened surface—John backing me into the bookshelf, the fear building inside until I might implode. Not only do the memories haunt me while I'm awake, but when I'm asleep, too. His presence looms over me and all I can do is curl into a ball and cry. He's too powerful. And I'm too weak.

When I wake up again, I remember John's hand on my throat, squeezing away my life force. I always imagined I might die by his hands, but I assumed we'd still be a couple when it happened. And for someone that loathes me this much, why does he fight so hard to get me to come back?

Jordan's Penny

One specific memory surfaces, but it wasn't what he did. It was the way the bulging vein in his forehead throbbed, and how his eyes turned cold while he demanded I come home. The angry snarl that curled his lips will forever haunt me. He reeked of disdain.

I try to sit up, but the room spins.

The sun no longer fills the space, and all the staff have changed shifts, but my one constant is Josey. She's never left my side. With eyes drawn and heavy, she licks her finger and flips another page of her magazine. She looks as if she hasn't slept in days.

I stir. With an exhausted grin, she scoots her chair closer to the bed and holds my hand, resting her head on my bed. Her warming stare comforts me.

"How long?" I mouth.

"Three days."

My mind sits on the news and after a few breaths, I worry about work. And Jordan.

"Job," I mouth. My throat is still too sore to talk.

"Relax," she reassures. She strokes my bruised knuckles. "I called Melissa with your phone and told her what happened. I'm sure she notified Jordan."

Everything hurts. Too overcome with emotion, salty tears burn my cheeks with their quiet power. I break down and sob into my hands with my best friend by my side. The dam broke. The weight of these emotions has become too heavy to hold in. After all the times I've woken up in a hospital bed, I've never wanted my parents as much as I want them now.

"I'm pressing charges."

She flaunts a tired grin, and a single tear slides down her cheek as she nods.

"Okay." She kisses the top of my hand and takes out her phone, along with a card. "Hi. This is Josephine Cordero. Penelope Matthews is awake, and she's ready to talk."

CHAPTER
TWENTY-FIVE

J OSEY DIDN'T LIE when she said she'd stay with me through every
step—she's never left my side. She held my hand while I ID'd John in
a photo lineup and stood beside me when I signed the order of
protection paperwork. Even though it's only a piece of paper, it brings
some comfort.

I'm not recovered, not completely, but I'm not helpless either. Each
day I rest, and an additional part of me heals, both physically and
mentally.

As expected, John paid bail, but he must refrain from making contact.
I pray he listens. Even though he hasn't called or texted, everyone agreed
I should change my number just in case. So, I did.

Once the doctors approve me for work, I put on my favorite
tortoiseshell sunglass and head to the office to discuss my future with the
company. The thick frames hide the bruising and stitches on my temple,
along with the blood-stained whites of my eyes.

With so much time on my hands, I've contemplated this decision long
and hard, deciding on a plan I can live with. Too bad things couldn't be
different, but after everything that's transpired, this is the best solution for
everyone.

As I walk through the hallways, my coworkers crowd around, asking
how I am. I never liked the attention and most times, I preferred to stay in
the shadows. Maybe they pity me, too, but today, I don't care because the
overwhelming support is comforting.

"What will happen to him?" Melissa inquires.

"Not sure. We have a court date in a month, but if he makes contact or
gets too close, they will revoke his bail, and violating a protective order
will only add to his charges." I shrug, hoping this nightmare will end soon,

so I won't spend another minute worrying about it. "I need to talk to Jordan."

She hugs me and I take a deep breath, rehearsing the speech in my head one last time before I enter his office. I glance toward my empty desk and the piles of folders stacked in the corner. Too bad I can't dive into them now, but the dull ache hums in my head, summoning me back to bed.

I walk into the doorway and Alec is sitting in my usual seat. I'll miss taking notes here. Jordan doesn't spot me right away, too enthralled in his own tirade about the temp assigned to him. Alec laughs and makes fun of his whining, a far different conversation than the last time they sat together, and the things I overheard. I'd be lying if I said I wasn't grateful they weren't talking about me now.

I tap on the door, and both turn their attention toward me. All whining ends. Jordan's eyes burn bright. His mouth draws open, and he stands up, ushering me in.

"You're here. Alec, get the hell out."

Alec laughs again, raking his fingers through his dark, slick-backed hair. "Damn. I know when I'm not wanted." He stands beside me in the doorway and puts his hand on my shoulder. "How ya feeling?" he asks.

"I'm good, Mr. Connall. Thanks."

Alec nods and gives a brief squeeze before closing the door behind him. A noticeable lump forms in my chest as I make my way to the chair. The distance isn't far, but it seems miles away, the longest journey I've traveled in some time.

The office is silent, except for the ticking of the clock on Jordan's shelf, the one that's always three minutes too fast. I need to get that fixed.

"So…" I start, lowering myself to the seat while Jordan walks toward me, propping the chair closer to mine. With him this close, all focus turns to shit, and my nerves run at warp speed. I clear my throat even though it didn't need clearing. I shouldn't be nervous, but beads of sweat form along my brow.

"Jesus Christ, Pen," he starts. "You disconnected your phone. I had no way to contact you." He rakes his hands through his hair like a nervous wreck as he leans in closer. "If it weren't for Melissa staying in contact with Josey, I'd be in the dark. Why didn't you talk to me?"

His concern appears genuine, borderline adorable, and it helps calm me. I rest my palm on his knee, needing him to relax, so I can relax, too. He stiffens at my touch.

"I'm sorry you worried. I should've called, but I needed some... time to get my head right. Josey updated Melissa, but you're right. I should've spoken to you."

"No. Don't apologize." He puts his hand on mine with such care, the heat from his skin warms me from the outside in. I'm reminded of all the times he's touched me before.

He pities you, Matthews.

The mantra repeats in the depths of my brain; it stops me from reading too much into his concerned gestures.

"I'm glad you're okay, Pen. You are okay, aren't you?"

"Yes." I pull my arm away and he eyes his lone hand, then busies himself by adjusting his tie, which was already perfect. "I'm good. But we need to talk."

Jordan inches his seat closer, grazing his knee against mine. It's as if I can still feel the electricity humming in his body from the last time we touched. An odd buzz tingles my knee as they barely touch. "You can talk to me about anything. Whatever you need, I'm here for you."

"I'm glad you said that because..." I start, but the nerves bundle in my throat.

As many times as I've rehearsed this conversation, playing both roles, even preparing answers for questions asked, sitting here with his knee on mine, clenches my heart. This is harder than I expected. Not only does he watch my every move, but he leans in like I'll reveal the greatest secret ever told.

Before he can inch any closer, I push forward. "I asked Melissa for a transfer. When I come back, I'm going to work for Tom."

Jordan leans back and scoffs at the idea. He opens his mouth, but I stop him before he can offer a rebuttal.

"I have your replacement. She's smart and a fast learner. I'll train her myself. Think of it like this, I'm merging what your old assistants used to be like but with my work ethic," I joke.

After a loud grunt or exhale, or both, he shakes his head, "No." With his head shaking like that, not only is he making me dizzy, but he resembles a deranged bobblehead or a child on the verge of a tantrum, and I can't take him seriously.

"Jordan," I drawl. "I can't sit outside your office and pretend nothing happened. You fought because of me, and I feel horrible about that." My head falls and I chew on the side of my cheek, tasting blood. "I'm not proud to admit this, but you're distracting." I turn to him, expecting to see that smug grin, but his face remains stoic. "And not just that," I drop my voice to a whisper, "we kissed. I can't pretend nothing happened or why you did it."

"What are you talking about? I kissed you because—"

"Like in the movies, where the universe is in shambles, the hero kisses the girl, or they make love when they should be running. I get it." Jordan's stare intensifies like I've gone mad, but I forge ahead, not letting his skepticism derail my point. "As the viewer, we're saying, 'What are you doing?' But I understand now. You witnessed me at my lowest, how my world was ablaze, crumbling all around me, so you kissed me. You helped me to forget what happened, if only for a second, because you know me. I would keep replaying the night's events in my head until I lost my mind. That kiss reminded me I wasn't alone. You felt sorry for me, and I don't blame you. I was pathetic, but I don't need your pity anymore. You may not be my boss anymore, but I would like it if we could be friends."

He scrunches his brows in disbelief. "Sorry for you?"

I remove my sunglasses and let him see the real me once and for all. All the pain I've endured—from the cut near my eye, still bruised and puffy, to the whites of my eyes now bloodied from broken capillaries. Let's not forget the bruised fingerprints lingering on my neck from John's tight grip where I teetered on the edge of unconsciousness. They're all remnants of a battle not won. This is me, even before I became his assistant. This was me.

He rips his eyes away, unable to stomach my truth.

"It's okay, Jordan. I overheard you talking to Alec one morning and said I was gross, and you felt sorry for me."

He drops his head into his hands, lets out another groan, leaning his elbows on his knees. "You don't understand, Penny." He combs through his hair with dramatic flair, shaking his head to himself.

"I'll be down the hall, not Mars. If you wanna harass me about music or need me to help you shop," I add with a wry grin, "you'll walk a little further, that's all. Oh, but you must run it past my boss first."

With his face tilted down, he asks, "Who's your replacement?"

"Josey. John's been harassing her, so she can't work at her parent's florist shop anymore. She has office experience, and she's done all her parent's bookkeeping since high school. It'll work out, you'll see. Tom and I already squared everything away." I put my shades back on and start for the door. Jordan remains seated, unmoved and sulking. "Jordan," I softly say, and he spins in the chair. "Out of all my jobs, you're the best boss and an even better friend, whether or not you meant to be. And..." I clear my throat as my body warms with the mere memory. "You are also the best kisser. So..." I hesitate as my embarrassing smirk forms. "There's that."

"Pen—"

"Jordan, please," I beg with a determined purpose, and he nods, accepting defeat and accepting my decision.

"I guess that joke about having an office tryst kinda played out after all, huh?" I tap my chin. "Now onto my next boss." I shoot a wink, forgetting he can't see the gesture through my dark shades.

For the first time, Jordan's sullen expression cracks. "At least it happened with your actual boss this time."

"Yeah, yeah, yeah," I deadpan. "That was a good joke until you ruined it with like, facts and stuff."

Now, his laugh isn't so silent. "Get out of here, Matthews. Get your rest so you can come back, break my heart, and leave me."

CHAPTER
TWENTY-SIX

IT'S TAKEN A while, but I'm getting used to my new surroundings. Not only at home, but work, too. Tom's office is decorated differently than the other partners. The difference is drastic, but I never imagined the decor would play a role in my work productivity.

Where Jordan's office is clean lines, brushed silver, polished glass, and black shelving, Tom's has more warmth with dark sycamore wood furniture and black accents. While both have modern touches, both are different. A large glass display unit sits to the side, donning decade's worth of accolades with Tom's name engraved on each. This office suits Tom's personality as much as Jordan's complements his.

As classy as Tom's office is, my workflow is off. Maybe the dark wood takes some getting used to, or perhaps Tom's slower pace is what's throwing me for a loop. One thing's certain, I won't have to worry about Tom pulling an earbud out and harassing me about my music. He stays in his office and out of my hair. Perhaps that's why I'm on edge. I'm expecting someone to bother me at any given moment, only for nothing to happen. But Tom doesn't complain. His desk is free of clutter, and I've arranged his schedule to something more manageable. Whatever work he gives me is done promptly. I must remind him of Grace because he's called me her name several times. Sadly, it wasn't the first time someone called me another woman's name.

Altogether, Tom is far different from Jordan. While Jordan wanted everything rushed, Tom's urgency differs; he's steadier, even-mannered, controlled, and precise. Tom is already twelve steps ahead, prepared to take an alternative route at any moment.

After working with Tom for a few weeks, I see what the partners mean when they refer to Jordan's age and inexperience, though I'd never tell

Jordan that. If Jordan changed tactics, it might ease the stress he puts on himself. There's no denying Jordan has an innate ability to wow the pants off any client, but if he studied Tom's approach, he'd need to do less work with more of a reward.

Josey is adjusting, too. She picked up the work with ease. Jordan has remained patient with her, and she has me to thank me for that. Every time he was about to throw a tantrum for one thing or another, I would turn to him and stare, blinking my widened eyes every second without a word. He called it my death stare, but it was more like a 'Are you for real right now, Jordan? You're a grown-ass man, so cut it out' stare. It was very useful.

Within a few weeks, we all agreed Josey could manage things on her own. And so far, she's handling him like a pro. Even swamped with work, he's been nice, not only to her but to others in the office, mindful of his tone. Perhaps I tamed the lion after all.

My life is normal again. Well, a new normal. The fear I expected to come along with my single status never surfaces. Sometimes I sit back and laugh to myself at how ridiculous I was to be afraid. What's terrifying about spa days or date nights with Josey? I put all of John's wants before my own, and he did the same, treated himself to everything and anything.

Now it's my turn.

All this time, I assumed I lost who I was in that relationship, but I don't think that's entirely true. Too busy being who John wanted me to be, it did not give me the chance to grow into who I am supposed to be. Each day, I'm finding out who the real Penelope Matthews is.

My new freedom has opened my eyes to the world around me. And I'm surprised to learn things I wouldn't have figured out if I didn't leave John. He always found ways of controlling various aspects of my day. I'm not sure why, but he limited my food; sushi was one of them. He claimed it was bad for women trying to get pregnant. And since he always wanted me pregnant, he forbid me from trying it.

On one of our business lunch outings with Josey, Jordan shoved raw tuna in my mouth. It took a minute to get over the texture, and Jordan's laughing. I enjoyed both. I liked everything Jordan asked me to try that day. And who knew heels hurt my feet less than flats? I needed to soak my feet every night after a long day wearing the shoes John preferred. He hated me in heels because I was taller than him. I also prefer sleeping with the television off. John needed the background noise, but I hated it. The late-night commercials would blare and wake me out of a dead sleep. But most of all, I love finding only my underwear in the laundry.

I open the trinket box, the one with the lone penny inside, reading the note my mother gave me the day I left. Not a day goes by, let alone a minute, that I don't remind myself of her words.

Never sell yourself short.

And I won't. I never will again. The days of letting others dictate my mood or tell me how to live are over. I won't ever settle for less than I deserve anymore, and I deserve it all. I love myself and the skin I'm in. Embracing my wings, flying free however I want and wherever I choose; I'll always choose fast, but I fly with more caution now.

"Hey, traitor."

His voice carries a unique force, a force so strong my insides feel like I'm wrapped in a silken cocoon of euphoria. "Hello, O.B."

A confused expression spreads on Jordan's mouth.

"Original Boss, like OG, Original Gangster." He shakes his head with an undeniable no. "Took it for a test drive. What can I say? They can't all be winners." I shrug. "Josey said you turned into a hermit, but as I live and breathe, here you are, standing before me."

He sits on the corner of my desk in that lazy, relaxed state he's done countless times, smiling over his shoulder. "It's called work. Maybe you've heard of it. Not gonna lie, I've been moping around. It's like I lost my best friend." He studies his shoes. "It's still a little weird, no? Or is that just me?"

So many things are weird. What's weird is being called Penelope or Ms. Matthews all day long and not Penny, Pens, or Pen. And then there's the occasional Grace. Is it weird that the sound of Jordan's voice somehow completes me? Or even at this moment with him sitting on my desk, is it weird that I still crave those lips?

The answer is yes to all the above.

He wears a smile so delicious, I want to taste it.

"You're so dramatic." I peer over my glasses, ignoring what he does to my insides. "How's Josey doing?"

"She's not as good as her predecessor, but she's in the top two of my Best Assistants List."

Tom's door swings open and once he sets sights on Jordan, his forehead wrinkles and brows furrow. "Oh no," he warns. "You get away from her. I'm just getting caught up."

"Ah, come on, Tom. I'll trade you my court-side seats and subsidize your youngest daughter until she's eighteen. You'd still need to raise her, but I'll pay for everything," Jordan quips, his voice void of sarcasm.

"Um," I chime in. "You know that kids get more expensive as they get older, right?"

Jordan shrugs. "I don't care. I'll do it."

Tom laughs and hits Jordan's arm with a stack of papers he holds before placing them on my desk. "Not a chance. I'm not giving up Ms. Matthews for all Tik Tok likes in the world."

Jordan busts a gut laughing while I chuckle. "What the hell do you know about Tik Tok?" Jordan asks.

"I'll have you know that Serena and I have a solid following. I guess you haven't seen our Shanty Tik Tok. That one has over ten thousand views. Or our second most-viewed video is us doing a little choreographed number to a song called, 'Renegade.' Can't have my kids thinking I'm an old fart," Tom finishes as he does some sort of dance move back to his office while giving Jordan a warning eye.

I sit with my mouth agape.

Jordan and I share a look. "I can't even comment on that, so I'll move on. How have you been?"

Even though he's asked more personal questions before, I can't help but get flustered around him now. Or perhaps it's his flirtatious glance over the shoulder, his sexy half-smile, and his manly-spiced cologne that turns me to putty.

He's a friend, I remind myself, an attractive friend that kissed me once and changed the way I'll view kisses for the rest of my life. Besides that, nothing should be awkward between us anymore. The buzz that hums in my body every time he's near, or how all my reproductive organs twerk once the heat of his gaze settles over me, that's not awkward either. Perfectly normal.

"I'm doing well. No news is good news."

He picks up my cellphone, reads the song playing in one of my earbuds. "That's good to hear." He presses the next song, not liking the one I'm listening to. "So," he coughs, clearing his throat, and presses for the next song again. "Want to go to lunch today? I drove past this new cafe the other day." He presses the button again.

"Hey! I liked that song." I snatch my phone from him.

He's always hated trying unknown places alone. As much as I revel in his invite now, all pleasure leaves in an instant.

"I, uh, I can't. I have a date."

His disappointment registers instantly. His shy grin sinks and his lips twitch downward. Even his eyes lose a little sparkle. Disappointment hits me, too. That anvil of unease sinks to my belly. I miss him and our lunch dates. Our conversation was effortless, and once our walls dropped, one topic branched off into thirty new ones, creating limitless possibilities and endless hours of talking and sharing. As much as I love spending time with him, I hate that my heart doesn't come with an operational turnoff switch.

As Jordan stands, he knocks over my paper clip holder, spilling mini clips everywhere. We scramble to scoop them up. As our hands touch retrieving the same clips, I could have sworn he interlocked our pinkies as his heat radiates onto me.

Any touch coming from him must remain off-limits.

"I'm having lunch with my parents," I add, no longer needing him to drag the information out of me. "Rain check?"

The smile he offers is even more delicious up close. "That's great. And yes, yes to the rain check."

"I'm excited, but nervous, too. It's been years since I've seen them."

I'm as anxious today as the day I picked up the phone and called my mom for the first time in years. After we both stopped crying, I told her everything, and the lengths I've gone to separate myself from John. I don't expect either of my parents to trust me right away; they've been down this road before, and I always went back to him. Over time, I'll earn their trust back and one day, Spencer and I will reconcile, too.

I've been an addict, in my own way, addicted to John. As many times I swore it was over, my need for love clawed at my better judgment until it overwhelmed me with self-doubt. Eventually, I would crawl back into his abusive arms. The high from making up with him became surreal. It was true and utter bliss. But once that fix wore off, I crashed hard. And sometimes in the literal sense. It would remind me why I needed to stay away all over again. The cycle was vicious, but I spun on that repetitive wheel for far too long.

"I found out my dad is having another lesson. If lunch goes well, wanna come? I'll show you my signature moves." My brows dance as my hands rub maniacally together.

"I'm not entertaining that with a response. Just tell me when and where. Plus, I'll need pointers for our next race."

Pfft. Too bad for him. There will be no more racing until Jordan Stephens makes good on his debt. He finishes picking up the mess he's created, but Jordan is acting weird and I can't put my finger on why.

"Word around the office is you're eyeing another company. Do you need an extra hand? I can help you and Josey, plus the overtime would come in handy. Tom's workload doesn't warrant late nights. I'm done by three on most days. Shh, don't tell him that."

"Yes, yes and yes," he exclaims. "When I accepted this project, you were still working for me. Once you left, I was hesitant because you're on Tom's team now."

Could he be that oblivious?

I'll always be on his team.

Jordan's entire body relaxes as if just receiving an hour-long full-body massage. He's about to say something, but I interrupt. "And yes, I'll be in charge of dinners."

He heads toward the door with a dumb smirk on his face. "Oh," he spins back around. "Before I forget." He digs into the pocket of his gray slacks, the ones that fit his trim physique to perfection. "To pay my debt, m'lady." He extends his hand, holding an old iPod and headphones.

I break into an open-mouth smile and snatch the device from his grip. "I expected a CD or something, but this works."

He holds the device in his hands, refusing to let go. "I'm not finished with the list, and I left off a bunch of my favorite songs, but this is a start. You'll see what I'm talking about when you get to a certain song. Penelope," he warns, and I'm not sure I like his tone. "Listen in order. Do. Not. Shuffle," he adds with his strictest voice to date—stern, forceful, and a bucket load of sexy. He forces his hands in his pockets again, moving something inside. A gesture he does a lot.

"If it doesn't even have your favorite songs—"

"Just listen. I labeled the list with your name. Promise me the second you finish, you'll find me. No matter what. I'm curious what you think." He pulls in the corner of his lower lip and chews on it. I'm not sure why he's nervous, but it only entices me more, so I agree. At this rate, I'd sign over my firstborn to hear what the heck he means.

Jordan releases the iPod. I plug the headphones in and pop one in my ear. "I promise. Now, scram. I've got some listening to do."

"I'll see you soon." He spins around and he's gone.

CHAPTER
TWENTY-SEVEN

NTICIPATION OVERFLOWS WHILE I scroll through his
playlists, spotting the one that says, "For Penny." My belly warms.
I'm already plotting. As soon as I'm done, I'm listening to his other
playlists. I don't care what he said.

The first song is Stevie Wonder's, "I Never Dreamed You'd Leave In
Summer." A slow song, not upbeat, but one of my Stevie favorites. Jordan
wouldn't have known, and I never told him.

The next one is more upbeat, Lucy Pearl's, "Dance Tonight." He
must've scrolled through my songs when I let him use my account. I skip
to the next and Zedd's, "Clarity," plays. The lyrics always got my
attention, relating one half of the verse to John. Our love was a tragedy,
but John would never be my remedy. Our love was insanity, but working
alongside Jordan became my clarity.

I bounce in my chair, working on a spreadsheet for Tom, letting the
song play out instead of skipping ahead. The upbeat songs continue with
Nikki Williams, "Glowing." I shake my head with disappointment. That
bastard must've copied from my playlists. Cheater.

The tempo changes. Robin Thicke, "Wanna Love U Girl." I listen for a
bit before jumping ahead. My curiosity overflows. I'm not sure I could sit
through any song in its entirety. I pegged Jordan for more classic rock or
rap, anything other than what's playing now.

Next up, R. Kelly's, "One Man." I stare at the device, brows pull
together, double-checking I didn't shuffle. With trepidation, I press for
the next song. Brian McKnight, "The Only One for Me." My heart
stutters as I put the theme of all these songs together like a puzzle.

Why on Earth would he put so many songs about love on his playlist?
And not just love songs, songs about wanting a person already taken.

Jordan's Penny

Don't read too into it, Matthews. You asked for his favorite songs, and now you have it.
Next. Jagged Edge's, "He Can't Love U". Next. Amber Run, "I Found." Song after song is about love or confessing love. I fast forward through more and there are no upbeat songs, no rap, no grunge or rock, only love songs.

I turn my head to the doorway when his sultry voice speaks my name, jerking upright as if Jordan caught me with my hand in the cookie jar. Confused when the doorway is empty, I stare at the device and read the name of the song, "Jordan's Penny," and the artist's name says, "Jordan Stephens."

Beautiful piano music plays in the background until he speaks again.

"Hey, Penny. You love movies and the music that accompanies them, so I've got an idea. Here's a piece I wrote that might complement a movie I came up with."

The piano plays while he remains silent, letting the music do the talking. He lied. He still plays.

I close my eyes, imagining him in front of a large, glossy black piano while his fingers glide over the keys and his foot taps on the pedals, staring at sheets of music he's masterfully created.

"The movie is about a superficial and conceited guy. Some might say he was pompous even, who for most of his life went through it with eyes closed, only opening them when he noticed something he liked. One day," he continues to play a lovely melody in the background, soft as if the heavens guided his fingers. "He walked into work and met his new assistant. He admits he didn't want her to work out. Decades of brainwashing led him to put stock in the wrong qualities of a person, but despite all that, her eyes..." he gushes before his voice fades away and beautiful music fills my ears. "They sparkled and burned bright like the sun. She had an air of destiny about her, not to mention her color-coded spreadsheets were killer. Ooh, wee." Jordan laughs to himself, while the harmonious music rings true.

His fingers key the perfect chords, plucking every one of my emotions with each string of beautiful notes.

"Weeks passed, and he tried to break her—he pushed her buttons—but she was forged from iron and showed no signs of weakness. When she divulged things, he enjoyed her company and ached to learn more.

Every day, his mission to get to know her better fueled him. He enjoyed her smile. He yearned for her voice even if she cracked jokes about him holding onto a childhood keepsake," he adds with a chuckle. "But he never stayed mad. He couldn't. When he found out she was engaged, something inside him changed."

Low chords play sullen notes that complement the tone of his voice and story. His fingers do all the talking, speaking to me through music.

"She belonged to another, but until he met the man she promised herself to, it wasn't real. Hell, that should've been the end of whatever intrigue he had for her, but he's never been one to stop when he wanted something bad enough. And he wouldn't start now because there was something indescribable between them, something he's never experienced before. He didn't understand what it meant, and he hated her because of it, but he needed to find out what *it* was."

The piano piece continues. His finger-work is precise and elegant. I close my lids and get swept away one note at a time. I imagine him swaying on the bench with his eyes closed as he creates this beautiful melody.

"The boss and the assistant's relationship got closer over time, and he would go home at night with her on his mind even though she belonged to someone else. He needed her and wanted her more than he could admit."

My vision becomes blurred from unshed tears. His tone, sinfully rich. The melodious voice has the power to make my toes curl. As he tells the story of us, his soft words stroke my skin, raising a shiver. Jordan is a maestro.

"Spotting her fiancé with another gutted him. The secret ate him alive. Her chipper mood stopped him from telling his secret. It'd tear him up if he were the one to bear the horrible news. He never wanted her sad; she possessed a mouth made for smiling, and a voice for laughing."

The melody of the song continues, a tortured beauty, explaining his turmoil in holding in his secret, much like the secret of my own tortured relationship.

"When he found out about her special day, he wanted to celebrate with her, make her day memorable. And he would be lying if he said seeing her dressed up didn't make his body react in ways HR would disapprove of. She was radiant, sexy, and so confident. He could hardly maintain a professional poker face. Little did anyone know, the celebration would remain memorable, but not for the reasons he wished. Her fiancé showed up. Again."

Low chords play as the song reaches its thunderous crescendo, chaotic like the scene that unfolded at the club, climaxing with brutal excitement.

"He fought for the girl he belonged with all along."

The speed of the keys amazes me, continuing its battle. My hair stands on end as I'm brought into the chaotic story of this musical journey.

"When they reunited, she looked broken, betrayed by someone she loved. But all that replayed in his mind were the nights they spent locked behind office doors—working and learning about one another. Her beauty, both inside and out, captivated him. How her eyes sparkled in the dim garage light, full of awe and wonderment, set his soul on fire. As hard as he tried, the woman with the honey-filled eyes consumed every one of his thoughts. He adored the way her left cheek dimpled when she tried to stifle a laugh, or the way she cut her tomatoes and whipped up a mean pasta dish. He ached to learn more, ached to kiss her lips, wondering if they were as soft as he'd imagined. So, he did what he needed to do, he kissed the woman he'd fallen for."

My heart is a stuttering fool, skipping beats as my palms sweat. The pit of my stomach wobbles like Jell-O, unable to contain my composure as the sweet tune continues in his silence. The melody envelops me.

Music has always been special to me. Explaining how one verse would melt my heart, or how one string of notes could send me to tears, was an impossible feat. How his love vibrates with each push on the keys is indescribable.

"When she didn't show up for work, he almost lost his mind; his gut told him something bad must've happened. Like always, he was helpless when it came to her. But when she returned, seeing what happened shattered his heart even more. Nothing prepared him to see those injuries. But it wasn't until she mentioned something she overheard him say once, that's when his world crumbled. As if someone ripped him apart, limb by limb, severing every tendon and nerve-ending, his heart bled devastation. What she didn't understand was, he couldn't explain to his business partner what he meant; that putz was incapable of understanding anything. But if he did, he'd say he felt bad for her because no one would ever appreciate her the way she deserves. She deserved the world, and the only man that could give it to her was him. It devastated him knowing someone as special as she wouldn't experience being loved, adored, and appreciated in that way; unless she chose him."

My tears fall. I do nothing to stop them. As the piano continues its journey. My heart clenches, drawing me deeper into the music he's created for us. The overwhelming emotions consume every fiber of my being.

His silky soft baritone voice speaks again. "Penny, this is where I need your help. The movie and song need an ending." I let out a brief sob/chuckle at his direct approach. "I'm unsure how things will play out. The assistant might reject him. He'll have a broken heart, but he would still love to be her friend. Or she might go into his office and tell him she cares about him too. They'd kiss again because that's what they do in the movies, right?" He releases another laugh all his own while continuing to play soft, sweet music in the background. "I've fallen for you, Penny. If that kiss meant anything to you the way it meant for me, you might have fallen for me, too. I've been a horrible man and you're too good for me, but you changed me without even trying. God," he let out a long whoosh of air.

The music stops. Only his exhales continue.

"I've changed because I want to be the man you deserve. I've never hoped for anything in my life, but I hope you'll take a chance on me. You're extraordinary and beautiful, from your silky chocolate hair to your sexy feet and everything in between. You're funny, incredibly smart, witty and charming, loving. And your soft lips…" He lets out another long breath. "I can't stop thinking about you. If you choose me, I promise to make sure you recognize how beautiful and important you are to me every day. Please choose me."

With that, the playlist ends, and the silence pains my ears. Already, I miss the music and his voice. Jordan asked me to go to him afterward, but my weakened legs wouldn't be able to hold me upright for long if I tried.

As I replay the last year, hell, the last decade, the only happy memories that surface revolve around Jordan. Everything else fades into the background as if irrelevant bits of my day. Since becoming his assistant, Jordan has been a permanent resident in my mind. I should've charged him rent.

While John forced himself on me, I fantasized about Jordan. All those nights I lay awake, I played out what questions Jordan might ask next, hoping he'd never stop. His deep voice would randomly ring in my ears when I'd least expect, making any time away from work so miserable, I contemplated calling his voicemail just to hold me over until Monday. Our blossoming friendship reeled me in hook, line, and sinker. And even though I shouldn't have, I grew to love him.

As hard as I tried to stop it from happening, I fell, too.

CHAPTER
TWENTY-EIGHT

THE CHAIR CRASHES behind me, and I rush to the bathroom. Tears ruined the minimal make-up I wear now. I can't confess my love while I'm a hot mess; although I doubt Jordan would mind. I blot the tears and try to salvage my mascara at all costs. The only thing that's not running down my face is my ever-growing smile. I may not be a supermodel, but he wouldn't write an entire musical score if he didn't recognize something in me, something I need to see in myself.

My strides are quick. I need to see Jordan before I lose all nerve. I clutch his iPod, holding the device with force to prevent my hands from shaking. Josey isn't at her desk, and when I turn my head, no one is in their cubicles. With Jordan's office door ajar, I suck in a quick breath and knock, swinging the door open before he can call me in.

I breathe, a panicked breath, through my teeth as both sets of eyes turn to me.

"Get out," Jordan commands.

But I can't. My shoes are like cinder blocks. John's quiet smile sends a prickle to my spine; he's back to his normal self—perfect clothes and hair, clean-shaven, unlike the last time we stood face to face.

"I knew you still worked here." He draws in a big, settling breath.

For a moment, my heart stops, then as if Jordan's eyes were a defibrillator, it starts again but with a harsh thud that pounds in my ears. My eyes dart from one man to the other, the man I love and the man I loved. Quiet chaos echoes in the room, or maybe it's just in my ears.

What is he doing here?

"Y-you can't be here," I stammer and bite off the urge to scream. But I'm no longer the weak person I was. I straighten my spine, determined to prove to John that he no longer controls me. "You need to leave."

Jordan's Penny

Jordan starts toward me, but I hold out my palm. His stare intensifies, face stern. "Penny, go!"

But it's John's eyes that burn into me, and only me. As fiery as his stares are, I'm running into this burning building. Head-on.

"I only want to talk," John says quietly.

"Jordan, can you please give us a minute?" Even though my voice is far from reassuring, Jordan doesn't need to worry about me, not anymore.

"No way in hell I'm leaving you in here with him."

With Jordan standing behind his desk, the ferocity of his glare puts me on pause. His jaw is tight and uncomfortable. If he doesn't let up, his enamel might shatter. Jordan balls his hands as if ready to leap over his desk in the blink of an eye. I can't tell who he's livid with more, John for being here, or me for not bolting the moment my eyes landed on John.

"I'll be quick, I promise." John steps toward me, slow movements narrowing the space between us. My eyes stay fixed on his hands, still tucked in his jacket pockets. "I wanted to tell you something." He pauses. An internal battle must be storming his thoughts as his eyes dart over me. "I still love you, but I know we can't be together."

With John uttering the words with such finality, it eases the stress in my heart. He gets it now.

"I've done too much to you, Pen. I don't deserve you. Maybe I did once, but I haven't deserved you for a long time now." His expression shifts and his lower lip quivers. "I'm sorry, Pen. I just needed to tell you that, face-to-face."

Whatever invisible hold still tied me to him, even in a minor way, severs. Everything around me is easier to do now—breathing, blinking, even the heaviness in my feet slips away.

"Thank you for the apology."

"You really loved me, didn't you?"

I nod. "We shared many beautiful moments." My voice is clear and calm, regardless of the tremors that roll over my surface. "You'll find someone that will make you happy, completely happy."

His cold, glazed stare, the one that's existed for years, has disappeared, finally accepting his fate.

"No one will ever make me happy," he concedes. His head tilts to his feet, hands still placed in his pockets. "None of those girls could hold a candle to you. I've done so many horribly cruel things to you," he sobs aloud. The dam that locked his emotions away has crumbled. "I deserve everything coming to me."

When his watery eyes find mine again, my heart sinks. Even after all that's happened, seeing the man I once loved accepting his fate pulls at my heartstrings. I inch toward him.

"Just give me time, John. Perhaps one day we could be friends again. We were always great as friends."

His shifting emotions play out on his face. "I'd like that."

I drift closer to him and can almost hear his heart stammering as his tears drip down his chiseled jaw. "I will forgive you in time. But please give me that."

Jordan's glares haven't softened, but I don't expect him to understand.

"I'll always love you, Penelope. No matter what."

I let out a quick snort. "You'll get over me before you realize." I swipe away a tear from his cheek. "You should leave before the police arrive."

He nods with a tenderness set in his face and a tremble to his hands. "One last hug?"

John opens one arm wide as his eyes pool again. Just as my heart knitted itself together, the image of the trembling man before me breaks my heart all over. We will never be together again, but I still miss how we once were—the best of friends, laughing, joking, and enjoying each other's company. It's been a while since we've done any of those things, but I've held onto a figment of hope that one day, we'd find that place again, together. But we won't. We can't. Too much has happened between us that can't be undone.

"Penny, don't," Jordan barks and I flinch. But this is our last goodbye, the closure John and I need to move on with our lives.

I wrap my arms around his neck. His masculine cologne fills my lungs and, for once, his scent is all his own. Nothing else foreign is mixed on his skin, just pure John. This is the end. He's letting me go and I can move on without the stress of worrying if he'll ever stop fighting for me.

He wraps one arm around me and hooks me in his embrace. "I'm so sorry, Penny." He sobs into the crook of my neck, and I let him have this moment.

His cries settle, and he takes his other hand out of his pocket to wrap around me.

A loud bang echoed in the room, like the backfiring of a car exhaust near my ear. My side burns, and an excruciating pain sears through my middle as tears begin well. I pull away and cringe.

A coldness returns to the base of his stare.

"PENNY!" Jordan shouts.

John watches me watching him as my realization forms. His lip curls, a grin that turns decidedly evil. The heaviness of my body pulls me down, but John holds me against him. As he leans in close, he says, "No one can have you... but me. Forever."

My eyes drift to where my hand clutches. My brain can't wrap around his words, too mesmerized by the red stain pooling around my cream-colored blouse until I face him again. A slow, wicked grin spreads over his brutal lips.

How could someone so handsome convey so much evil with a single expression?

He raises the black gun to his mouth and pulls the trigger. We both collapse to the floor.

Chaos and pain.

The burning inside me amplifies everything—blacks are darker, light is brighter, and noises are deafening. Jordan drops to the floor beside me, his hand presses down over mine and I gasp.

"Call an ambulance!" he screams. "Penny?"

My eyes flutter hearing his voice. When I focus on him, seeing the terror in his eyes darting from my middle to my face, sheer panic sets in. Even riddled with fear, I can't help but admire how handsome he still is.

"Jord..."

"Don't talk. Help is on the way."

Coldness creeps in like a slow-moving frost even though his hands and my blood are hot against my skin. Outside, more panic ensues, muffled in my ears, but loud all the same. With his iPod still clutched in my hand, I replay his music. I already ingrained the melody in my mind and soul. It is my first thought when I find his tear-filled eyes in my blurred vision again.

"I wanted your..." My eyes fall shut as tears still spill down my temples. The pain is excruciating, taking my breath away, but I need to tell him. "Ending." As loud as my voice sounds in my head, his face doesn't look comforted.

Can he not hear me?

I can't find the strength to repeat it. I gulp quick, shortened, pained breaths.

"Penny, stay with me."

I reach for his face. The warmth of skin on mine can fill me one last time. My hands, stained with red, leave his beautiful cheeks streaked. Jordan holds my hand against him, tilting his head into my palm while he presses down on my side with the other. He's my sun, always warming me.

"Penny, don't leave me." He kisses my hand and somehow, I feel it in my toes. "Please."

I close my eyes as he cries out my name over and over. His voice is like an echo, dying slowly, softer and softer with each word and breath. But that song of love, his confession of love keeps playing as loud as ever. I love you, Jordan.

PART THREE:
JORDAN

CHAPTER
TWENTY-NINE

I PACE THE same set of bleached tiles for the past two hours, wearing down the linoleum. Josey slumps in an awaiting chair, wiping away stray tears. We wear matching crimson stains on our hands and clothes. The metallic odor of blood, Penny's blood, weakens my stomach. My heart sinks, a dark heaviness I never experienced before while the unknown awaits us. One thought, my only thought, replays in my mind— our story can't end.

A woman with flaxen hair, reddened eyes, and black eyeliner streaming down her cheeks barrels into the room, with a familiar-looking man rushing behind her—Penny's father.

The resemblance between Penelope and this woman is astounding, making it more difficult to glance in her direction. Faint spots freckle the tops of her reddened cheeks and nose, and her lips have a similar curvature around the cupid's bow, just like her daughter.

Josey springs to her toes, throwing herself into the woman's embrace while Penny's father soothes the two women, offering me a quick bow. I'm barely keeping it together; I can't fathom the pain they're enduring at this very moment.

No one would peg me as a hugger, but dammit, I need one now. Penny's father ushers them to sit, and the two clutch their hands together and share a whisper. My nerves run rampant as her father approaches me.

Mr. Matthews extends one of his wide, capable hands, and I stretch mine. His breath hitches when he scans my clothes, crusted with his daughter's blood.

"Mr. Stephens," he says before dropping his hand and stepping away. With few places to rest his eyes without reminders of why we're here, my insides twist again.

"Still no update on Penelope?" I ask.

With one quick shake of his head, his eyes fall before retreating to Mrs. Matthews as another man burst through the swing doors. Another familiar face. Penelope's uncle throws her dad in a tight embrace, whispering something in his ear. Feeling useless, I sink into my empty chair and hide behind my palms.

Why didn't I stop her? Why didn't I force her to leave?

I stood by and let this happen. I did nothing. Nothing.

My tears spill. I might lose her forever, and it's all my fault. I'm not prepared to lose Penny.

Images from before the paramedics arrived flash behind my closed lids, but it doesn't matter if my eyes are open or closed. I'm haunted by them, regardless. Her skin, ashen, void of her usual glow, eyes closed but lips parted as if she fell asleep mid-sentence. That's not the way I want to remember Penny. Fuck. I don't want to *remember* her at all. She needs to be here with me. Forever.

A low sob grows, and its seconds away from reaching the surface. I jolt upright when a hand rests on my shoulder.

Josey. She remains silent, soothing me with circular motions on my back, sniffling between breaths.

"Penny must pull through, Josey. She has to." I swipe at my tears with the balls of my thumbs and lean back.

With one glance in Josey's direction, my vision wavers behind unshed tears. Hers, too. I wrap my arm around her shoulder and pull her close as she weeps. No inhale is deep enough to soothe my nerves; especially when Josey wears the same perfume as Penny.

A silver-haired gentleman with a bleached coat hurries into the waiting area, carrying an extensive file wedged between his rounded torso and arm. A storm of worry hits my gut.

We stand at full attention. As he approaches Penelope's parents, Josey and I hover nearby, eager to receive any updates on her status. Josey clings to my arm as if I'm the only thing that'll keep her standing.

"Mr. and Mrs. Matthews?" he asks, and they nod.

Penelope's mom swipes underneath her eyes, smearing her black liner across her temples. Her father comforts his wife as best he can, pulling her close to him.

"Ms. Matthews is out of surgery. Good news first. There is an exit wound. The bullet nicked her spleen and rib. She's stable," he advises, and we all take in a relieved breath. "But she's lost a lot of blood, so, we aren' out of the woods yet, but we're monitoring her closely."

"When can we see her?" Penny's mother pleads.

"Once Ms. Matthews is out of recovery, we will allow her visitors Family only. She'll be in the ICU for a few days before we discuss releasing her. Ms. Matthews was extremely lucky the bullet didn't hit her stomach."

Her parents nod while Josey's head drops, but Penny's father is quick to console her. "We'll get you in inside, too, kiddo. Don't worry."

My stammering heart drowns further in my chest. The idea of being alone with my horrible images replaying on an infinite loop terrifies me. I need to be with the woman who captivated my fumbling heart, and she needs me.

I sink back into an empty armchair and toss my suffering into my palms again.

Why didn't I make her leave my office? Would he have shot us both if I tried? He should've shot me instead.

Hours pass since the surgeon visited us. Despite harassing the staff for updates, they only repeat the same line—she's still in recovery.

"I can't take this anymore. I'm going to lose my shit." The words slip from my tongue.

"Makes two of us." Josey's strained voice makes me sit at attention as her nails dig into her palms. Her eyes never leave the hospital floor when she speaks again. "Maybe after they change shifts, we can tell them you're her brother. That way, you can visit her, too."

"Where is Spencer?" I ask.

She inhales deeply. "Her mom said he's driving down from college now. They only told him an hour ago, too afraid…"

Josey doesn't need to finish. The pit in my stomach already knows why Penny's parents might not want him here.

"Josey," I summon with a quiet tone, but her eyes stay locked on the worn white tiles. "I'm not sure what she's told you about…" I release a faint breath. Saying what we had doesn't quite equate to a relationship, but the connection that grew between us is the closest thing to one I ever experienced. Hell, I wish I knew the perfect term for what we share. I shake my head with hope the blinding fog clouding my mind will clear, but it doesn't. I try an alternative approach. "Did Penny ever talk about me?"

This question gets her attention, and she raises her eyes to meet mine. A smirk pulls at the edges of her lips.

"I never took you for a nosey person, Mr. Stephens." She chuckles to herself as she breaks our eye contact. "You already know the answer to that."

I do.

Josey gazes off into the distance. "Penny loved working, even before you became her boss. But once she worked for you, that job was her escape. She told me how rude you could be, but Penny's resolve far exceeded yours. She is a force, that's for sure. We joked that if you replaced her, your future crappy secretaries would turn your hair gray. Real fast. She became accustomed to John's abuse, so whatever you threw at her, she handled like the powerhouse she is. But Penny has this way," Josey starts but becomes silent. She's willing herself not to bawl. "Effortless. Penny never tried to be funny or nice, she just was. To meet her is to care for her. She's warm-hearted, personable, kind, selfless, charming, and genuine. To know her is to love her. I told her she would change you, and you would bend to her will. Per usual, I was right."

"What?" I choke.

She waves me off. "Body language studies are my secret hobby. Besides your sulking, how you two interacted while training me was more personal than business. Anyone who didn't pick up on those cues is a moron."

Josey sits across from me, body less tense than before, but her expression still oozes sadness. Heart-crushing sadness.

"Am I that obvious?"

As a person inexperienced with feelings and then suddenly feel something, I didn't understand how to deal with these newfound sensations. It was a foreign presence in my body. I tried denying and hiding it, not just from myself, but from everybody around me, too. But these emotions posed even more complex to maneuver because we worked together. Add to that, she was engaged to a man that didn't deserve her. The entire situation stressed me the fuck out, but no matter how hard I struggled to dismiss the growing attraction, both to her outer and inner beauty, one simple smile or joke reignited that flame inside me all over again.

It became confusing, infuriating almost because once those emotions grew like roots in my soul, nothing could stop them. Her smiles and laughs were like fertilizer, making the bond between us stronger and stronger. It was wrong, but I didn't want it to stop. For once in my life, I enjoyed caring about someone other than myself. I craved it. I craved her. All this time, I assumed I hid it well, but I was wrong.

"Don't worry. She's pretty obvious, too." Josey raises her eyes, and we share a smirk.

All conversation drops when the doctor enters the small waiting room. His stoic expression makes my stomach plummet into my intestines.

"She's waking up," he announces, and his former exterior lightens.

Penelope's mother takes a deep breath as her hand clutches her heart. "Ms. Matthews asked to speak with a…" He peers down to a notepad. "Jordan Stephens, but from what I'm told, the police would like a word with him first."

"Can we see her while he speaks with the detectives?" Mrs. Matthews asks.

"Of course."

It guts me I can't be with her. She even requested to see me. She needs me. I've spent hours sitting in this room, plenty of time for the authorities to ask me what happened today. Of all times, now they want to talk?

Josey rests her palm on my arm. "I'll inform her you'll be in soon."

Two detectives enter the room, one in an ill-fitted chocolate suit, and the other in khakis and a white polo, ready to take my account of today's events. As they near, the doctor escorts everyone else to the one place I should be—Penelope's bedside.

"Mr. Stephens?" The man dressed in brown asks, reaching into his jacket pocket and reveals a pen and small pad. "I'm Detective Kennedy, and this is Detective Payne." He points to his more casually dressed partner.

I nod.

"We're aware you wish to see the victim." He glances at his notebook and starts jotting something on the tiny paper. "Ms. Matthews, but we need to know what ensued in the moments leading up to Ms. Matthews getting shot in your office."

"Ms. Matthews was my assistant until she transferred to another partner in our firm. My current secretary, Josephine Cordero, Ms. Matthews' best friend, barged into my office slightly before noon, frantic. She spotted Penelope's ex, John, in the hallway searching for Penelope."

"Why did she transfer to another colleague?"

"Penelope requested the move. One reason stemmed from a scuffle at Mavericks between John and me. The following day, well, there's already a record from her attack at the bookstore," I add with mounting frustration.

The detectives show no knowledge of Penny's assault at the bookstore, nor do they show interest in doing any research to get it.

After a long and aggravated exhale, I continue. "A few days before Mavericks, I caught Penelope's fiancé in a restaurant making out with another woman. When John found her at the club, and then me, he assumed I told Penelope about his cheating because she moved out of their house. But I never shared what I witnessed, and she never informed me she left him. He assaulted her at the club and that's when I found out about his abusive history with her. After Mavericks and the bookstore, our company issued orders to all personnel in the event John was to call or enter the building. We instructed everyone to say she no longer worked with the company. After his arrest, he called and visited the office multiple times, so I started a log. I can have someone send you a copy. Over time, his attempts dwindled until they stopped altogether. I'm assuming we didn't inform our new receptionist of our protocol, because Josey spotted him in the hallway. I ordered her to lock Penelope in Tom's office and call 911 while I summoned John into my office."

Detective Payne asks, "Why call him into your office if you're aware of his violent history? You already got into a physical altercation with him once. Another one might have occurred, no?" He folds his arms across his chest with a dumbfounded expression written on his face.

"Penelope's safety was my only concern," I blurt, as if it wasn't clear enough. And I would lure him again if it meant protecting her from him, gun or no gun. "I'm guessing Josey didn't locate Penny in time because…"

My throat constricts reliving this dreaded moment all over again, but aloud. I swallow the sadness and continue replaying the events for the detectives. Detective Kennedy jots down my account, while his partner stands with his feet a shoulder's width apart, arms still crossed over his chest, checking his watch. He asks a few questions but is less interested in listening to my answers.

By the time I'm finished, I'm emotionally drained and in desperate need of three drinks. The only true remedy would be Penelope's hand in mine or for someone to tell me it was all just a dream and when I wake up, we'll be back at work, together.

The detectives are satisfied with my statement and leave me with their card, noting I'll need to go into the precinct at a later time.

Left alone with these haunting images, I'm engulfed with emotion and spiral out of control. A hand settles on my back, startling me, and I spring to my feet, quick to wipe away my hot tears.

It's Josey.

"I didn't mean to startle you," she purrs.

We both sink into the uncomfortable chairs, and I release a weary breath. I prop my elbows on my knees, supporting my head in my hands again.

"Is she still awake?" I inquire.

"Yea, for now. She gave strict orders to the nurses to escort you in. Penny is adamant," Josey jokes. "I told her if you didn't see her soon, you're threatening to buy the hospital and turn it into a blueberry smoothie shop."

"Don't tempt me."

We share a brief laugh before her parents return to the waiting area. I spring to my feet, ready. A nurse gives me a nod and I follow, cracking every one of my knuckles. As we weave through the staff walking the halls, I'm fixed on the nurse's path and continue close behind.

As we approach a closed door, she urges, "Don't stay too long, she needs rest."

I slowly push her door open.

Penny is alone in the soft-lit room. The low beeping of her heart monitor is music to my ears. The most amazing song ever created by man. For the first time in hours, the gnawing despair inside me eases.

She relaxes her head on the pillow as if she's comatose, but that doesn't deter me. Nothing can, not now. Even if she's asleep, I'm staying until the hospital staff kicks me out.

I park myself in the cushioned chair pulled beside her bed and, with the slightest movement, her golden gaze freezes on me.

God damn if her eyes aren't the most welcoming and warmest pair in this entire universe.

The edges of her lips curve upward, and with that, I surrender control of my emotions and let them run wild. Tears, so many tears, spill. And I don't care if she sees every single one of them. My soul screams for me to hold her close, and it's killing me that I can't.

As if magnetic, our hands reach for one another. She squeezes with ample pressure to weaken me.

How is she still so strong, while I'm so weak?

"Jordan," she whispers, voice hoarse and scratchy.

But I don't lift my eyes to find hers again as much as I could use the warmth. I settle my forehead on our entwined fingers and unravel. She does nothing.

Once my tears run dry, I muster the power to raise my eyes to her, and she gazes back, endearing, wearing the same half-grin as before.

"I need to confess something, Jordan." Her voice doesn't waver, she remains as relaxed as ever, most likely riding the high of whatever pain-reducing drug they've put her on, but now her smile fades.

"Anything. You can tell me anything."

She closes her eyes, and for a moment, I turn cold. But I needn't wait long before she opens them again, replenishing all the warmth I need.

"I was hoping you'd say that." Her head shifts to the ceiling, eyeing the tiles for a few strained breaths. "I'm giving my two-week notice," she announces. "I've done it again. My boss is in love with me and I'm in love with him."

My jaw drops open until it hits me. A grin pushes up my cheeks and I break out into a modest chuckle, planting another peck on her delicate fingers.

"You have this knack for mixing up your bosses." My smirk grows and her grip on me tightens as her beautiful lips widen into a weak grin.

As she closes her eyes, her smile doesn't fade. I plant more kisses on our locked hands and watch her chest rise and fall. When she opens those golden gems again, she turns and searches for me.

How can a single expression make me whole?

She's lit a fire inside me, igniting life. My life.

She's nowhere near recovered, but she'll pull through this. She must. I'll give her any help she needs.

Penelope's lids become heavy with sleep, but that alluring smile doesn't budge. I nuzzle my cheek against her hand. Her warmth is astounding.

"I can't explain it, but your song played on an endless loop in my head. I hung onto the melody and trust me when I say, it helped me find my path." Penelope pulled in one tired breath, one that appeared painful. "I'm so tired," she murmurs. "But I need to confess something. For real this time." Penny squeezes my hand with one last burst of strength. "I choose your ending," she utters in a sleepy tone. "Because I love you." The words may have been mumbled, but they are music to my ears.

I plant one last kiss and declare, "I'm so in love with you, Penelope Matthews."

Want more Jordan's Penny content?

Subscribe to my website for an exclusive
scene sent straight to your inbox!

Plus, you'll stay up to date with blogs, upcoming
releases, content, offers and giveaways.

https://bit.ly/StefanieStratton

Thanks for reading!

Please add a review on Amazon
and share your thoughts!

Amazon reviews are extremely helpful for
authors. Thank you for taking the time to support
me and my work. Don't forget to share your review
on social media with the hashtag #JordansPenny
and encourage others to read the story too!

Don't forget to check out my other works!

Acknowledgments

The first person I need to thank is my beautiful, amazing, talented, funny, intelligent daughter, Olyvia. Love you, munchkin. You make me so proud to be your mom. I wish to thank my Mom and Dad, all my family and friends for their constant support. My Sparagna fam, no words could ever express how grateful I am that you all are in my life. Maura, my loverrr...and my biggest cheerleader, I love you. Many hugs and thanks to Rachel G for always being a great sport and friend, reading the very first and usually horrible draft of my works, and the many revisions thereafter. A big thanks to Mary K for joining my test-reader team. To my coworkers who hear me rant about projects and support me with every one of them, hugs and kisses. Michelle B for promoting my books far and wide. Love you! And to you guys, the readers, who have bought this book or Behind the Canvas, you'll never understand how grateful I truly am for the continued support. So many thanks, hugs, and kisses!

Made in United States
North Haven, CT
01 June 2024

53200401R00157